GOOD DEEDS

A REVERSE HAREM ANDROID ROMANCE

KATHRYN MOON

BY

KATHRYN MOON

Copyright 2019 Kathryn Moon
All Rights Reserved

Cover by Covers by Combs

No part of this book may be reproduced or transmitted in any form or by any means, electronic or mechanical, without written permission from the author.

This is a work of fiction. Any names or characters, business or events, are fictitious. Any resemblance to actual persons, living or dead, or actual events is purely coincidental.

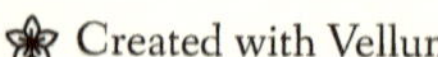 Created with Vellum

Emma... you know what you did.

ONE
NÖTCHKA

"YOU'RE LOOKING FLUSHED, MISS UUMIAN," the woman across from me said. Everyone in the room just called her 'Duchesse,' but I thought it sounded like a made up name.

"I'm... I'm alright," I said, ignoring the way sweat was starting to drip down my back and between my breasts. Now was not the time to start telling people to turn their environs down to a less tropical temperature. All I had to do was make the sale, and get out of here.

And ignore the urge to strip off all my clothes and dive into the orgy taking place in the corner of the room.

Duchesse smirked at me, lips stretching and contorting strangely, eyes glinting beneath an enormous poof of starlight white hair. The woman was like a work of art. Not the kind of art I *enjoyed*, but there was definitely craftsmanship involved. Her face was tiny and full of sweetness beneath a cloud of glittering hair, strands illuminated in pastel shades of light. Her body was an abstract exaggeration of a woman, petite and curvaceous in a way that made me question her structural integrity. She was an organic woman who was more cybernetics than natural materials by now. There *was* a beauty in it, although I wasn't sure if that was just the amateur engineer in me.

"You're welcome to partake in anything my house has to offer," Duchesse said with a sweep of her hand, wrists gilded with golden wires that ran like veins up to a bare shoulder. Cleavage overflowed from the top of a gown made of something like the material used to make weather balloons, three gigantic puffs of silver with lightning flashing over the surface.

I glanced around the room and regretted it immediately. There was bare skin *everywhere*. It had been worse downstairs. Duchesse's pleasure house was full to the brim with what seemed like every race in the universe. Through most of the house, on my way to the office, there hadn't been clear lines of who was with who. An orgy that writhed and expanded to fill the space of its container. Even here in the office there was a group on a couch—which might as well have been a bed— enjoying each other *noisily*.

I wasn't shy about sex. I was Dendärys, after all, a race seemingly built for pleasure. I'd actually been looking forward to coming to Bandalier, planning to take a few days off to enjoy what the planet had to offer.

But something weird was happening. My skin felt like it was ready to crawl right off my body. I was hot when no one else in the room seemed to be. If the woman on the couch-bed was any indication, it might even have been a little chilly in here. And while a big part of me—my entire physical body— wanted to take Duchesse up on her offer and simply jump into the closest available set of arms and lose myself in a Bandalier sex haze, there were warning bells in the back of my head telling me to get out and get back on my ship.

I was picky. I was Dendärys, which meant pretty much every other being in the universe would have sold their valuables for a night in my company. I was never *desperate* for sex. Not unless...

Shit.

I swallowed and mustered a smile for Duchesse. Make the sale. Get out. Get to my ship and then... would I make it somewhere safe in time? Not if the throb between my legs was any indication.

"I appreciate the hospitality," I said, trying to remain diplomatic. "I am looking forward to some... sight-seeing while I'm on ground."

"Of course," Duchesse said, with a coy bat of her eyelashes. "We'll take care of the business before we get to the pleasure. Conmar?"

A dark figure stepped forward, a dim shadow in comparison to Duchesse's glittering spectacle. He was a Thimean, from a desert planet, bipedal with four arms. He held a scanner in one hand, a deposit credit in the other, a small metal case in the third, and held the fourth out to me.

"The Proto chip," he said, voice layered in a tone that grated away at some of the arousal I'd felt rising like a tide.

I pulled it out of the collar of my suit where I'd tucked it against my breast. Up close to Duchesse I could see Conmar's patternings, dark jewel tones speckling up his neck and across his cheeks close to the compound eyes, facets mirroring me hundreds of times in iridescent lenses.

He scanned the chip I'd found a month ago, Duchesse leaning in and craning a long, pristine neck to watch.

I'd been scavenging through junk on an outer planet and while I'd found a good enough haul for some of my usual sources, I'd also picked up a chip of a Proto Pleasure model. I hadn't expected much interest in the chip—pleasure models had evolved well beyond the Protos by now—but I'd never found AI material before and was looking forward to studying the programming in my downtime. I loaded it in my sale stock data because I loaded *everything* in my sale stock. I was operating a scavenging business solo. I needed every unit I could scrape together.

Then I'd gotten the notice from Bandalier. A purchaser

willing to pay three times what I'd marked the Proto chip worth if I brought it to them straight away. Pay day on the pleasure planet.

Conmar nodded to Duchesse, passing her the chip and me the deposit credit which I promptly loaded onto my ID bracelet.

"Wonderful, Ms. Uumian," Duchesse said, beaming, teeth so bright they almost glowed as much as the rest of her. Maybe she *had* replaced her original set with bulbs. "How long do you plan on staying on Bandalier?"

My original answer would have been a day or two at most. Now, with this warmth crawling up my neck and chest tightening, the answer was either that I'd make it back to my ship and out of the atmosphere or I would be stuck on Bandalier for weeks.

"I'm not sure," I said, swallowing hard and trying to block out the cries of the group on the couch by sheer will alone. It wasn't working, and I tried to press my thighs together in a subtle, invisible way.

"Well I may have you do a little hunting for me if you stay," Duchesse said, leaning back in her chair, something between a throne and a nest, robotic hands unfolding from the structure to reach out and caress her skin. She pressed herself into their touch, eyes heavy lidded and breasts heaving with a sigh. "And of course if you ever find any more Proto chips, please contact me directly. I collect them."

"Of course," I said, nodding and looking for a spot in the room where there wasn't some kind of erotic influence. There was none. Even the window curtains depicted bodies entwined. "I'll keep an eye out for them from now on. You have my contact."

"I do," Duchesse said, and I wondered if I was imagining the way she drew out every word, like little sensuous caresses.

I was too far gone. I'd never make it back to my ship.

"Enjoy your stay here, Nötchka."

I tried not to shiver as I stood, every little shift of my suit creating a kind of friction my skin now craved.

"Thank you very much, Duchesse," I said, uncertain exactly how to make my exit politely. I started a bow, felt ridiculous, and gave it up immediately, hurrying toward the door.

"And don't forget to come back and visit while you stay," Duchesse called out. But I couldn't stop my feet now, I was too close to the lovers on the couch, the ripe scent of them turning to perfume in my head. I was afraid I might not make it out of the room. "The doorman will remember you. You're always welcome."

"Thank you so much," I answered without turning, blessedly close to my exit. I shut the door behind me. The hall was nearly empty, just a couple fucking up against a wall off to my left. I turned my head in the other direction and took a long breath. It was time to face the facts.

I was going into heat.

I'd gone twenty five years. Even at seventeen, just before I'd left home, I'd been considered a late-bloomer for never hitting my cycle. But to go another eight years? I'd begun to think I was immune. To dream that I might never have a heat, fall into a mating bond. And now, here I was, surrounded by sex and blooming into my first ever heatburn.

Fuck.

I needed to get away from other organics. It was rare for a Dendärys female to form a bond with a different race, but that was mostly because it was rare for a Dendärys female to make it off planet without one. The last thing I wanted was a bond that tied me down to a house. Or to anything other than my ship and my business and my life as I liked it, solitary and free.

In my desperation to get out of Duchesse's office, I'd forgotten what was waiting for me downstairs. A vekking orgy in full swing. The sight from the top of the stairs was something beyond erotic, almost violent and strange—all the bodies clustered together, faces twisted with a painful looking ecstasy. It didn't matter if it was something I might wrinkle my nose at on another day. Today it was *destroying* me.

I covered my body with crossed arms and tried to keep my eyes on the ground but there was enough in my periphery to leave me aching and trembling. My knees were weak by the time I made it to the bottom of the stairs. The front door was in sight, but the path there was riddled with sex, hands reaching out to me as I tried to make my way without any contact.

Someone brushed against my back and I twisted away from the touch, facing a room on my left. Three figures were strapped to racks, naked and stretched for all the eyes in the room. An enormous, pearl white man stood in front of them, the switch of a whip flicking against the floor as he stood as still as a statue. All at once, there was a snapping sound ringing through the air and the woman on the middle rack was crying out, body straining against the clamps that held her up. The audience to the scene cheered as the man in charge glared around the room. He had eyes as bright and red as a warning light. A Rough model droid. I shivered, body leaning in the android's direction.

"I can smell you, cub," a voice purred from behind me. "You'll throw me in rut, if you're not careful."

I glanced over my shoulder and my frozen feet stuttered forward. Now, more than ever, it was vital that I *not stop*. A Dendärys male stood behind me, pale sapphire skin bare of mating tattoos, body already half unwrapped for me, like a gift. A scar ran down one cheek to his mouth, and even the gruesome stretch of his smile made my belly clutch with need. I could have him... he could turn the heatburn that was coursing through me into something exquisite if I just-

"I *am* careful," I said, weaving through the crowds, feeling his heat at my back. "Spend your rut somewhere you're wanted."

His laugh chased me to the door, growing fainter. Getting

off planet was out of the question, I'd burn up before I made it out of the atmosphere and probably end up crashing and getting myself killed.

I broke out of Duchesse's open house, running into the street, thick clouds hanging overhead, reflecting the neon glow of the city. I needed a solution. I needed a *fuck*. But one that was safe, without any chance of mating.

I needed...

Two men approached me on the road, bodies big and cocks already tenting their pants, clearly about to head into the pleasure house I'd just left. Behind them trailed an exquisite doll-like woman, eyes a brilliant, glowing emerald. She was a pleasure model.

The thought struck like a meteor.

I needed to get the vek out of the organic district and find the androids.

TWO
NÖTCHKA

I SHOULD NEVER HAVE TAKEN that Proto chip. I shouldn't have put it up for sale. I shouldn't have come to Bandalier. I was fairly sure the pleasure planet was to blame for the sudden springing of my biological trap, the heat cycle.

Everywhere flesh winked at me, distracting my feet and drying my mouth. The planet environment was kept cool to help dampen the smells but still my skin burnt with need. A Vasulier female brushed past me on the arm of her host for the evening, clad in an iridescent illusion tech that might as well have been nothing, and I nearly dropped to my knees and begged to join them.

My vision was blurring. I could just strip in the street right now and surely some reveler would take me, rut away some of the fire in my blood.

Too Risky, Nötchka. That Dendärys male was somewhere on this soil and if he found me...

I didn't want to end up saddled with a stranger who'd strap me down to a dinner table. I was not fond of gravity. Not unless it came from the switch of a dial on my ship's control system.

These next couple weeks were going to be a trial enough as

it is. If I found some moon-damned place to stay and fuck and nap and didn't just blaze up with the heat.

Look. Look.

"Hello little Dendärys, come inside and play. I can't wait to taste you."

There was a Sparkle Boy hanging out of a Cozy's window, gold hair glittering and cheeks shining. Next to him, another sinuous and limbless Alternative model—for the universe's more exotic species or the very adventurous— coiled itself over his back, undulating at me in invitation. I almost leapt on top of them both, but it would cost me my entire ship to steal even one heatburn with one of the luxury models, let alone the days or weeks of the full cycle.

"Is this the Droid district?" I rasped, trying not to rub myself on the window frame.

"I hear Dendärys can come for hours, pretty cub," the Sparkle cooed, lips nearly falling onto mine.

I hissed and yanked myself away before I ended up indebted to a Cozy house I couldn't pay.

He sighed and pouted, drawing back, as the Alternative took off in search of a more likely client. "Yeah, and if you want to find your kind you're on the wrong end of town."

"Where's the cheapest place in the district?" I needed to stretch my units as far as they could take me.

He sniffed and rolled his eyes, and I thought he might leave me to wander around alone again. "Three gates down," he said, flat and bored if I wasn't going to offer to share my heat burn with him. "Bunch of broken parts and good luck with them."

As long as there were a few key parts, I would manage.

I kept my head down and eyes fixed to the debris on the road as I passed the next few gates. Cozy houses did nothing to mute the sounds coming from inside and as needy as I was the whimpers and moans echoed in my ears as if they were being amplified. My skin was goose-bumped and feverish and I was already aching and wet between the thighs, the stretchy fabric clinging and sticking in a terrible tease.

The lumo-plates hanging over the street were flickering blue and green, light almost dying by the time I reached the end of the block. I stood in front of the last Cozy in the district. Instead of glittering window displays, the enormous building stood gray and drab with dark holo-lenses facing me like empty eyes, just a flicker left on the door. Was the business closed? Or did they specialize in something that couldn't be advertised? Whatever the reason, I was too far gone to take my chances trying another house.

I stumbled up the walkway, the front door blinking and dying at my approach. I pounded on the glass with the flat of my palm, leaving a foggy handprint smeared across the pixelating holo-words that announced the house as *Cozy Nuts and Bolts; The first Droid Cozy on Bandelier*. In the back of my head a little snort of amusement broke through the haze of lust.

The glass slid open and a giant appeared before me in the dim, bare hallway. He was beautiful—the pleasure models usually were—with flossy blonde hair and spark-blue eyes, and tall enough to leave me almost tilting backwards. He stood fully dressed, unusual in this district, hanging back in the dark of the hall, right shoulder pushed into the shadows.

"Dendärys," he said, words flat, eyes glittering as he skimmed down me. A whole new dew of sweat broke out over me, even under his sterile gaze.

"Heat," I said, feeling myself shiver just at the sight of him, nearly landing on my knees but catching myself against the doorway. "Please."

"Verify units," he said, without any of a Cozy's usual charm. He held his wrist out and I lifted my own for my ID bracelet to face his scanner, almost shaking too much for him to get a decent reading. He frowned at the results. "I don't have a model available that you can afford."

"Please, please," I whimpered, my feet inching closer. Could I just touch him? It might even be enough. (It wouldn't, I knew enough about a heat to know better.) "I crossed half the vekking market."

"You'd have better luck in the open houses. No cost and you might find another Dendärys to throw into rut," he said, stepping forward. And my vision, which had started to water pathetically, fixed onto the shoulder he'd been hiding. It ended in open wires peeking out from the sleeve of his shirt, the right arm completely missing from the shoulder socket. The fact that he had a socket at all dated his model way before my time.

The glass started to slide shut and my hand snapped out, holding it open.

"I'll end up mated in an open house," I said, still staring at his arm. "I can fix that for you."

"Fix?" he asked, although without any tone it almost sounded more like a statement.

"Your arm," I said, teeth gritting as my arm wobbled, trying to keep the door from shutting on me.

The droid froze and the glass slid back to open. "You're a-"

"An engineer. Scavenger. And a pilot but I know my way around anything with a circuit. I'll fix your arm and... and you can have my units."

"You're shaking too bad to fix it before-" he started, the first expression appearing on his face with a faint furrow between his brows.

"After," I said, staring up at him. Could he scan me for signs of honesty? He might be too old a model or I might be too off-kilter to tell. "Just think of it as a- a good deed!"

There was a saying about those, right? I couldn't remember through the dense fog in my brain.

His eyes narrowed, illuminating brighter with internal activity, and his head tilted in what was probably a programmed gesture to exhibit thoughtfulness. "If you're lying

I will take the units. If you're not, you can hold on to them after you fix the arm."

Free sex? I almost broke into relieved sobs.

He stepped to the side and I fell in after him, the glass door catching at my heels as I pressed myself against the AI's front, moaning at the contact, my hands fisting in the shirt he wore. Heat blistered up my skin where we made contact and when a hand appeared on my back I hissed at the scorching sensation that followed, twisting into the touch as he braced me against him. My stomach cramped and my body crumpled into him.

"I've never serviced a Dendärys before," the AI said, words still even and cold. "I'll upload the files."

"Fine, that's fine, just don't make me wait," I said, tone broken with need. I was rolling my hips into his when the hand at my back slid down over my ass and then I was scooped up against the droid's chest and carried down the hall.

"Is that for me?" a voice called from overhead.

I tilted my head back and found myself looking into an upside-down face leaning over a balcony. Even from the funny angle it was clear. A Sparkle Boy. His skin was gleaming brown with inky black hair swept back from his face in waves that looked nearly liquid. His cheeks were a shimmering rosy hue and there was a tease of stubble around his jaw, making his preternaturally beautiful face more mature than the one I had seen out on the street.

"She can't afford you," the droid carrying me said while my throat dried at the sight of the face above me.

"You're not letting-"

"I'm handling it."

"*You're* handling it? You don't service."

The droid ducked us down and then the Sparkle Boy was gone and we were hurrying down a short flight of steps. The room we entered wasn't a Cozy guest room at all. It looked more like an office, with shelves cluttered with broken tech and circuitry and the house controls mainframe although there was decent looking couch pushed against the far wall. That was where he dropped me.

I was scrambling out of my clothes, wishing I'd thought to change into something less constrictive on my ship, as the droid stood in front of me.

"I can't find the usual mentions of preparation in your species files," he announced, and I stilled, my piloting suit half peeled off my shoulders, skin stinging with every brush of air.

"I'm not- I'm already prepared," I said, feeling an unexpected twitch of a smile at the corners of my lips. "I don't think a heatburn requires much, but... you know, the usual."

The droid blinked, his eyes brighter in the dark room. "You don't think?" he asked.

"It's my first."

"The files say a first heat should be at home with your tribe," he recited.

"Those files sound old-fashioned," I said. Over his shoulder I noticed the missing arm, waiting on the top of a shelf. "What's your name?" I asked, pushing the suit the rest of the way off my chest. The room felt icy and I wasn't sure if that was how he kept it or I was just too feverish from the heatburn.

"Avan-8," he said, eyes studying me as I wiggled the clinging suit off my wide hips. It had been a pain to find a pilot's suit that would fit a female Dendärys form and I'd finally settled for trimming up a too large garment around my shoulders. The hips were still a squeeze. "Would you like me to keep the shoulder covered?" he asked, shrugging the empty socket, two wires swaying with the gesture.

I blinked. Was that why he didn't service? Were women generally skittish of a little wiring? That seemed silly to me. Or could a droid just be a little vain?

"I'd rather see you," I said, staring up at him. My eyes widened as I added, "Mostly I just want to hurry and fuck."

For one, I was cold. For two, now that I was undressed

every little breeze that brushed my skin was making my pussy clench on nothing. The cramps in my stomach were coming faster too, a punishment for not having found any relief already.

Avan-8 took the instruction, tugging the shirt over the back of his head and revealing startling pale skin and a stunning plating pattern down his chest, the seams of musculature almost decorative. The engineer in me wanted to trace the design of his body. The heatburn did too but for entirely different reasons. My knees shook and I barely noticed the empty shoulder, although I caught the way he twisted his stance to keep it tucked away.

"Your kind kiss," he said, stepping forward.

I didn't want to kiss. I wanted him to press me down into the couch cushions and fill up the gaping void inside of me over and over again until my skin stopped crawling and my belly stopped cramping and my legs stopped working altogether.

But he bent forward with all the delicate practice and programing of a pleasure model. His lips brushed down over my cheek until they landed over my mouth, pulling me into a gentle, introductory kiss. The softness of his lips was a direct contrast to the plating over his chest, which was cool to the touch as my hands greedily began to map him. The burn under my skin flashed hotter and with a quick lift of my bare hips Avan-8 was following me down onto the couch, mouths linked, his tongue flicking out with surprising little sparks of electricity.

"Please," I tried again, word muffled in the kiss. "The burn..."

His hand disappeared from my skin and my eyes opened at the rustle of fabric hitting the floor. It was dark in the room, but there was enough light coming off the mainframes for me to see that the droid was hard—the cock jutting out from his hips the most natural looking thing about him. Long and thick and reddened as if with desire. I wondered if I imagined the almost visible pulse along the length or if that was an intentional effect. He carefully pushed my legs apart, first one draping off the edge of the couch, and then the other, stretched up to prop my heel against the wall.

"I'm out of lubricant," he said, as if he'd just realized, eyes flashing bright.

I stifled a wild giggle and reached up to draw his hips close, my breath hitching as the head of his cock tapped against my swollen, needy clit.

"We're good," I said, looking down between us to see the way I was already starting to slick up the tip of him.

He made a little hum and beneath the sound I heard a fascinating buzz of machinery, his skin warming under my hands to an almost matching temperature. With the first nudge inside of me my eyes fell shut again, lips parting on a low, needy moan.

"Ah, I see," he said, with a brief, easy pump.

I stretched my legs further apart and he fell into me, a wave of electric heat rushing up from my core all through my blood. I came before he was even halfway inside of me, whimpering and shaking, fluttering and squeezing him for every inch he slid deeper.

I'd always been told that everything would be stronger during my heat but I'd never expected my head to spin this way, my lungs feeling like I'd run a marathon in double gravity as I panted, the waves of pleasure still rolling in.

"How many times do you like to come?" he asked, as he nestled against me. His hand was braced above my head against the arm of the couch, his chest now warm as it lay over mine, pressing comfortably against my small breasts.

"Never had a heat before," I said, eyes opening to find his watching me. His head tilted again at that. "Usually a few, but this might be different."

He nodded and without a hint of teasing he said, "Just say when."

I started a laugh but it transformed into a moan as he began to fuck me in a steady pace—long, deep strokes that ended with noisy slaps of skin, never failing to grind himself into my clit with every thrust. The sting and ache from earlier transformed into a heady rush, my body feeling liquid and expansive. I wrapped my arms around Avan-8's back, hands clenching at his shoulders and lifted my chin for a new kiss, catching his mouth as a second wave started.

"Do you want to hear your name?" he asked and I nodded without thinking. "Nötchka. You're very soft, Nötchka. Soft and warm. You hold onto my cock tighter than any I remember."

The words had a strange pace, too steady to be natural, but his voice was coaxing, a programmed sweetness that gave some sincerity to the declaration.

"Tell me what you like, Nötchka."

"Harder," I hissed, and he followed the order straight away, the wave finally breaking over me, my hips rising to meet his in quick snaps as I panted and whined through the orgasm.

Avan-8 lifted me up, slipping out of me and turning me over onto my hands and knees before pressing in again, deeper than before. The cushions sagged under me and I rocked, working myself on his length, already impatient for more. The burn in my blood was a steady, pulsing thing, never worse but still demanding, not yet fully fed.

"Yes!" I shouted, as his fingers tangled into my hair, lifting my head and arching my back as he began to pound into me again, faster than before, the sounds of our bodies meeting echoing in the room.

"The file has finished uploading," Avan-8 said behind me. "I see why your species is so popular on this planet. Now let me try..." he pulled me up, my back to his chest and every thrust was a strike inside of me against a Dendärys' most sensitive nerves, leaving me melting and trembling in his hold as I came apart with lightning quick bursts of ecstasy.

"Don't forget to say when," he repeated in my ear, hand reaching up to tweak at a nipple and then slide down my stomach to play over my clit before buzzing in a soft vibration.

I twined my arms back around his neck to hang on, fingers digging in to the synthetic flesh and then stopping at the plating underneath. I didn't think I would be able to say anything before this was over, but beneath the curling explosions of my orgasming was something like a black hole, sucking up the pleasure and whisking it away, leaving only the craving. The heatburn wasn't satisfied yet.

"Avan. Avan, don't stop," I begged as his hips jerked unsteadily beneath me for a moment.

"Bad joint," he said, words amusingly steady while I was huffing and puffing for air on top of him. "Keeps sticking."

I jumped up from his lap and turned around to face him, lining him up at my entrance again before sinking down. "I can help with that too," I said before beginning to ride him, my hands at his shoulders. His arm wrapped around my waist, holding me close and helping me bounce, the slide and rock of him inside of me growing to a pounding pressure.

"Usually in service-" he started.

"Call it sex," I said, grinning at his puzzled face.

"The women prefer we do the work," he said.

"This woman is grateful for any help," I said.

I took his chin in one hand and tilted it up to kiss, our tongues stroking together, his causing shivery electric thrills that ran down my spine. I stayed pressed close, every rise and fall of movement creating friction between our chests. Avan-8 brought his hand between my legs again, fingers working in firm circles to bring me to another release, eyes watching my face with a focus that had me shifting from shy to fascinated.

The endless hunger of my body began to transform from

an unquenchable emptiness to something rising up, ready to overtake me.

"Oh starshine, here it comes," I breathed out, eyes falling shut and head dropping back.

"Yes, I feel it starting. Do you know, your body has a curious malleability-"

I dove forward again, swallowing any further observations with a clumsy kiss, hands fisting in Avan-8's fine blonde hair. My hips surged and crashed down again urgently, trying to fill every inch of myself with the droid. The heat was swelling and it was all I could do to keep moving, unsure if I was trying to stall or rush to the end. Avan seemed to have recovered from his hip joint as he began to rut up inside of me. The vibration of his touch on my clit increased, audible even under the rush of my breathing and the chorus of our fucking.

"Fuck! Fuck yes!" I didn't recognize my own voice, I'd never sounded so desperate before.

The heat burst, spiraling out of my blood, ringing in my bones, running over my skin until I felt as if I was changing into something larger than my own body, than even the room. Avan-8 was humming loudly as I shouted, fingers and cock never faltering until I could not even feel an edge between us and my head was beautifully blank of anything but the heart-burn's explosive finish. Light flared behind my eyes and my blood felt like an electric current, ceaselessly running.

And then the switch flipped.

Avan-8's touch stopped as I started to fall backwards, his arm catching me just in time and turning us on the couch so that he was laying on top of me again. I knotted my legs around his hips to keep him in place there, feeling too much like one giant nerve to be moved more than I had to be. He was a soothing kind of pressure on top of me, a reassurance that I wasn't about to completely dematerialize with the slowly fading sizzle under my skin.

"You're right," he said. My head was still spinning, but I

thought he might have had his hand in my hair, fingers brushing soothingly through the knotted strands. "You would have ended up mated in an open house."

I grunted my agreement and happily accepted the gentle kiss from Avan as he ducked his head down. I unwound with his lips on mine, electric tickles of his tongue tasting me.

THREE
NÖTCHKA

AVAN-8 CLEANED me up with careful touches. I wasn't sure if his concern was that he might hurt me, or work me up again. I remained collapsed on the couch, eyes begging to fall shut and let me sleep now that the worst of the first heatburn was over. There would be more soon enough.

"You can bring your arm over," I said, lips feeling numb from kisses.

"The files say you need rest," he said.

"I promise not to mix up any of the wires," I assured him, fighting a smile. As robotic as he behaved, the concern over Dendärys heat protocols was a strange and particular kind of touching. I pushed up on my elbows to prove that I could move and said, "We agreed I'd fix your arm after. Now's after."

He hummed again, head tilting, and rose up from the couch, crossing the room to pull the arm down from the shelf. He tucked it under his working arm and then grabbed what looked like a crude kind of tool box, the contents making a metallic rattle as he carried it over. It would serve me well enough. I scooped Avan-8's discarded shirt from the floor and slid it on over my skin, ignoring the first stirrings of warmth at the brush of fabric over my nipples. He turned and blinked at my makeshift outfit, the shirt pooling over my lap, considerably longer on my small frame.

"Your heat's going to last longer if you aren't mating," he said, eyes narrowed slightly.

I chewed at my bottom lip and kept my eyes fixed to the arm he was carrying. I could see where some of the connections had been carefully separated, and also those that looked like the product of damage. It wouldn't be the hardest repair job I'd done and with a little bit of help from a manual I'd have him sorted out.

"I know," I said. "But mated Dendärys don't run their own scavenging businesses and fly solo on their own ships. I appreciate you agreeing to this trade. I didn't realize how bad it was going to get."

"Your units won't see you through the day in the other houses," he said, sitting down on my left so I could study his shoulder. He seemed relaxed enough to stay undressed while I worked.

"I'll figure something out," I said, although for the life of me I had no clue what that might be. Maybe I could see if anyone on planet needed work done on their ships? It would be risky to take jobs when a heatburn might sneak up on me at any moment, but how else was I going to make the units I'd need to have Avan-8 service me. I winced as I realized his terminology was sneaking into my vocabulary. And there was no reason why it had to be Avan-8.

We sat in the quiet while I studied the craftsmanship of his shoulder joint with a kind of lust that had nothing to do with my heat.

"My arm isn't the only thing in the house that needs repairs."

I looked up from the impressive machinery in front of me. Avan-8 was staring out across the room, expression as empty as ever.

"Like the lights?" I asked, thinking back to the hall and the front of the Cozy house. Without the holo-screens running ads the house didn't even look open for business.

"Yes," Avan-8 said."The holo-screens. Most of the guest suite environment software. Our automatic sterilization systems are working now but they'll probably be down again in a week or so and we'll have to close till the repair comes. Some of the other models need work too. All of them. Except the Sparkle, he's brand new."

I blinked at that assessment. The entire house was in disrepair. How had it gotten so bad?

Avan-8 turned to face me. "I can give you a room for the duration of your heat in exchange for repairs. I'll service you. And you can make arrangements with the others who need repairs. I don't take debt accounts from my staff so that will be between you and them."

"Just to be clear," I said, eyes widening. "You're offering to let me work here through my heat as... an engineer... in exchange for sex?"

"Service," he said automatically and then he blinked and amended, "Sex, yes. My personality chip was fried. Can you fix that too?"

"Probably, I don't know much about AI coding but if it just needs a clean up, I could manage. And I learn fast. I'll need better tools than this," I said glancing down at the box he'd brought me. These were practically vintage. They'd work fine for the arm but something as delicate as a personality chip— and that being broken made a lot of sense now—was going to take a decent kit. "I'll have to go back to my ship for those. And I should find somewhere safer to store it."

"There's an empty garage here you can use," Avan-8 said.

"I really appreciate your help," I said. Now with the heat-burn faded I could really *see* the droid in front of me. He was... classical almost. With fine and traditional features and not a flaw to be seen aside from the missing arm. Later models put in intentional flaws to keep clientele from being unnerved or overwhelmed. I wondered what kind of personality he'd been programmed with. Probably something flawless as well.

"It's just business," he said, matter of fact.

I frowned and focused on the work in front of me, mapping out what connections needed repairs before I could set the arm back into the socket. I realized after a moment that his cool response to my thanks had rubbed me wrong, some little burr of offense scraping at my feelings. After another minute the sting transformed into amusement. Pleasure models were typically all flattery, *especially* where it concerned business. No wonder Avan-8 hadn't been servicing before our arrangement.

In truth, I think I preferred the honesty to the empty flattery and flirtation of a Sparkle Boy hoping to ride the high of a heatburn with me. Those models felt their client's pleasure. And no one felt pleasure like a Dendärys female in heat.

"How did this happen?" I asked.

"A rough guest," he said, and my fingers froze as the words sunk in, but when he glanced at me I forced myself back to work. "At first it was just sticking, like my hip. Then the control went in and out. I couldn't afford full repairs. Cutting it out was the cheaper option. My model is too out of date to bring in any guests now, anyway. I take care of the house. My staff takes care of guests."

"You own the house? I thought they were all owned by the Bandalier government," I said, digging around the tool box for the laser to reattach wires.

"I own the house. Bandalier owns me. For now."

No, Nötchka. But the warning was coming too late, my chest was already squeezing. It didn't matter if he was a droid, *anyone* striving for independence was someone I could feel empathy for.

"You said you don't take debt accounts from your staff," I said. "I thought that was how Cozy houses operated."

"Gloss, the Sparkle, I... purchased him for the house,"

Avan-8 said slowly. "But the others were going to be decommissioned or recycled. The house takes a cut for their service and the rest is theirs to keep."

"So they stay for fun?" I asked, liking the thought.

"They stay because a Cozy house is what they were built for," he said, and if there was an emotion in his voice, which I doubted, it had a bitter edge.

"Can you turn your own sensors off? I'm not sure how this will feel to you," I said, ready to do the real work of the repair.

"I had them turned off with the removal," he said. "I may need you to turn them back on again."

I nodded and took a steadying breath, rubbing my face on the inside of my elbow to try and wipe away some of the drowsiness lingering at my corners. "Alright. Let's... let's get started." How did one prepare a droid for a bit of mechanical surgery?

Avan's back straightened, face pointing forward again and body going completely still.

Just another machine, I told myself. Not surgery. Repair.

I focused, his broken arm propped up in my lap, close enough to his shoulder for me to rewire and fuse any frays. I'd made a few robots to help me in my ship. Nothing as sophisticated as a droid, least of all a pleasure model, but it pleased me all the same to see I had some of the same structures and connections.

"You're much more careful than the men who took the arm off," Avan said, words quiet so as to not startle me.

"In my experience, I'm much more careful than men in general," I mused absently.

Avan-8 made a noise that might have been a snort of amusement if I didn't know his personality was missing for the moment. He sat in silence for the rest of my work, occasionally turning to watch me. When I finally began to fit the arm into the socket he reached over, helping me with the dead weight of the arm until it was fastened. It hung, still for so long that I thought I'd done something wrong until I looked up into Avan's face.

"Can you move it?" I asked, nerves bubbling in my stomach.

The arm lifted, twisted, and then swayed through the air. "Feels smoother than the other one now," he said, blinking down at the hand, fingers waving in a testing motion. He clenched a fist and his eyebrows raised. "You found the sensors?"

"I was pretty sure I did," I said, with a shaky grin. "Now I'm certain."

My grin transformed into a long yawn, so full my jaw let out a weary cracking sound. Avan-8 hummed and stood up from the couch, pulling his slacks up from the floor and working his fixed arm through the air.

"Rest here," he said. "I'll get a room ready for you and let Kino know your plans. He can escort you to your ship and back."

I was grateful he didn't mention anything about taking back his shirt. The room still felt too cool for me, but not enough to stop me from stretching down the length of the couch, eyes falling gratefully shut. I heard Avan-8 padding quietly across the floor, but by the time a thin, soft fabric was draped over me, I was too close to sleep to see that he'd covered me with a blanket.

FOUR
NÖTCHKA

KINO, or KɪNo as he was labelled with silver over a pillowy dark chest, was the most cheerful AI I had ever met. If it weren't for the enormous, bright smile spread over his cheeks, I might have screamed after waking and finding him towering over me.

"Purple is my favorite color, you know," he said, eyeing my violet leg hanging over the edge of the couch.

"Um..." I rubbed a hand over my eyes and sat up. Avan-8 was nowhere to be seen in the office.

Kino crouched as I got my bearings. I flushed at the memory of the heatburn and tried to look anywhere but at the couch it had taken place on. My gaze settled on Kino's chest. Even folded up to half his height, I still had to look up to meet his eyes.

"Haven't seen boss-man so relaxed in a long time," he continued, still beaming, the exact opposite of Avan-8's blank neutrality.

"I'm going to fix up the house," I said, voice rasping.

Kino was wearing long white pants out of a rustic kind of fabric, but his chest was bare, dark with curling hair leading down his stomach in a tight line. His skin had a metallic sheen, like polished bronze and I fisted my hands under my thighs to resist the urge to touch and see how he felt. There was a close cropped black beard over his face and swirling patterns shaved into the side of his head.

"You, Nötchka," he said, in a grunt, brow furrowing as he reached out a hand. "Me, Kino."

I stared blankly at his mimicking frown for a moment before breaking out in a snort. "That's an old joke."

He grinned again and nodded. "I collect them."

When he stood up, I realized he was a Rough model, built for safe thrills. They were meant to be stern faced and threatening. And while his size was certainly intimidating—even standing I wouldn't make it up to his chest—nothing about that smile invited fear. The combination of dominating form and friendly demeanor was doing giddy things to my insides already.

"Come on," he said, reaching out one huge, warm hand and pulling me up from the couch. "Let's go get your ship and then you and I can make a deal." He winked at me at that and I felt my cheeks flush as he bent so his face was just in front of mine. He even smelled nice, something natural and woody that reminded me of the forest reserves back home. "Feeling feverish, Nötchka?"

My blush worsened at the glitter in his gaze, but my skin didn't itch and burn. This wasn't my heat. It was just plain old attraction, a pretty common situation for one of my race.

"Not yet," I said, drawing up a smile for him. "Let me get some pants on and I'll meet you in the hall."

He straightened and shrugged. "Shout if you need me."

Save it for the heatburn, you space-dumbed fool, I told myself as I watched his back shifting with every step he took out of the room.

I wormed my way back into my piloting suit and then tied the sleeves around my waist, not bothering to change out of

Avan-8's more comfortable shirt. I'd give it back when I had my own clothes to wear. Maybe. It was very soft.

Kino was leaning up against the wall in the hallway, another AI at his side, a slight and pale model with delicate features and soft, feathery black hair.

"Here she is, Romeo," Kino said, grin widening as I appeared. Romeo shifted anxiously as I appeared and a faint flush washed over his cheeks and nose as his eyes stared somewhere over my shoulder. "Romeo's a Lover Boy."

"Hello," he said, eyes glinting silver as he ducked his head. On his chest read ROM-Eo in the same silver lettering.

I'd heard about the Lover Boys, a precursor to Sparkle Boys, pleasure models who developed emotions for their clients. Their production run was cut short when it was discovered that an AI whose emotions outweighed that of their client could become... problematic. Never dangerous, but too obsessed for short-term affairs.

"Nice to meet you," I offered, watching the color deepen over his cheeks as he ducked his head a little lower and stepped back, hiding in Kino's shadow.

"I'll bring her back safely for you to swoon over later," Kino said, clapping Romeo on the back roughly before making a sweeping gesture with his arm for me to lead the way.

Romeo's face lifted, eyes huge, and he darted down the hall and up a flight of stairs away from us.

"You shouldn't tease him," I said. "He can't help what he is."

"No, he really can't," Kino said, laughing. "Just remember that when he's leaving you love notes on your pillow."

Outside of the Nuts and Bolts Cozy the world was clearer without the fog of heatburn hanging in my head, although the building was as bleak as I remembered.

"It's a diamond in the rough," Kino said as I looked over my shoulder at the house.

The yard around the building was cleared of the usual

refuse of the planet, probably some attempt on Avan-8's part to make the place look presentable. Unfortunately it backfired and the building looked even more abandoned than it might have with scraps of clothing and drink cups tossed about.

"I'll do what I can to get it shining again," I said and Kino beamed at me for my effort, slinging a heavy arm over my shoulder.

"I like the open districts," Kino said as we made our way past the droid houses and into the Intox district where the pleasure exchanges were made between equally willing parties and without any formality. "I worked for awhile at a drink hall, after my last Cozy."

"You served drinks?" I asked, craning my neck back to stare up at him. I'd never heard of AI crossing out of what they were built for into a different field.

"No, I could never remember the recipes. I was there to keep patrons in-line," Kino said. "But I got fired. Cracked too many jokes."

"I didn't know they made Rough models with senses of humor," I said.

Kino grinned. "They aren't *supposed* to. *I am a creature without mold or model.*"

"Garmond the Gargantuan!" I said, clapping my hands and twisting under Kino's arm. He had just quoted one of the more dramatic characters from my favorite series. "I watch space epics constantly. Best thing to keep the brain occupied when you're in deep space with nothing to do."

"I sneak them whenever I can," Kino said. He leaned down and whispered, "Velocious is my favorite."

I broke into giddy laughter, catching stares from the staggering Intox patrons around us. Velocious was the most tawdry, melodramatic, nonsensical space epic currently in production and I *loved* it.

"*Uneeda, my prize, my precious-*" I started

"*Our passion is destroying the Cadulian Empire,*" Kino

said in a low, erotic growl, sending a surprise shiver up and down my spine even as I fell apart in a new round of giggles. "This is good. With Romeo we should be able to outvote any of the others for what to watch during down time."

"Hey! *Cochie*!!"

I almost turned my head reflexively at the call, a familiar Dendärys endearment, but Kino squeezed me closer to his side.

"Don't look," he said. I looked up and found his face suddenly hardened, shoulders broader than before and me tucked safely beneath one. "It's a pack of Dendärys males. They've been following us a ways."

"Following?" I asked, some of the flush of heat that was building at Kino's scent and warmth now turning bitter on my tongue.

"Not close," he said, glancing down at me with a shallow smile. "They know they can't take me on. Avan said you don't want a mate yet." I shook my head and Kino nodded, "We'll be alright. No heatburn yet, right? Can't throw them into rut?"

"Not yet," I said, although it was lingering in the corners. "My ship isn't far."

"Cocheana," one of the men called behind us, a crooning tone I'd heard men use with their mates and sweethearts back home. "Come home with us, cub."

"We can smell you, sweet and ripe," another called.

"Now *that's* romantic," Kino said in an undertone, breaking the strange daze building in my head at their voices and drawing out another laugh from my lips. I grinned gratefully up at him but the firm set of his face over our shoulders was almost as good a lure for my heat as my own kind's call.

"Ummm, my ship is... close," I said, recognizing the area I had arrived at, already dewy with sweat, earlier in the day before my meeting with Duchesse. "But I... wasn't feeling well and I can't quite remember where exactly."

"There's a ship lot in that direction, and one farther off to the left," Kino said, still watching the men behind us. "They are starting to get brave, aren't they?"

Chewing on my lip I looked in either direction, but the streets looked nearly identical. Better to guess and hope I got lucky. Especially with a pack of men working up the courage to fight Kino for some kind of rights to me. They would find me a surprisingly unwilling participant in the competition if it came to it.

"This way," I said, seeing the closer ship lot in the distance. I wrapped my hand over Kino's arm on my shoulder and we picked up our pace.

"Unmated Dendärys women are rare around here, aren't they?" Kino asked, eyes focused on the people around us.

"Most mate in their first heatburn," I said. "And we're generally outnumbered two to one at home."

"No wonder this planet is littered with the men," Kino noted.

"Cocheana," they chorused behind us.

I hissed as my stomach cramped at the entrance to the ship lot. But right at the entrance was a Imerial 480 with tech-glass wings, such an impressive ship that I'd nearly stopped to ogle it on my way out the first time.

"It's starting, isn't it?" Kino asked.

I nodded, nearly glancing back to the pack of men behind us. My insides froze as I recognized one of the males as the one from Duchesse's pleasure house. "My ship is three rows back. Definitely here."

"Then I hope you don't mind me doing this," Kino said and then he picked me up off the ground, holding me up to his chest and hustling down the aisles. Over his shoulder I got a quick glance of three sneers spread over blue-green faces. But they trailed to a stop at the ship lot gates as Kino ran us around the corner of a decrepit looking battleship and out of sight.

I squirmed a little in his hold, but only so that I could press closer to his warmth, my fingertips learning the unfamiliar texture of his skin, smoother and firmer than flesh. When I tapped my nail over his shoulder the sound was something like silk over metal. I caught him smirking at me as I looked up.

"Avan-8 said you all needed repairs but I can't see anything wrong with you," I said, grimacing as I realized I hadn't meant to say that particular thought out loud.

"Can't you?" Kino asked, eyebrows raising. "It's my personality glitch, of course. I need to be reset."

"I like your personality!" I said, frowning. "Oh wait! We're here. Put me down."

Kino put me back on my feet, ducking down so he didn't crash his head into the belly of my little solo ship. I scanned my ID bracelet at the door before it slid open over my head. Kino lifted me up in through the opening and I scrambled back to give him room to squeeze in, although the fit of his shoulders through the doorway was not unlike watching myself trying to get into my pilot's suit.

"This is a very small ship," he grunted.

I laughed, leaning back against the wall as he wiggled his way inside with me. He was right. My ship's size kept the fuel costs down and the speed fast when I wasn't hauling something along with me, but even on my own it was a squeeze. I had to hook up most of the scrap in a pod outside and what was small enough just came in with me for short trips.

By the time Kino closed the door after him, he was balled up in a knot and my belly hurt with laughing at the sight of him. Or maybe those were the heatburn cramps. I groaned, trying to pull myself up the wall, and set a hand on my cheek, feeling the feverish heat lingering there.

"Ohh," I groaned. "I was hoping we'd make it back to the Cozy house before it got bad again."

Kino stood, or attempted to stand in the entrance, his back bent forward and head scraping against the roof.

"Did you mean what you said?" he asked. "About my personality flaw?"

"Telling jokes is *not* a flaw," I said.

"It's not what guests pay for with a Rough model, though," Kino said with a smile and a shrug.

I leaned against the wall so I could stare up at him. It would be a waste to erase a personality so bright. I certainly didn't have it in me. "Maybe I could tweak your programming? For every spank you give, you get to tell a joke."

Kino laughed then, a raucous boom that echoed around the narrow space.

"Come on, I have a slightly taller room I think you'll like," I said, turning around and pulling him by the hand through the doorway at our right.

The hand came down with a sharp crack, a brilliant sting on the skin of my ass answering the sound, and then flaring out from the spot, stealing my breath.

"Why did the sun go to school?"

My jaw dropped and my throat tightened, the slap still ringing under my skin, warmth gathering between my thighs. "Whaa?"

"To get brighter!" Kino said, grinning, body looming over mine in the doorway to the main entrance as I stared dumbly up at him. "Turn around, and I'll give you another one." His eyebrows waggled and my mouth dried.

And then I turned and crossed the small room in three steps, bracing my hands on the low bed pallet. It was far too small for the pair of us but for this...

Smack! I cried out, already laughing, as Kino soothed his palm over the spot he'd just sent up in flames. On the wall in front of me I could see his shadow hulking and it made my insides flutter.

"How do you organize a space party?" he asked, his body nestling over mine, large hands stroking up my sides beneath Avan-8's shirt.

"Umm." I couldn't even think of an answer, the edges of the room already going foggy in my sight.

"You plan…et," Kino said, voice happy and proud, hips jutting forward to bump against my ass. Then he retreated and, without hesitating, spanked me again.

I grunted, falling to my elbows, grinning stupidly and waited for the joke.

"Why did the meteor crash?"

"I don't know," I said, giggling and trying to push myself back into Kino's touch, but even at my very tippy-toes he was too far up.

"It was tired," Kino said.

My laughs turned into hysterical cackles as I turned around and found him grinning and, surprisingly, starting to tent the pants he wore with an erection. I'd thought pleasure AI only operated under specific orders but maybe I was giving clear enough signs, or maybe a Rough model was meant to be the aggressor.

"How can you tell when the moon has had enough to eat?" Kino asked.

"You forgot to spank me," I said, raising an eyebrow.

Kino grinned, taking my hands that were resting at the edge of the bed and pushing them back against the wall so that my back arched and my breasts were pushed up towards his face. His body curved over mine and when he patted my hands I left them where he'd put them. His fingers hooked into the waistband of my pilot suit and he knelt down on the tile floor in front of me.

"When it's full," Kino said, looking every bit the predator even with his warm grin.

He tore the suit off my hips, fabric tearing down the center and snapping against my already aching center. He left the shredded clothing hanging off my legs as he pulled my hips to his mouth, throwing my thighs over his broad shoulders and latching his lips onto my clit. I fell backwards onto the bed with a long moan, my head knocking against the wall and I could feel his beard scratching against the too sensitive skin of my pussy as he laughed against me.

"I won't reset you," I said, just in case this was supposed to be part of Avan-8's deal with me.

"My pinky toe has been malfunctioning," Kino said, lifting his lips just enough to lick a long stripe up my center. He flicked his tongue over my clit again for good measure and added, "So when you fix that we'll be even."

Then his hands slid up my stomach and squeezed hard at my breasts, drawing out a guttural sound from my throat and making me writhe against his mouth as his tongue studied me with expert attention. When his fingers pinched and pulled at my nipples in time with the sucking kisses over my clit, I came with a shout, my hands clamped around the back of his head to hold him close. He licked me clean and then pushed up from the floor, kisses trailing up my stomach on his way.

"Who stole the martian's spaceship?" Kino asked, resting his chin on my stomach.

I caught my breath, blinking up at the ceiling of my ship, thoughts flip-flopping about how to get Kino inside of me, and the answer to the joke.

"Um, an Exarvian fleet?" I tried.

Kino's tongue dipped into my belly button and then he rose up over me, teeth shining bright in his smile.

"A thief, silly."

I started to laugh and tell him his jokes were stupid but he had distracted me. With a quick touch to line himself up, Kino thrust forward, hands lifting my hips to bring them flush against his.

"Oh, fucknuts!" I shouted, and then bit my lips shut with a moan.

"Fucknuts," Kino mused, his cock stretching me wide as he mulled the word over. "I like that one. I have an idea now."

I was wiggling against him. My awkward position of half on the bed and half held up in his hands was making it difficult for me to take any control, and I paused, panting and staring up at him. Our bodies were knitted together, my legs spread wide to accommodate his size, but he seemed entirely too patient to get the show started.

"What might that be?" I asked, trying to muster calm.

"For every time I make you come, I get to tell a joke," Kino said, head hanging down, our foreheads pressed together.

"I love that idea," I said, nodding. "Let's start now."

Kino grinned, one hand reaching up to cup at the back of my neck. "So you don't hit your head," he said.

Then he started a brutal, pounding pace inside of me, hand anchoring my spine and lifting me just so, every stroke of his cock inside me dragging perfectly over all my nerves. My mouth parted on a silent shout, eyes falling shut, and hands pushing against the wall, trying to take *more*, and harder, and *faster*. A rush to the end now that I knew how it felt.

"Nötchka," Kino grunted, a frown knotting between his eyebrows. "I may not be a Sparkle Boy but I know how good you feel. Your skin is burning up. How can you stand it?"

"I can't," I said. "I can't. But I don't want it to stop. Please, Kino. Please keep fucking me."

His hand on my neck squeezed tight and the other wrapped over my hip, slamming me onto his cock and when I shouted he echoed it with a grunt, sounding every bit the part he was designed to play. Sweat was breaking out over my back, and I could feel myself soaking mine and Kino's thighs, a new rush building up in my cunt. Kino leaned back and his thrusts hit a sweet, swollen nerve, turning me into a thrashing, gasping creature, his hips barely able to move as I squeezed around him.

"Do you know why you can never trust an atom?" Kino asked, pulling me up against his chest so our noses brushed and turning so that he sat on the mattress with me on his lap.

My body was still singing and craving all at once so I rocked gently on top of him even as I caught my breath.

"Why?" I asked, voice torn and a whimper rising up.

"They make up everything," Kino said, wrapping his arm around my waist and trying to fit us both on the bed, him stacked on top of me, legs hanging off the edge.

I snorted and squirmed. "Where do you get these? And you're going to break my bed."

"You'll fix it later," he said, pushing my thigh that was pressed into the wall up to my shoulder and then covering me completely with his body, warm and smooth, hairs tickling at my belly and clit.

He was a heavy weight and it felt wonderful, crowding me head to toe and fixing me to the mattress. His hips rolled into mine, pelvises grinding together and suddenly that strange firmness to his skin felt even more wonderful. He had no give and my body was forced to mold to his as he worked himself into and on top of me.

"I like the way you feel," he said, sounding a little surprised.

I smiled and opened my eyes, having to tilt my head back into the mattress to find his face. He was stroking the thigh he'd pushed back, fingers digging into the soft flesh experimentally, golden eyes brighter.

"I like the way you feel too," I said, squeezing his cock inside me and making his eyebrows raise in surprise.

"You're too far away to kiss," he said, grinning. "Are all Dendärys women so little?"

I snorted at that and rolled my eyes. "No."

I was short, even for my race. I turned my cheek and bit at his chest where I could reach, although there was no point. He was too hard. But he laughed at my effort and began to rut against me in a quick beat, hips rocking against mine, our bodies pressed so tightly that the pressure was constant and the friction heady. I curled my other leg up over his hip and reached around his back, raking my nails over a back impervious to harm.

"Tickles," Kino grunted, thrusts deepening. "Ah, I've just thought of another joke."

I was too wired to laugh, and maybe a little too buried beneath him to catch my breath, but I hung on as he rutted in a wild rhythm, drawing fractured noises out of me with every beat of our skin together. When I felt it start, the expanding heat rather than the constant hunger, I clung tighter.

"I don't care how many jokes you tell in a row, just don't stop. Don't stop till I beg you," I warned him, the words broken in time with his rhythm, every thrust catching my breath.

He made the bed rattle on the wall with his force and I thought for sure we were about to crash onto the floor at any minute. But I was just as sure that the fall wouldn't stop him, not while I was shouting and clinging and struggling beneath him, lightning licking through my blood and stars exploding behind my eyes.

There was a joke, at least one, somewhere in the crescendo. Something about black holes, and I think I might even have laughed until I cried, but mostly there was the heat, flashing through and transforming me.

Kino was still fucking me when I finally settled, although now it was in slow, smooth strokes. He was being gentle. And when I looked up his face was buried in the red strands of my hair, an engine sound coming from his chest that was almost a purr. I unclenched my hands and stroked them up and down his back and the purring got louder, vibrating into my chest. It felt nice actually, a pleasant buzz in my skin, little echo flashes of the heatburn still tickling my center.

"How does the moon cut its hair?" I asked.

Kino rumbled on top of me, his body rolling over mine like a wave, an almost breathless hitch in his throat.

"Eclipse it," I said.

Kino groaned, arms wrapping around my back and squeezing me against him in a long hug, hips circling in steadily shallower thrusts until he stopped altogether. It was almost as if I had made him... but no. He was a droid. He turned us, his back thumping hard against my mattress, my bed frame creaking.

"That was a good one," he said, eyes glittering, grin wide. Then he pulled me up his chest, and tugged at my hair until we were kissing. His mouth was soft, lips pliant, and I nibbled and pulled at them until the purring engine sound started again and Kino shook beneath me.

FIVE
AVAN-8

GLOSS WAS HOVERING in the doorway to my office, glittering dully in the hall. The city's glow filtered in through the dead holoscreen windows, just enough that a guest might see the shadowy edges of their surroundings. Enough to be "kind of creepy," according to most that visited. That would need to be fixed soon. I added it to my internal list for Nötchka.

The Sparkle had been waiting for my attention for the better part of ten clicks, underestimating my lack of interest in finding out what he wanted. If the Dendärys woman did fix my personality chip I wondered if I could revise the program to keep this trait. It was already written into the programming I'd been working on for when I left Bandalier.

"Are you taking a break or going back up to the door to watch for guests?" I asked when his shifting and pacing out of the corner of my eye continued. He'd finished with a guest before coming to hover in front of me and generally his habit was to lounge at the front of the house, hoping to find the next one. A Sparkle was bound to find the quiet of the house too dull without work.

"KɪNo should be back with her by now," GLoSS said, taking my question as permission to join me in the office.

"She probably had another heatburn," I said, shrugging my shoulder. The one she'd fixed. Just to test it again. "They come in irregular patterns."

GLoSS released a soft mechanical whine at my back, barely audible. "Aren't you worried he won't take payment?"

I spun in my chair to finally face him, finding the Sparkle draped along the couch right where I had spread Nötchka out hours ago. His hands were skimming over the fabric. Was he tracing for leftovers? Hoping to catch some of that rare heatburn? It would make sense that such an overwhelming arousal would be an experience a Sparkle craved. They rode the high of their client's pleasure. Nötchka's had been *extreme* in my experience although I'd never had another Dendärys to compare to. And likely never would again. Dendärys females did not want for sexual partners and most were mated without ever landing on Bandalier.

I had considered it while she was riding over my lap, what it might feel like to have a Sparkle's capability to feel her pleasure with her. I had never felt a satisfaction beyond knowing I'd fulfilled my function for a guest, and for the past decade not even that. With her... there had been a new kind of signal in me, sensory and environmental and comprehensive all at once. I'd enjoyed myself.

"She doesn't have payment to give," I said, warning GLoSS. "And you don't have anything for her to fix."

"What if she leaves the planet with him? You did just give her a pleasure model, after all," GLoSS pointed out, ignoring the warning. "She doesn't need to come back for her heatburn if KɪNo is there to take care of her."

I... hadn't thought of that. My head tilted and GLoSS folded his arms, raising a dark eyebrow at me.

"Then I will take his place until I can find another to join the house," I said. "She fixed my arm. That was all she owed me. And K1No is in charge of himself."

"You're never going to get your deed back if you run this house like a charity," GLoSS said. I regretted ever telling him my goal of leaving the planet. He was constantly offering opinions on how to run the house. He could have it once I left for all I cared but I wish he'd stick to his guests' business and stay out of mine.

"You've been watching too many of K1No's epics," I said, but there were footsteps coming up the back steps from the kitchen and I was more interested in who it might be than any accusations from the Sparkle Boy.

ROM-Eo peeked his head around the edge of the doorway, cheeks blushing already while his eyes landed over our heads, unseeing. "They've just landed."

GLoSS was up off the couch at the announcement, darting into the hall.

"She can't pay, GLoSS," I repeated, but he was already on his way to the kitchen, where K1No and Nötchka would enter from the garage.

While I didn't have a say in most of my staff's down-time, I *had* purchased GLoSS for the house, even though it went against a code I'd developed in my later years. But he was right, I was too lenient and guests hardly wanted anything but the Sparkle models these days. In another handful of years a new model would roll out and even GLoSS would be old news.

"Should she meet KEV-1?" ROM-Eo asked, ears turned in the direction of the kitchen, looking ready to chase GLoSS there.

"He knows he's not allowed to service," I said.

I doubted even Nötchka could fix that particular problem. KEV-1 was a Proto model, like me, from the same production roll of models. While he had no definable errors in his operations, and nothing that needed direct repair, something... happened when he was alone with guests. He seemed happy enough to keep to the kitchens and keep guests fed without going back into the work he was designed for, and I didn't see the worth in recycling him when it cost me nothing to keep him on hand. We were probably the last two Pleasure Protos in existence. Or at least on Bandalier.

ROM-Eo made a rattling sound in his chest and then disappeared from the doorway. I hesitated, staring around my office for a moment before deciding that, of everyone in the house, I didn't trust GLoSS enough yet to leave him alone with Nötchka. It would be against his programming to engage her without payment but his interest was too high and I had a habit of finding AI who didn't follow their programming.

I followed ROM-Eo down to the kitchen. The lights were off, but I could see KEV-1 organizing the cupboards, oblivious to the rare congregation taking place in the room. GLoSS was turning on some of the smaller battery lamps we kept around as the door to the garage opened and K1No entered, Nötchka stumbling sleepily behind him. She winced as a light flickered on overhead before giving up again, leaving the room in the soft orange glow of the little lamps at the corners of the room.

She was still wearing my shirt and I ignored GLoSS's raised eyebrow, instead watching her stretch, the hem brushing at the tops of her thighs, revealing dark golden bruises on the soft flesh. The file had said Dendärys bruised easily, but almost never suffered more serious injury due to how flexible and elastic their bodies were. Had I left those bruises on her or K1No?

What does that matter? It didn't. I pushed the question out of my system.

"Oh," she said, noticing the collection of us waiting for her, one foot curling around her ankle as she leaned against K1No. "Hello." She shuffled back as she stared at the room, cheeks blushing to a deep pink.

"Hello," KEV-1 greeted with a nod before going back to

his cupboards. I'd given him the suggestion that when he was not cooking, he could organize the kitchen, and it was what he spent ninety percent of his time doing when K1No couldn't lure him away to watch epics.

"Kev this is Nötchka. Notchka, Kev-1. He stays in the kitchens away from the guests for now," K1No explained.

"Hello," KEV-1 repeated with the same nod and the same return to his cupboards.

Nötchka nodded slowly, eyes running over KEV-1. Another reason we kept him out of sight was because he seemed to be especially appealing to guests. There'd been a few who tried to talk him out of his orders to keep away and I'd caught them just in time. I wasn't sure if it was the glasses they'd designed him with, or the benign smile, but I wasn't designed to understand attraction either.

"You've met Romeo and the boss man of course," K1No continued. "And the Sparkle Boy is Gloss."

"Hi," Nötchka said, although the word was transformed by another one of her enormous yawns. She made a small wave, either to greet us or excuse her yawn.

"Hello," KEV-1 said again, with his nod.

"I've arranged a room for you," I said, stepping forward. "It's not much now, but once the guest environments are repaired you can design it to your liking."

Nötchka shrugged, eyes drooping and another yawn interrupting whatever she was trying to say. "I doubt..." yawn, "...I'll notice."

"Come on, Cocheana," K1No said, swatting Nötchka on the rear and making her eyes pop open again. "I'll tuck you in."

GLoSS was probably right then. K1No wasn't bothering with a trade. Nötchka was leaning into his side as he directed her past us, looking already asleep as she mumbled, "I still have to fix your pinky toe."

"Pinky toe?" I asked.

"It's stuck," KiNo said, his strong face doing a poor impression of innocence.

"Stuck pinky toes," GLoSS said, mouth pursing in a sour pout. "Sounds bad for business."

"Not all of us can be brand new, problem-free models," KiNo said in a taunting sing-song, eyebrow raised.

"Guest room eight," I told KiNo. "And she *sleeps*."

KiNo said nothing and I had a rare urge to give him an order, give them *all* the order to go look for their own guests and leave Nötchka—and her heatburn, and the matter of payment—to me. Instead I returned to my office and decided to focus on the list of what needed repairs. If Nötchka was going to keep my androids busy then I was going to keep her equally busy in exchange.

SIX
NÖTCHKA

IT WAS night when I woke again, on a wonderfully soft mattress in a dark, plain room. At least the beds were in good condition. My guest room was the last down the hall and Kino said it was hardly ever touched. With the Cozy house only having three androids in service, eight rooms had been more than plenty.

"And we're hardly ever busy even with the three of us," he'd confided, pulling the sheets back for me before following me under them with a grin.

He was gone now and I found my bags at the foot of the bed. I bit at my smile, touched that he'd thought to bring in my things while I'd slept. I dug around until I found my clothes and pulled on a skirt for easy access—I wanted to look halfway decent but I was still in heat, after all. I decided to keep Avan-8's shirt on. Just to tease him, if that was possible. It was difficult to read the stony house owner. I'd caught glimpses of warmth while we were fucking but it could just as easily have been practiced behaviors for his work as a pleasure model.

Dressed and with my hair up and out of my face, I threw my toolkit over my shoulder and tiptoed down the hall to the elevator, catching the rapid, breathy sighs coming out of one of the rooms.

"Oh! Oh! Oh! Oh!" A woman was squeaking, the sound of flesh slapping in the same quick beat, although I couldn't guess which of the pleasure models was with her.

There was a louder, longer squeal and I bit my lip to keep from giggling, ignoring the flare of warmth the sounds lured out of me. According to my bracelet I'd only slept a couple hours again, and I was sure to fall into another heatburn. This time, I didn't want to be running on credit. Also, it would be nice to walk through the cozy house with lights on.

Downstairs, Gloss was draped across the open doorway, staring with a coy smile at the crowds in the street.

"Any takers?" I asked.

He turned to me, skin shimmering like gilt and fully on display, with him dressed in nothing but a pair of skin tight black shorts. "Not yet. Maybe once you spruce the place up a bit."

His eyes were tracing me with the same interest as the Sparkle Boy from the cozy I'd passed earlier. I wondered if a Sparkle Boy had ever felt a heatburn before. They'd clearly heard of them and coveted the thought. I imagined Gloss under me, equally as overwhelmed by the shattering climax and felt a flare of arousal again. He would be exquisite, the pair of us amplifying the experience back and forth to each other.

Watch it, I reminded myself. This one was off limits.

I'd always resented the heatburn, even before it first struck. I loved sex as much as the next of my race but I preferred the experience on my terms and under my control. Landing on Bandalier and having fire start threading through my veins at Duchesse's had proven to me exactly how easily that control could vanish.

But I'd made it here safely and Nuts and Bolts was a stroke of luck. My units would have vanished in the first cozy I found and then I'd be left for days—or worse, still craving and *broke.*

"I'll see what I can do," I told Gloss, heading down to Avan-8's office. The Sparkle was welcome to covet the heat-burn, but unless I came into a surprising fortune and felt like wasting it, he'd never get a taste. I'd manage fine with the others. They seemed sweet anyways.

Well, most of them.

"Not jumping back into service?" I asked Avan-8 upon finding him at his desk, working figures on a small holo-screen.

"Without the personality programming, I am unnerving," he said, matter of fact and flat, without turning.

I smiled. "Who, you?"

That had him spinning, head tilted. "Who else? We're alone."

I coughed, disguising my laugh, and nodded. "Right. Dumb question. I came to see if I could turn the lights on."

"Are you in... flux, again?" he asked, eyes fixed to my chest. Or his shirt, maybe.

"No, but give me ten minutes and I might be," I said shrugging. "For now I'm awake and not rubbing up against anything, so I might as well get some work done, right?"

"It would be ideal," Avan agreed. He stood and crossed to me. "The panels are up here. Can you reach?"

He was standing at full height in front of the wall at my left and still reaching up so the answer was no, I could not reach, because he was a giant and I was... the opposite. But instead I said, "I'll handle it," and he left me to it with a brief glance.

I found a metal box to stand on and pried off the cover of the wall panel, plugging in my systems and firing up diagnostics. There was an alert at the top of my tablet. *Missing woman reported* with her picture and details.

"Someone's gone missing." I studied the picture, trying to remember if I'd seen a girl with wings while I was out in the streets, or at Duchesse's, but both times were too hazy.

"You'll get half a dozen alerts a day for those," Avan-8 said, looking over at me. "They lose track of whoever they landed with. But they turn up, usually whenever they've run out of units. If she comes to the droid district, one of us will report the sighting."

I chewed my lip, looking down at the alert again. Commonplace or not, a woman going missing felt like cause for concern. I memorized the woman's face and details. I would keep an eye out for her at the very least.

I swiped the alert aside and looked at what I'd found in the house. The coding was nonsense, as if it had started degrading from the beginning and then just been left to carry on that way. Now it looked more like the programming for a washing machine than a lights and display system.

"This has been... broken for awhile?" I asked.

"It's gotten worse." I snorted at that assessment and heard Avan-8 approaching behind me. "Can you fix it?"

"We're gonna be better off deleting the entire system and starting fresh," I said, watching the chaotic code streak by.

"The programs are very expensive," Avan-8 said.

"They are if you *buy* them. But there are free ones we can download and adjust. They won't have displays already programmed but they'll turn the lights on in a room when someone walks in." I turned on my self-appointed stool and found him almost close enough to lean against. He didn't bother exuding the fake body heat like the others did, making it clearer that he was not an organic. Instead of leaving me uncomfortable, I wanted to press up to him, soothing my flesh as the fever built.

I was starting to stare as he read the code over my shoulder. "It looks like a virus," he said, eyes meeting mine for confirmation.

"It looks like there was a virus eighty years ago," I said. "Now it's a parasite. It's probably been funking up your environments the entire time too. Do you have any idea how it got on here?"

"Funking up," Avan-8 mouthed, head tilting and still watching the strange code. "I bought the house from the previous owner sixty years back. The repair issues started not long after." He looked up and nodded. "Alright, delete it."

The first part was easy and with a few commands the program was off the server. Since the lights had already more or less given up, no one would notice for a few minutes before I got a new system up and working. I just had to chase down all the traces of corruption through the rest of the house. Less easy. I jumped down from the box I'd been standing on and Avan-8 went back to his desk. He pulled up a new screen with a tidier looking code.

"What's that for?" I asked, glancing for a second at the program. It didn't look like it belonged to the house. Although at the moment the programs *in* the house didn't look like they belonged either.

"I'm writing a personality code for myself," Avan-8 said.

I almost missed a bit of corruption when I looked up to stare at him. I shook off my surprise and tried to focus on my work again. He could write his own personality. Did androids do that often?

"The failsafes will still be in place," he said. "We can't unwrite those." Failsafes kept models from doing damage to organic beings. They were the first core of programming AI and impossible to tamper with. A droid didn't turn on if the failsafe wasn't running.

"I can still fix your dead chip," I said, wondering if he was concerned about not having his personality running so he could get back to work.

"I know. This isn't for service. I'm writing this for after, once I've bought my deed and I can leave Bandalier," he said.

Oh, vekking star-gas. When he talked like that, my chest hurt with a problematic sweetness. What would I have written in and out of my personality when I left home so young? I might have written out homesickness, although I was glad I felt it now. It was good to go home again, even if it was better to know I could still leave when I wanted. But I wasn't designed for one kind of function like a pleasure model and I suppose if it were possible I would have deleted the heatburns out of my system.

Although I was less convinced of how terrible those really were now that I'd spent a couple with Avan-8 and Kino. A small part of me was already looking forward to the next wave, or maybe that was just heat brain at work.

"How close to finished are you?" I asked, glancing over. The program looked huge from what I'd seen.

"Just tweaking," Avan-8 said. "It passes time."

After running through all the extended programming in the house, and freezing up a few more programs that were likely to cause issues before I got the chance to work on them, I sat on the box and watched Avan-8. The early pleasure models were designed with similar traits and coloring, golden skin and fair hair and eyes, broad shouldered and narrow hips. I suspected the funny one in the kitchen was another older model, although he had a warmer look than Avan-8, with a little less going on between the ears. Or wherever an android's main operating system was.

Avan's feet were bare, toes wiggling absently against the cool tile floor as he worked, and he'd yet to replace the shirt I'd stolen from him. Maybe now that his arm was reattached he didn't see the point of covering up, like most other pleasure models. I certainly didn't mind ogling those chest plates.

"Your heart rate has been increasing slowly since you entered the office," he said, glancing up and catching my gaze. But unlike any other male I'd met, he didn't gloat or preen or tease me for staring. "It's been more than ten minutes. Is your heatburn returning?"

"I think so. Let me get your lights up first," I said, turning back to my tablet, and starting the search for a good starter program that would work for the house.

"You shouldn't wait for the cramps to start," Avan-8 said, rising up from his chair. "The files say it's painful."

I rolled my eyes, pulling up a database of useable programs for the house. "You and your files."

"They're *your* files. Dendärys files," Avan-8 corrected, crossing the room and towering above where I sat.

"Here, do you want a slow dim by command or on an automatic control?" I asked, ignoring his attempt at looming. He couldn't boss me into sex for my own sake.

"By command," he said. "Stand up."

Well...maybe he could. I jumped up at the order but held the tablet up between us as if it might be enough to stop him on his mission. "I'm supposed to fix things first, remember?"

"You deleted the faulty programming," he said, pushing my hands aside and bending forward, taking the hem of my skirt in his hands.

I started laughing, trying to dart out of his hold, but with the first skim of his fingers on the skin of my thighs I already knew it was too late. It felt like sunlight stroking my skin as he pulled my skirt up my legs, knuckles brushing over flesh.

"Avan, wait! I have the program, just let me-"

The fabric popped up over my hips exposing my bare skin to the cool air in a sudden rush that left me gasping. I stared at Avan with my jaw dropped as he took the tablet out of my hand, tapping in the download code and then placing it on a shelf well above my head.

"You're getting awfully bossy," I said.

It seemed impossible but even in the perfect neutrality of his expression I couldn't help but feel like he was teasing me.

"I'm efficient," he said. The smirk was in his tone if not spread over his face. He stepped forward, hands still on my hips, and I edged backwards until my back was against the wall, bumping my head as I tried to look up at him.

"You don't even know if the program works yet," I said.

There was no reason why it wouldn't, but he was jumping the gun a bit this way.

"That's true," he said, head tilted, still leaning in until our chests were pressed together and his face was hovering over mine. Was he going to suggest a kiss again while we were standing here like this? With my skirt bunched up around my waist?

No. His hand traced to my front and dipped between my legs, stroking at the lips of my pussy and causing a shiver to run down my spine.

"Well the heatburn's starting *now*," I hissed, my lungs tightening as I tried to catch a breath. I took small steps, parting my legs and trying to rub myself against his hand.

"I think it's better like this," Avan-8 said in a light tone that I envied while I was busy sucking in air like I'd been running a mile when we'd barely fucking started. "You can have immediate relief."

He dipped two fingers inside of me to the first knuckle and I wrapped my hands around his upper-arms. He set his thumb over my clit and then held himself still while I worked myself back and forth against his fingers, whimpering and panting all the while.

"This doesn't feel like relief," I said through gritted teeth. It felt like a tease, even if it *was* wonderful at the same time.

His thumb began to vibrate and I moaned as his head ducked down, cheek nuzzling against mine. "Better?" he asked, lips against the shell of my ear. He lowered his face a little more and licked along my pulse, that flicker of electricity shocking me and making me clutch him tighter against me.

"I'm wet, I'm ready," I said, my hips working in uneven jerks as I tried to chase ahead of the heatburn to my first release.

"The lights haven't come on," Avan-8 said, and now I knew he was definitely teasing me. Apparently an android could be an ass even without a personality.

"I *told* you to let me finish the install. Now I'm telling you to let me finish this too," I whined.

My feet were slipping on the floor, toes curling and Avan-8 was keeping his hand carefully distant, fingers just barely inside me, thumb just grazing my clit, vibrations as light as bird wings. He sucked at my pulse, those electric nips zinging through me and making me twitch and lose my rhythm. I growled and tried to snap at his shoulder with my teeth but he only made his touch lighter.

Over our heads there was a bright chime from my tablet. The download was ready.

"Lights!" I shouted. "Lights on! Now!!"

Overhead the lights flared bright under the urgent command and from somewhere deeper in the house I heard a confused exclamation.

"You fixed it," Avan-8 said, pulling back from my shoulder.

"I did," I snapped, glaring up at his face as he looked at the suddenly illuminated ceiling, his skin pale and stunningly perfect under the bright light. "Now fuck me."

He turned back to me, glancing down between us to where I was trying to grind myself onto his hand. "Very well," he said.

With one organized movement he pushed the waistband of his pants down his hips and lifted me up from the floor. I grabbed onto his shoulders and watched as his cock went from soft to stiff and ready, and then it was sliding inside of me. My back was fixed firmly to the wall, legs spread until my knees touched the flat surface and were held there by his hands.

"I do appreciate the way you stretch but still hold such a grip on me," Avan said cooly while I moaned and went nearly limp in his arms. He nestled into me until we were all but glued together at the hips and I blinked through a haze of foggy desire at him. "It is almost like our engineering but I do not think even the pleasure companies have invented some-thing like it yet. Another time, in a bed, there are some positions I would like to try. Given your flexibility, I think you would appreciate them."

I swallowed hard and slipped one hand up into his hair, taking a tight grip. "If you stall my orgasm for one more minute I am going to write a code that makes this entire house smell like old cheese."

"Guests won't like that," Avan-8 said, head cocking in confusion.

"No, they won't."

And with that he took mercy on me, or took the threat to heart, hips snapping into mine until I was shouting praise up into the illuminated ceiling.

SEVEN
NÖTCHKA

I WAS BACK in my dark room, waking with the heatburn already crawling up my legs, taking the same path as a careful set of warm fingertips. I held my breath for a moment but when the unseen touch skimmed over the back of my left knee I buried a whine into my pillow.

"Sorry," the culprit whispered.

"Forgiven," I said. We remained still and silent for too long so I added, "Keep going."

The hand transformed into a body, curling up against my side. Another hand appeared at the nape of my neck, sifting through my tangled hair, careful not to pull.

"Light at ten percent," I said, blinking as the room turned from black to shadowy. I rolled my head on the pillow to find Romeo at my side, eyes unfocused around my shoulder. "So you can see what you feel," I told him.

"I can't see," he said, fingers running back and forth over my dimpled thigh like he was memorizing the pattern. "Lost sight capabilities three years ago."

I turned onto my side to face him and his hand learned the curve of my hip, the other brushing strands of hair out of my eyes.

"Avan-8 wouldn't help pay for the repairs?" I asked.

"He offered," Romeo said, silvery blank eyes widening. "But I decided to leave it. I thought it might help me not... fall in love so much. If I couldn't see them, it would be something I didn't have to remember later."

I bit my lip and held my breath, fisting my hands against my stomach to keep from tackling Romeo back to the bed. Aside from avoiding any chance of mating, the one thing I'd felt certain of being safe from in the android district was *feelings*. Instead I was being bombarded by them.

"It didn't work," Romeo added with a thin, sweet smile. "I'm used to it now."

"Not seeing?" I asked.

"That too." My chest burned as his hands continued their study, tracing around my jawline, sliding up my belly and down between my thighs. I shifted to give him more room. And also because I was a greedy Dendärys female in heat and I couldn't help myself. "All pleasure droids have sensors in their touch for mapping and memorizing. They just don't usually rely on them."

"I think, in a way, that's true for organics too, although maybe we don't gather the same imaging as an android would."

Romeo hummed in agreement, the sound stopping abruptly as he found the slick waiting on the lips of my pussy. He spread the wetness in a slow swirl, smiling as I released a shuddering breath.

I chewed at my bottom lip for a moment, shifting in little ways underneath his hands so that I could soak up his touch in the needier places. When the fingers of his other hand travelled down from my collarbone to skim between my breasts I reached to guide the touch, covering his hand with mine over my breast until he squeezed me, massaging the tender flesh. I sighed and rolled onto my back, arching up into his hands.

"Do you still love them all?" I asked, wondering if the love his model was programmed with was temporary.

His lips twitched and he shifted from my side to hover over me, sitting up on his knees. One hand rolled my breast and the other abandoned my wet cunt to run the backs of his fingers along the insides of my thighs, barely skimming against my sex.

"I remember them all," Romeo said. "But most of the feeling fades with time."

"Do you want me to fix your sight?" I asked watching his silver gaze roam aimlessly over skin he couldn't see.

Maybe he wouldn't. Maybe he wouldn't want to make the same deals with me that Avan-8 and Kino had and then maybe I wouldn't have to feel terrible that an android fell in love with me over a span of minutes. Of course if that were true, if it wasn't too late, he probably wouldn't have gotten in the bed in the first place.

"Later," Romeo said, hands sliding off my skin and bracing on either side of my head as he leaned down, trailing feathery kisses across my temple and over my cheek until his lips were grazing against mine.

"You don't have to," I whispered, searching those silver eyes even if they did stare without seeing. "If it will make you... if you don't..."

"Don't worry about me, Nötchka," Romeo said, eyes fluttering shut. "Let me help you first."

There was a fragile sound at the back of my throat as Romeo relaxed on top of me, delicate hips falling between my thighs, arms circling my back to hold me close to his chest. He didn't have the spark to his kiss that Avan-8 did, or the rumbling engine purr of Kino. Instead we made small sighing sounds together and when I scratched my nails up his sides lightly he shivered against me. His hands roamed, urging me closer and mapping not just my shape but my reactions. When he found a ticklish spot on my ribs he teased there until I was pulling away, squirming and gasping out with tight laughter.

"You taste sweet," Romeo crooned, tongue licking stripes up my throat.

I wrapped my thighs around his hips until I felt his cock nestled between the lips of my pussy, hard and hot. I twisted beneath him, sliding the head of him against my clit, feeling him growing slick and slippery from me.

"You process flavor?" I asked, surprised, my brain wanting information as much as my body craved contact.

"Mhmm. And you sound like you're singing as you come," he said, body sliding down mine until he was kissing across my collarbone and over my chest. "I could hear you with Avan earlier. Even from my room."

I could feel my skin flushing and I wasn't sure if it was the heat or embarrassment but both were distracted the moment Romeo wrapped cool lips around an aching, pebbled nipple. I cried out and he pulled off my skin with a 'pop!'

"Yes, just like that," Romeo said, cheeks dimpling with the biggest smile I'd seen him wear yet.

I reached up and carded my fingers into his black hair, fluffing it and feeling my chest warm at the happy, boyish expression on his face.

"I'll keep singing if you keep touching," I said to him, pulling him back for another kiss.

He grinned and our teeth bumped together for a moment before our lips softened against each other. His fingers toyed with my nipples, and then soothed every little aching pinch away with his thumbs, all while he swirled his hips against me, soaking his cock in my wetness without ever entering me.

"Are you going to make me beg, Romeo?" I asked, nipping along his jaw. When my head landed on the pillow again his eyes were brighter.

"Could I?" he asked, face openly excited.

Since he couldn't see my smile I didn't bothering trying to hide it, stretching up to peck at his lips again before pressing a kiss to his ear.

"Please Romeo," I said, not even having to fake the whimper as he nudged at my clit again with the tip of his cock. "Please. Please, fuck me. Be good to me. Be sweet and make me come. I want you to make me come."

There was a faint, high-pitched, whirring sound from the back of Romeo's throat, his eyes wide and almost lamp-like. Then he was nudging at my opening in soft thrusts, my body trying to rise up to meet him.

"Please," I said again, hearing the little noise again behind his firm lips.

So I chanted the plea and his name together, watching his throat bob in a swallow that must have been a programmed gesture rather than an actual physical need. His skin was flushing pink and his hips were kicking in small quick motions, sinking into me slowly.

"You feel so good," I said. "Romeo, I want you. I want you to make love to me."

The whirring turned into an honest whine and then Romeo had my hands pinned above my head, filling me up in one last thrust, swallowing my moan with a hard kiss. He kept our mouths fused, lips and teeth and tongue dominating mine while he rocked against me in the slowest, most agonizingly gentle pace. When I tried to speed him up he spread my legs apart by locking our ankles together, leaving me under his control.

I didn't know if I was doing him more harm than good but I wanted him to feel needed, desired, the way he felt about the people he'd slept with. If I had to take his heart with me, code-written or not, the least I could do was give something back. Even if it was only temporary. So while I couldn't speak, only doing my best to follow his kisses with my own, I let every sound he conjured with his body working mine fly free, filling up the room with my cries.

He released my hands only to hold my face, fingers tangling in my hair as his tongue stroked against mine, slowing to the pace of his pumping cock. I traced the planes of his back, doing my best to memorize him in turn.

"Say more," he whispered, finally releasing me. His eyes were shut, brow furrowed in a knot, and his shoulders were curling up to his ears as he waited for me to answer.

"You're beautiful," I told him. "You- oh, fuck, that feels so good. You make me feel so good. You're so good, Romeo. Don't stop, please."

He deserved better words, something sweeter, but I was having trouble thinking straight, the heat building, that cavernous need growing again.

He kissed me. "Thank you, Nötchka. Now come for me." He ground himself against my clit, thrusting fast and deep, lips sucking at my pulse as I came with a shout, body curling under his. Even as he squeezed he continued to fuck me through the shuddering waves.

"Don't stop," I rasped as he started to slow.

"I won't," he promised, peppering kisses over my jaw and cheeks and lips. "I just want to draw it out. I'll make it good."

I licked into his mouth, fingernails combing through his hair, pressing my breasts into his chest so he could pick up my pounding heartbeat.

"You're doing more than good, Romeo," I told him, grinning as his smile broke out. "Mmm, I think you like teasing me."

There was another orgasm waiting at the edges but I was fairly certain Romeo was delaying it, rocking shallowly, just teasing at my opening and making sure not to brush against my clit.

"Don't want to rush," he said. "Don't want you to forget this."

You're in such deep shit, Nötchka, I thought.

"I'm not going to forget you." I kissed the corner of his jaw, pressing the reassurance into his skin, "I'm going to remember you."

His lips made a firm line as he whined and swallowed hard again and I pulled him back down, soothing kisses against his lips until he relaxed against me. I came again—although I would have delayed it for him if I could have—and I sighed and whimpered and moaned into his ear.

When he tried to pull away I clung to him. "Roll over, Blossom," he said and I knew my cheeks turned magenta with the name. He slipped out of me and turned me onto my belly on the mattress, and when his body covered mine again I felt suddenly nervy. This was how Dendärys mated, the men fitting in from behind and the heads of their cocks rubbing at our most sensitive spots, sending us into those last frenzies.

But Romeo wasn't a Dendärys, I reminded myself. And even if he was...

No. No 'even if's.

My worries died as Romeo lined himself up and slid home again, stomach pressing against my back. He nudged my legs apart and my swollen clit scraped against the bedsheets. I fisted my pillow in my hands until Romeo reached up and linked our fingers together.

"Does this feel good?" he asked.

I could barely find the words to tell him, yes, yes it felt better than good. The weight of him, heavier than I would have expected, was a comforting kind of a pressure.

"You feel fucking amazing," I said, squeezing his hands tight in mine.

He rewarded with me a searching shift of his hips until I was shouting, body spasming beneath his. Tears gathered at the corners of my eyes at the burst of ecstasy, white hot and flaring up my spine and down to my toes. He set the slow, dragging rhythm of earlier, but every beat ended in the same *bang!* note of pleasure. I was sobbing nonsense words, begging and praising and thanking in jumbled phrases, wanting to race to the end but also savoring every prolonged second he gave me.

He kissed patterns over my shoulders and up the back of my neck, little exhalations of air puffing into my hair.

"Nötchka, my Blossom," he whispered.

There were words in my throat and I bit them back, trying to bury them under shattered, aching cries.

When the pressure broke and I was finally taken under the enormous wave, body quaking, I thought I heard him speak again but my ears were flooded with a rushing roar, my eyes covered in stars. Romeo twisted our arms around my chest, holding me tight enough to stop my shaking as I came down again. He turned us to the side and tucked our legs up high, his cock still buried inside me.

I listened to the sounds of my breath steadying and my heartbeat slowing and Romeo's happy humming. He pressed a kiss into my shoulder and somewhere in the back of my head I wondered if I should have felt guilty for using him this way, knowing what he would carry for years after. But I couldn't muster guilt, I only felt safe and happy and a kind of sated I'd never known before.

"Romeo," I mumbled and he nodded, chin tucked against my shoulder. "Thank you."

He hummed again, face nestling into my hair, probably sweaty and tangled into a nasty nest again. "Wanted to be good for you."

"You were wonderful," I said, squeezing his hands again.

If he *had* been a Dendärys male...

Stop it, idiot.

It would be easy to fall asleep and avoid thinking about it, I was already feeling the drowsiness sneak up on me again.

"I'll fix your eyes when I wake up," I said, words slurring.

"I'll be here."

Fall asleep before you say something stupid.

But in the back of my head I kept wondering if I'd heard it, just at the end, just as I was crashing through the last wave of the heatburn. *Keep me.*

EIGHT

NÖTCHKA

KINO HAD BROUGHT me breakfast in bed and, even better, good reading material. Manuals on house programing and each of their droid models were uploaded to my tablet while I slept. I dug in straight away when I woke, fitted between two surprisingly comfy bodies given how firm they were, being hand fed bites of an old fashioned hot breakfast. There was, to Kino's disappointment, no hint of heatburn lingering under my skin. I promised him it would come back soon. A two day heat was more or less impossible for my kind.

With a better idea of what to do for the house, and a full read through on how to fix Romeo's sight, we went down to the kitchen as a group to work under the brighter lighting.

"Are you sure it doesn't hurt?" I asked, wincing as I accidentally scratched the inside of Romeo's head again.

There was nothing like opening the secret latch behind an android's ear and swinging half his head open on a hinge to remind you that he was made differently than you. His head was full of layers of hair-fine wires and the most exquisitely elaborate integrated circuitry I'd ever seen. I was worried I'd end up doing more damage than good with a wrong move, but secretly, I coveted the experience. Romeo was the most amazing machine I'd ever worked on.

"You turned the sensors off," Romeo said, making sure not to move as he spoke. With his head open his normally whispery voice had a hollow echo, turning tinny.

"Yeah, I know. Just seems like you should at least have an itch or something."

"Would you like a snack?" Kev-1 asked me.

He'd been drifting back and forth between where I sat on the counter and reorganizing his cupboards. This was the fifth time he'd asked me the same question and I was beginning to see why Kev-1 didn't service guests. Of the group he was by far the most robotic. Still, there was something almost infectious about that enormous grin of his and he was pretty enough to be distracting.

"I'm alright, buddy," I said, nudging his thigh with my foot.

His hand wrapped around my ankle in a firm grip and I held my breath, pausing in my fiddling with Romeo's circuits. Kev-1's fingers stroked along the thin muscle above my heel and when I glanced at him he was staring where he touched me.

"Kev," Kino said, almost chastising, but with a nervous watchfulness. His body was tensed as if he was prepared to step in.

Kev-1 released me with a beaming smile and went back to his cupboards. I raised my eyebrows at Kino.

"He forgets sometimes," Kino said with a shrug, relaxing back against the counter opposite me.

"Is it just the... you know, repetition thing?" I asked. Because I could maybe fix him up and then... I mean, it really was a waste to have an android built with thighs like that and not let them serve their purpose. And repetition had its place. I could think of a few good things that required repetition, actually.

Kino watched Kev-1 pull everything down from the

shelves, line them up along the counter, and then put them back in the cupboard again. Apparently he'd been coming up with new organizational logics for every time he re-shelved, which was kind of impressive, I supposed. If you didn't mind looking for ingredients based on food-coloring formulas.

"It's not that he's dangerous," Kino said with a faint frown. "He's never hurt anyone. But he just... loses control. Stops responding to directions and... usually his guests pass out before he stops."

My brain went a little funny at that explanation, stalling out and leaving me staring with my mouth open at Kev-1's benign smile.

"After making sure there was nothing really *wrong* with him that could be fixed Avan-8 decided it was better to keep him in here than risk a guest filing complaints against the house. *Nötchka*," Kino said in a cooing tone until my eyes snapped back to his and found him smirking. I shut my mouth. "Don't get ideas."

Too late.

Had any of those guests Kev-1 lost control on been Dendärys? Our sexual tolerance was *high*. I was willing to bet that even if I passed out, there'd be a big damn smile on my face. And he didn't need to follow directions. I wouldn't be thinking straight enough to offer any if he was just going to town on me.

"Are we close?" Romeo asked and I jumped, shaking myself out of my haze. "I'm excited to see you."

"Super close," I said, focusing back on my task as Kino laughed at me.

"Prepare yourself E-O," Kino said. "She's prettier than she sounds."

"Watch yourself," I growled at Kino, flicking a pair of zoomers down over my eyes so I could get the best view of the last details.

"I've *felt* her," Romeo said with a warm reverence that I rewarded by cuddling closer to his back.

"And you should be prepared too," Kino said to me, grin growing. "Poor boy's probably going to lose his speech functions after you've finished."

"I know someone who's going to lose his speech functions if he's not careful," I grumbled.

I squinted through the zoomers as I peeled back the little maze of circuitry with a delicate pair of pliers, finding the frayed wire, curling off its panel. I put the pliers between my teeth and picked up the laser that would refuse the wire and heard an audible click off to my left.

"Just capturing the moment," Kino said.

I ignored him, filing in the back of my thoughts the need for some light revenge at a later date.

"I can see!" Romeo announced, as I sealed up the vision chip again.

He tried to turn and I lifted my knees to squeeze around his sides, holding him in place. "No moving yet! I wanna close you back up before you get dust in here or something."

I set everything back to rights and turned Romeo's sensors back on just before swinging him shut, triggering his safety seal that kept any damaging elements—like water or dust— away from his programming. He was spinning around with the last lock click.

I smiled as I saw his eyes again, a warm caramel color now, black pupils dilating fast as he stared at me. When I took the zoomers off my nose the whirring whine from the night before returned and I reached out to squeeze his hands. The pink flush of his blush started on his cheeks but quickly darkened and spread farther, turning from pink to the same pale purple of my own skin.

"You're changing colors!" I said, laughing.

"*Nötchka*," he breathed, the high whine at the back of his

throat, violet flooding down his throat, eyes huge and black, absorbing every inch of me.

I released his hands and took his face in a gentle hold, pulling him close and pressing a kiss to his stunned lips, slightly parted. He responded after a moment, the mechanical whirr softening.

"Hello, handsome," I greeted, pulling back slightly and trying not to fidget under Romeo's stare.

"You're beautiful," he whispered.

"Thank you," I said, popping a kiss on the tip of his nose.

"Hey, boss man," Kino announced.

I leaned away from Romeo and found Avan-8 standing in the doorway of the kitchen, watching us with his head tilted. There was a guilty twinge in my belly although I couldn't place exactly why. I'd repaired Romeo, after all. And Avan had said any arrangements between myself and the other androids were strictly that, between us. Maybe it was the lingering guilt of knowing that Romeo was built to love. Every kiss I offered, every scrap of affection I accepted from him, would make my leaving worse for the android, no matter what I told myself.

"We got Romeo seeing again," I said.

Avan looked non-plussed but he answered, "Good."

"Look at her," Romeo said, without tearing his eyes away.

I blushed as Kino snorted in the background. I nudged Romeo's side with my knee, hoping to shake him out of the reverie. That only made him look down at my knee in a kind of rapture.

"I also think I know what I need to get your displays perked up," I said to Avan-8. "And clean up the environments systems. I'm just going to go scavenging for some parts today."

"Do you need one of us to go with you?" Avan-8 asked.

I thought he might be about to offer to come with me himself, but Kino beat him to the punch.

"We'll go with her, boss man. You couldn't pry Romeo off her even if you wanted to."

Romeo nodded a little at that but I thought I might have caught him with a hint of a smirk. They were conspiring together.

Avan-8 hummed in the doorway and we all waited in silence. Would he really be willing to let me run off with *two* of his working androids when that meant there'd just be him and Gloss for any guests that might show up?

"There's not going to be a rush before we get back," Kino said, raising an eyebrow, following the same line of thought.

Avan-8 finally shrugged. "Your time is yours. You know that."

Kino grinned in triumph and Romeo lifted me up from the counter. "Let's get dressed, Blossom."

"Be discreet," Avan-8 said to Kino in an undertone as we passed him on our way into the hall.

SANDWICHED between Kino and Romeo on the speed train's bench seats I saw less of Bandalier than I had on my other outings. Given that we were leaving the more reputable districts on our way to the junkyards, out past the main city, that was probably for the best.

"I've heard there's a good haul out here," I said. "More or less untouched."

"Scavengers don't come out to the planet?" Kino asked, his eyes sweeping over our heads. The cozy, casual, jokester was tucked underneath his more formidable mask the longer we travelled. The train wasn't packed but it was a rougher crowd now than it had been we'd boarded in the center of the city. Gone were the buzz-happy revelers. We were heading past the Intox manufacturers and into the regions of Bandalier that specialized in what couldn't legally be advertised.

"They come to Bandalier for fun not for work," I said, peering out the window at our stop, staring up at the massive, glowing factories. "Or they come for work but then forget to do any when they find the fun. Either way, we'll find what we need if we don't mind sifting through less appetizing fare first."

When I looked up Kino was staring back behind us to where new passengers were loading in. His arm, wrapped over my shoulder, grew heavy, pushing me down a little in my seat.

"Nötchka," he said, in a heavy tone. "I'm going to take a picture and I want you to tell me whether or not the men that just got on at the back of the train car look familiar. I'll send it to your tablet. Don't turn."

I slouched in my seat and Romeo, with a brief glance behind us, leaned in toward Kino, making it appear as if it were just the two of them together. Kino turned stiffly forward and my tablet glowed softly in the bag on my lap, his incoming file received. I peeked into my bag and frowned at the image, waiting for the faintly familiar faces to click in my memory.

It took a moment, the train firing up again with a soft jerk of momentum, and I remembered.

"It looks like the pack of Dendärys that was hollering at us yesterday," I whispered.

"Yes," Kino said. "I thought so. They've sat behind us a ways and I want to make sure they don't spot you again."

I stared at the picture, studying the men. I could only really see one of their faces but it was the one who'd called me Cocheana at Duchesse's—I remembered the ragged scar on his cheek. The others might not have been the same group, but it was pretty common for unmated Dendärys to go 'hunting' for females together. Now they had a woman with them. She wasn't Dendärys, but from one of the hotter planets, a gold sheen to the scales framing her face and running down the sides of her throat. She leaned against one of the men, eyes half-lidded, and hands digging into his collar.

"Is she... does she look like she's safe with them?" I whispered.

Romeo looked this time, just a brief glance, and the violet

color he'd borrowed from me earlier flushed over his cheeks again. "She's... they all look pretty willing."

Kino glanced back, grinned, and turned forward again, eyes widening in mock shock. "Her vitals are... normal. For what they're getting up to back there, anyway."

I chewed up my lip, debating turning to see. But I couldn't afford to kickstart a heatburn in the middle of the speed train and this *was* the pleasure planet after all. It probably wasn't unheard of for a group to be partaking on public transport.

What *was* strange was that Dendärys males *didn't share*. They'd hunt for mates together, but when they found one, what had once been brotherly camaraderie almost immediately became vicious competition. Maybe because she wasn't a Dendärys too, it didn't kickstart their possessive tendencies?

"You definitely think she's willing?" I asked, wanting to be sure.

"Definitely," Romeo and Kino chorused, glancing at each other over my head. Just as they spoke a high, feminine exclamation of 'yessss!' echoed down in our direction. I pressed my ear to Kino's chest to dim the sounds that followed.

The group got off the train two stops later, where there were cheaper rooms to rent than the ones in the central city. Cheaper company too if you had the right kind of currency. Kino and Romeo stiffened as the group got up but they left out the same back door as they arrived in. I was finally able to look as the train doors shut and the engine groaned to life again.

The woman was pressed between two of the men, their hands traveling under her clothes, her head tilted back with an expression of wide-eyed bliss. I caught the gaze of one of the unoccupied men as we started to pull away. His skin was a dark shade of azure, eyes startlingly pale, and mouth surprisingly grim for how pleased she seemed to be. That mouth twisted as he stared at me, eyes narrowing, and then he smirked. Rather than shrink back against Kino, I remained sitting up, watching him until we slid past. Let him recognize me from the day before. What could he do now? Better her than me if she was happy with them.

"Our stop is next," I said, relaxing as we left the pack behind.

I didn't like knowing that they were still on planet. Even if I *was* safe. Even if I never ran into them again. They were exactly what I was trying to avoid by coming to Bandalier. Or maybe they weren't. Maybe they were on this planet together making sure they didn't mate either. Then we could happily avoid each other for the rest of our stay. I hoped at least the woman would have a good time with them.

Before the train reached high speed again, an enormous silvery building that stretched all the way up to the low cloud cover appeared after a curve on the tracks. Every window was framed in lightning blue light, but there wasn't a hint of advertising anywhere on the surface.

"What's that building?" I asked.

"Development," Romeo said. "Where they come up with new versions of us."

"What company?" I asked.

"*The* company," Kino said, voice dark and eyes fixed narrowly on the building as we rounded the curve. "Ecstatic Entertainment Empire. The only company making pleasure models. They own the Intox manufacturers and most of the Cozies and all the Pleasure houses. They basically *are* Bandalier."

I frowned. There was only one company for all of Bandalier? And Bandalier was the biggest pleasure planet in the galaxy. Which meant whoever that CEO was, they all but owned the planet. And that meant they owned Avan-8's deed too. No wonder he was having such a hard time buying it back, if every repair put him further in debt with the same company.

"How long do we have before your next heatburn?" Kino asked as we neared the junkyard station.

I shrugged, rising with them on either side of me. "There's

no telling. But we'll have time to get back to the cozy when it does. I'd rather not make a public thing out of it."

"It's better that way," Kino said, sharing a look with Romeo. "There are those who wouldn't want to leave a Dendärys to enjoy her heat with androids."

"Back home there are people who try to mate the females *before* a heat even comes in," I said, frowning. "They can all eat dicks as far as I'm concerned."

Kino barked out a laugh, hands wrapping around my hips to steady me as we walked to the doors. The rubble was rising like mountains, the outlines foggy against the thick reddened cloud cover over head.

"Do you ever see the *sky* on Bandalier?" I asked as the train started to slow.

"The smog *is* the sky on Bandalier," Kino said, frowning with me.

"How are we going to find anything in that mess?" Romeo asked, nose wrinkling at the sight of the refuse rising up against the invisible electric wall of the Junkyard gate, a dense curtain of trash.

"It's more organized than it looks," I promised. "And I've got a scanner that should do a little leg work for us. Come on."

I led my way to the door, pulling the collar of my shirt high up over my nose. I hoped for their sake that androids didn't have a sense of smell or that they could turn it off. Even through my shield the wave of sour and musk and metal and grease and rot hit me straight in the gut. I huffed out the first breath I'd taken and waited for the initial nausea to pass. I'd spent enough time in junkyards to know how to survive a worse stench than this.

"Well that's just not great, is it?" Kino asked, face twisting in horror.

"Let's get in there," I said with a cheer that was only half a joke. Disgusting and unappetizing though it could be sometimes, I really did love my work.

"WE'RE NOT GOING to need this," Kino said, holding up the flexible socket strip and shaking it in the air, extensions swaying like arms. "No one needs this. No one ever did. It went directly into that garbage dump upon creation."

"That might be *just* the thing I need at some point," I said, defending my choice of grabbing it up upon sight. "I can think of at least eight different uses."

"Name them," Romeo said.

We were on our way back to Nuts and Bolts and my skin was already crawling, warmth sneaking up my neck and down my chest and biting at the backs of my thighs. Kino had seated himself and Romeo across from me, careful not to touch and tease. Seeing them sitting there together wasn't much easier. Even loaded up with the haul of parts I had collected, they were a beautiful contrast, Romeo's delicate perfection and Kino's aggressive handsomeness.

I crossed my legs, sighed, and shivered at the friction of my legs rubbing together and then repeated the action in the other direction, as if it might be enough. It wasn't. Kino raised an eyebrow at me. They were trying to distract me from the heat-burn with silly chatter.

"I could use it as a doorstop," I said, pulling up the first thing that came to mind.

They both stared at me with baffled expressions and I grabbed onto the ledge of the seat to keep from launching myself over into their laps.

"You could use almost anything as a doorstop," Kino said, frowning. "What do you need a doorstop for?"

"How did you know those men were unmated?" Romeo asked, changing the subject.

I blinked and Kino elbowed Romeo's side. "Don't get her started on mating *now*," he hissed.

"They weren't tattooed," I said, shrugging. Because despite

what Kino thought, mating talk did shake me out of my stupor enough to think straight.

"As far as we could see," Romeo said with a smug glance at Kino.

"You don't hide a mating tattoo," I said. "The point is that everyone sees it. It's marking territory for the female and a point of pride for the male."

"Who tattooed you?" Kino asked, nodding to the serpents and dragons that surrounded my arms.

"I did," I said, lifting my chin. "It takes some fancy machinery, I'll admit, but a Dendärys female doesn't take a tattoo from anyone else."

Romeo leaned forward and I twisted to let him look longer at the one silver and black dragon that twined around my upper left arm. "Not even your mate?" he asked.

I bristled for a moment. I didn't even *want* a mate let alone want to let one mark me permanently. But Romeo didn't know how rare that kind of exchange of trust was, he was just asking simple questions.

"Some do," I said. "Not many. It's not uncommon for a Dendärys female to leave her mate and find a new one. And I guess we're rare enough that some males count on it."

Kino was watching Romeo without any expression and I wished I could read whatever thought or process or information he was working through. Romeo tended to be constantly expressive, although that expression was often admiration or reverence. Avan-8 was the constant lack of expression. Kino seemed to fall between them, often projecting his humor and delight and even his protective habits, but just as capable of turning all of that openness off when he wanted.

"We're almost back to the central city," Romeo said, eyes drifting away from my skin and out the window to where the cloud cover was becoming luminescent overhead, shining and mirroring the wild colors of the city below.

"You'll make it back," Kino assured me and I realized I'd been sliding my hands between my legs.

I clamped them back onto the edge of the seat and held Kino's stare. "What do I get when I do?"

"Whatever you want," Romeo said, sweeter than sinful, but that was its own kind of lure for me apparently. I wanted to reward him with affection and continue until he had me back on my belly, sliding in and-

"You get us," Kino answered, catching my attention again. He'd thrown everything I collected at the junkyard into a bag and strapped it to his back, leaning forward on the bench. His legs were spread wide, the outline of his cock clear in the crotch of his pants, taunting me with the memory of how full I'd felt while he was buried inside me.

"Both of you?" I rocked a little in my seat at the thought, wondering how the contrast of gentleness and force would play out.

"If that's what you want, Cocheana," Kino said, grin growing.

Romeo's hands twitched in my direction and then settled again, his eyes brightening as he looked out the window and found us nearly back again.

"Definitely what I want," I said, swallowing hard. I just needed us to make it back to the house before we started.

NINE
GLOSS

THE ROUGHIE and the Lover Boy returned with Nötchka just before nightfall, running through foot traffic in the district as I stretched across the doorway of the Cozy. KɪNo was carrying the little Dendärys woman, thick arms wrapped under her full hips. She was wiggling against his chest and I thought at first she was trying to get down, with KɪNo laughing at her efforts.

No. She was trying to undress herself, and him. Flashing violet skin as she tried to ruck up her own shirt, the pink ends of her hair whipping back and forth against the base of her spine.

"Almost there, Blossom," ROM-Eo said, reaching a hand up to stroke her back.

She arched in KɪNo's arms, moaning at the touch, skin flushed a deep reddish pink. *Blossom.* It suited her, she looked like some kind of exotic bloom, lush and heavy, body turning into the sun... if the sun were two undeserving pleasure models.

"The three of you smell like garbage," I said, nose wrinkling.

"We won't trouble your delicate Sparkle senses long,

Gloss," K1No said with a laugh as Nötchka whimpered and stretched in his hold again.

They reached the door and I got a whiff of her perfume, the sweetness under the smell of the Junkyard, my systems firing wildly at the scent of her pheromones. A little closer and I'd be hard and ready to perform for her and strictly uninvited to do so.

K1No's laugh died with a glance at me, even while Nötchka nuzzled into his neck, taking nips and making small, pleading squeaks and whimpers. "We need to get her upstairs," he said.

"Why not have her right here?" I asked. "She wouldn't mind."

"She would. We promised her," ROM-Eo said, frowning and petting at her side again, nearly causing her to throw herself out of K1No's arms and into his.

"He just wants a taste of the heatburn," K1No said, shouldering past me, keeping Nötchka out of my reach.

The flavor of arousal was so strong on the air it felt like a vicious grind inside of me; the need to pin her against the nearest surface and service, let the pheromones buzz through me as I took us both apart. One little brush against her skin and I would be ready.

She whimpered, legs balling up to her chest with a cramp and K1No moved quicker, loading them together in the elevator, ROM-Eo close on their heels. They squeezed in tight, the elevator only meant for two, and Nötchka slid down K1No's chest, fitting between them, body already working in the rhythm she was craving, toes curling.

There was a bitter, metallic flavor in my head, an unfamiliar feeling and completely unrelated to Nötchka's syrupy pleasure. I needed to find a guest to entertain and shake the residue of her flavor out of my system. But looking out at the crowds on the street I knew that nothing would compare. I was built to enjoy my guest's pleasure, to share it with them, but right now I *craved* Nötchka's to an extent that felt almost selfish, something nearly opposite to my programming. I didn't want to create another's ecstasy, I wanted to chase my own.

When the elevator hit the floor again I let the front door close behind me as I rushed into the small compartment instead. Avan-8 was happy enough to whittle away at his projects in his office, almost entirely disinterested in what went on in the house as long as no one had complaints and we didn't go too long without work. Kev-1 was unlikely to leave his kitchen if no one called for him. I may not be allowed to service Nötchka but maybe I could take something for myself as long as no one caught me at it.

The elevator door sealed shut behind me and my body began to quake, cock stiffening in my pants, sensors soaking up the cloud of arousal and pheromones and release. They'd gotten her off before they even made it out of here. Or she'd managed for herself. Her flavor was as strong on my tongue as it would have been with my face buried between her thighs, a dense kind of sweetness. Blossom's nectar.

That bitterness was at the back of my throat again as I thought of those older, malfunctioning models getting to share what I wanted so badly.

The hallway upstairs was worse. They hadn't even made it down to guest room eight. The closest door, normally K1No's room, was cracked open, the bed creaking and a whispering rustle of clothes being shed. Nötchka was crying out, her voice muffled, ROM-E0 whispering romantic nonsense as K1No made a low groaning sound I'd never heard before. My chest vibrated as I crossed the hall, pressing myself against the wall by the door, a quieter version of K1No's almost animal growl.

Jealous.

That was the word, the harsh flavor in my head. A *feeling*. I was *jealous*.

"If I don't get a cock in me in the next three- ohhh!!" Nötchka made a breathy, quaking sound. Another burst of her scent flooded the room in front of me, sneaking out into the hall and leaving me taut and burning and aching, my fingers clawing at the wall as my cock throbbed.

My vision adjusted to the dark of the room without even having to think of the command. ROM-Eo held her wrists pinned to the bed, the door cutting off my view of her breasts, until she arched with a moan. KıNo's head appeared, kissing a wet trail up to her neck. I was watching Nötchka's face, the way her lip trembled as she bit down on it, her brow furrowing with a whine. It wasn't until KıNo was standing in the doorway blocking my view that I realized I had been caught. The door snapped shut and KıNo's laugh was the last thing I heard from the room.

I hated them. I needed her.

I knew of cruder, organic ways of dealing with this feeling. I reached my hand down, slipping it beneath the waistband of my shorts, wrapping my fingers around my stiff length and giving an experimental caress. Nothing. I squeezed harder, but it was only sensory data, none of the dizzying code that turned the world sideways.

This was her pleasure, not mine. I could share it with her or I could have no satisfaction.

———

I RETREATED TO THE KITCHEN, uncertain if I was imagining the sounds of Nötchka crying out for more or if her voice was really bleeding through the walls and into my ears to torture me. I suspected the latter because after an hour or more of me leaving dents on the countertop with my grip—and Kev-ı painstakingly pressing them back into place—the house went quiet again, a dull ringing lingering in my ears.

Shortly after, Nötchka came flouncing into the room, blessedly washed clean of her own aroma. She had a bag on her hip with mechanical odds and ends hanging out and she had finally taken Avan-8's old shirt off. Except now I suspected she was wearing one of K1No's that he never bothered wearing. It acted as a dress on her, belted at the waist and rising higher on her hips, revealing fingertip bruises on her hips and the faint impression of a bite mark on the back of a thigh.

"Hello! Want a snack?" Kev-1 asked her as she jumped up onto the island counter, bag clanking at her side.

"I do," she said, beaming back. I wondered if she realized yet Kev-1 had a few wires loose and then some. With a glance at me she added, "Hey, Gloss."

I unground my teeth from their clench and nodded at her. "Nötchka. Where are your paramours?"

"Resting," she said, grinning wickedly, and flipping her damp hair over her shoulder. "And it seems like I'm riding one of those upper waves so I thought I'd get some work done while I could. Any requests?"

That you let me bend you over this counter top so I can share your burn until we both collapse.

"I'd like the environs working," I said, trying to turn my speech patterns back to seduction instead of snappish. "It's difficult to make a fantasy out of a dark shabby room."

She grinned, eyes following Kev-1 as he bent over and pulled a bizarre combination of ingredients out to work with. Pickled fruits and dense breads and heady cheeses. "You got it," she said, without looking at me.

I wanted to reach out and take her by the chin, force her to look at me. I wanted her to see how much better I was than the others, prettier and brighter and better equipped to please her, please us both. I wished androids weren't prevented from self-harm because I think I would have ripped my own arm off to have her fix it. I wondered if I could trip down a flight of stairs...

She pulled a tablet out of her bag and a handful of programming discs, waggling her eyebrows at me. "Found these in a pile of stuff from an old travel agency office. Thought we could pick out some exotic planet environments along with the usual stuff. Wanna help?"

She patted at the part of the countertop that she hadn't already covered with little scraps of tech, a spot right at her side, and I jumped up without thinking. I couldn't decide if it was a relief or a disappointment there was no lingering heat-burn clinging to her. She still left a faintly sweet flavor on my sensors. I was a larger model of Sparkle, not as big as K1No or Avan or Kev-1, but broad and tall enough to scoop her up and frame myself around her. If that were something I was allowed to do. Which I wasn't.

Nötchka dropped her tablet into my lap. "Pick out five locations for us. I need to clean up a few more of these discs."

There was a water planet staring up at me from the screen, mossy islands freely floating, and I swiped. There was a time and place for humidity but never *that* much of it at once. I glanced over at the tech Nötchka had piled in her lap, a little basket made there out of K1No's shirt. Sitting on her knee, waiting for her attention, was a bright red disc with electric yellow circuitry.

"Is that an Ero-Experience chip?" I asked, uploading the image and finding the match. Ero-Experience houses had been popular on Bandalier for awhile, before my time. Virtual Reality offered a more private option for those who wanted the sexual experience without any physical company.

"I found a few while we were scrapping," she said.

"We don't have the right tech for you to use them." And if K1No and ROM-Eo were doing a lousy enough job that she wanted Ero-E over them I was going to start seriously glitching.

"I'm not going to use VR," Nötchka said with a snort, rolling her eyes at me before going back to work. "I'm just tweaking some things so I can run through them on my tablet and steal clips for your holo-screens out front. These are all back-dated enough that there shouldn't be any imaging rights issues and Avan won't have to pay for new ads."

"So you're just going to watch it later?" I asked. "Do you need help with that too?"

Nötchka set the disc on her knee, lifting her chin and meeting my eyes, hers an almost indigo-black. A small smirk appeared on her lips and then grew wider, cheeks so full I was ready for her to start laughing at me. I didn't like to be laughed at but if it meant my sensors catching her breath on my skin... well, I'd survive.

"While I appreciate the offer of *help*," she said, emphasizing the last word with a wobbling twitch of her smile, "I think that might not be the best idea given that you're off limits while I'm in heat, 'kay buddy?"

She was leaned in, chin nearly resting on my shoulder, close enough to kiss. Kissing wasn't directly against Avan-8's orders, right? I could kiss for free. Just a taste. Some Cozy Houses offered samples.

"You're awake."

That cold-wired bastard. I hated him.

Nötchka leaned forward, ducking out of kissing range, pink tips of her hair tickling along the tops of my thigh. She smiled fully at Avan-8 as he lurked in the doorway of the kitchen like some vintage horror villain.

"Come pick out some environs," she said tipping her head in our direction.

I refused to look at the other android, to be caught mooning over a guest I couldn't have. Avan-8 appeared in front of me, lifting the tablet out of my hands. He flipped through the stream of travel images with a blurry flicker of his fingers and when he turned it back to Nötchka I saw that he had already picked out a handful. That was *my* job.

"Ohh, nice choices," Nötchka said, lips parting as she zoomed in on a balcony scene of a planet with an arch of moons hanging like lamps in the sky. "I'll start loading these up for you along with a few others I found, yeah?"

Avan nodded, and if I wasn't so completely sure his face was broken and no longer made expressions I'd have said he smiled at her. "I'll add it to the favors I owe you."

Nötchka blushed softly and jumped down from the counter just as Kev-1 brought her a plate of something that looked like a sandwich in the wrong order. She shoveled her things back into her bag and carried the not-wich out of the kitchen with her, moaning at the first bite and flashing Kev-1 a grin and a thumbs up as she left. That recycling can of a droid got a thumbs up and she didn't even glance at me.

I was going to throw Avan-8 in a compactor. It was time to turn him in for scrap, if it weren't for Nötchka's recent help he'd be *completely* useless. She was repairing his entire black hole of a Cozy business *and* he was getting to savor her heatburn. He couldn't even taste her. Not like I could.

I wished I was broken.

"Is this going to be a problem?"

I turned away from the kitchen door. He'd caught me staring, and staring too long after she'd left the room. Avan-8 stood in front of me, arms braced on the counter behind him, head cocked in that glitch he'd adopted as intentional.

"Sparkle models don't have problems," I said, finally finding that confident, sinuous voice in my programming again. If only it'd reappeared while Nötchka was still in the room. "Isn't that why you purchased me?"

Kev-1 made a strange sound, something like a click and a cough, until I realized he was laughing. Avan-8 didn't laugh or smile, if anything he looked... worried, a downturn at the corner of his mouth. He hardly ever projected for us. Maybe he was relearning the habit for her sake.

"New models never have problems," Avan-8 said. "But they always invent a next model. That's when the glitches start."

I jumped off the counter and left the kitchen without answering. I didn't want to become one of them, but at the moment a glitch might be the only thing to get me what I wanted.

A giggle drifted down from the balcony on the second floor.

Nötchka.

TEN
NÖTCHKA

THE TABLET CHIMED at my feet, my work on the house forgotten in the face of Velocious playing out a spectacular battle on the screen in the 'staff room,' a spare guest room that had been transformed into a recreational space for the house. Kino had his arm draped over my body as I leaned into his side, my legs stretched down to Romeo's lap as we watched the epic together.

"You have an invitation," Romeo said, looking down at the screen of the tablet.

"An invitation?" What would I be invited to? And who on earth would be doing the inviting? My toes scrambled, trying to pick up the tablet without me having to move my position. I was too comfortable spread out over my- the droids like this.

Romeo huffed a laugh, passing me the tablet and then working his fingers into the tired arches of my feet. I hummed, pressing into the touch and swiped at the screen.

!!Midnight Masquerade Masturbation!!
Darling Miss Uumian,
You are cordially invited to-

I snorted and deleted Duchesse's invitation back to her pleasure house.

"No orgies for you, Cocheana?" Kino asked.

I reached up, linking our fingers together and let the tablet drop to my lap. I was enjoying the lull before my next heat-burn, too drowsy to concentrate on work and too comfortable to want to be in my own bed.

"Who needs an orgy when you have junkyard adventures and a threesome chaser?"

Kino snorted and Romeo blushed, taking special care with my tired heels as I purred my appreciation.

The tablet chimed again and I glanced down with a frown, a prickle of irritation at the persistent interruptions.

!!CONGRATULATIONS!!
You've WON a FREE All-You-Can-Fuck WEEKEND
At Diamond's Sparkle Resort
CLICK HERE TO RSVP

"Scam," I muttered, deleting the notification.

"You think?" Kino asked.

"No way a Sparkle resort gives out a pass like that," I said, staring hard at the epic on the screen without absorbing what was happening.

"I get the orgy, cause you don't want to bond, but at least with Sparkles..." Kino said, voice softened as Romeo stared hard at the both of us.

I shrugged. "If I had accepted it probably would have made me jump a million hoops and sign up for a bunch of subscriptions of weird ero-flashers."

I wanted to say, 'I don't need a Sparkle resort. I like it here.' But what would that mean to Kino and Romeo? What would it mean to me to admit as much? Maybe at the start of this all, before the deal with Avan-8, I would have taken the free weekend. Maybe it would have been safer than here where the droids made me covet sex for reasons other than my heat. Either way I now wanted nothing more than to continue laying curled up with these two droids.

"I'm happy here," I said, trying to sound light, easy. Uncaring.

Romeo's hands stilled for a moment on my foot, and then he very gently set it down and started the process over again on the other, a delicate smile peeking at the corner of his mouth. Kino's face was in my hair, missing the explosive finish of the episode on the screen. When his fingers clutched the strands at the nape of my neck there was answering spark of arousal, not as insistent as the start of a heatburn, but enough to make me consider twisting around for a kiss.

The thought was interrupted as Gloss stuck his head in the room. "Girl's night out just showed up. Four clients. Avan-8 is jumping in too. Come on."

The three of us on the couch tensed, my eyes falling to my lap, another notification chiming on my tablet.

"Blossom?"

I forced myself to smile at Romeo. "Go on. I'll go get my work done in my room." I turned and caught Kino's frown. "Velocious just ended, anyway."

"They're waiting," Gloss prompted.

Kino ducked down, leaving a kiss on the top of my head and Romeo's hands squeezed briefly around my ankles. I curled up, wrapping my arms around my knees and giving them room to leave.

"We'll see you later, Cocheana," Kino breathed into my hair, and then rose up from the couch.

I ignored the dull ache in my chest and flashed them both a semblance of a smile as they left with Gloss out the door. The notification flashed on my tablet again.

Spend the night with Bandalier's BEST droids
A SPECIAL OFFER JUST FOR YOU!!

I should have taken the weekend with the Sparkles. Maybe a change of scenery would shake some of the creeping feelings out of my thoughts. I was getting too comfortable at the Nuts and Bolts. I'd only come here to avoid a heatburn bond. I was becoming less and less certain that I'd succeeded in that goal.

Another invitation popped up, something along the lines of the others. Free service with androids, and I frowned at the screen. Had I accidentally triggered some kind of advertisement bait with one of the programs I was running? Or was all of Bandalier offering specials today for some reason? If I was really serious about avoiding tangled emotions while I stayed here, then I needed to take advantage of one of these deals.

I deleted the notifications and hurried to my guest room before I could pass any of the others in the hall with their clients.

It was decided. I was fully committed to being a complete idiot.

IT HAD BEEN a bad decision to comb through the Ero-Experiences alone. Worse, I was in bed. Worst of all Kino, Romeo, and even Avan-8 were busy with guests and I was soaking in a simmering possessive anger when I thought too long about that.

Which was just unacceptable. I was not allowed to be possessive over androids. The point of coming to the Cozy was to avoid...

I wasn't even going to think the words.

So instead I watched lovers on screen, moaning and clutching one another, my heatburn boiling in my bloodstream. I would notify Avan-8 if I had to, although I was craving time spent with someone who *wanted* to be with me rather than kept a tally of favors between us. I wanted to wait for Kino or Romeo to be free.

No feelings. No feelings. No feelings.

I caught the VR and clipped out a snippet of a mouth closing around a taut nipple and sucking. My breasts ached at the visual and my pussy wept. I bit my lip and uploaded the clip into the cycle that would flash over the front of the house, trying not to think about the fact that these ads would bring *more* clients to the house, more work for the droids I was feeling selfish over. I started up the video again, watching the man kiss and nip his way down the woman's stomach, tongue tracing patterns that left a wet shine on her skin.

My belly cramped and I hissed, dropping the tablet to the mattress and trying to bury my whine behind my teeth, a pained squeak escaping.

"Are you hungry?"

My chin shot up up from my knees and I found Kev-1 in my doorway wearing his usual mild smile but this time with a furrow between his eyes, a glimmer of concern.

"Hey," I said, throat tight with the subsiding ache. "Not for a snack. Sorry, Kev."

I went to curl up on the bed, tucking my head against my chest, knowing I should have Kev-1 send a quiet alert to Avan-8, but stubbornly refusing to. I didn't want to interrupt Avan-8 with a client and anyway I wanted my... Kino and Romeo.

"You need fucking."

My eyes widened, head lifting again, slower this time. Kev-1 was inside of my room now, still near the door, his eyes studying me, hands in pockets, smile flashing on and off again.

"I- yeah," I said, eyes catching on the thick build of his arms. I wondered what kind of machinery was disguised by the appearance of muscle. Androids were generally stronger than they looked and I wondered if a form like his, built to mimic muscle, was a deception or a warning. Or a promise.

"Avan-8 asks me not to do that," Kev-1 said and he took another silent step forward. "I don't like to stop."

I grinned through the next cramp of my belly, and pushed myself up on my elbows. "Yeah. Me neither," I said. Because I could at least *flirt* with Kev-1, right? I mean, he hardly seemed to get it but at least it distracted me.

Kev-1's head tilted at that. "Would you like me to find Avan-8 to assist you?"

"I'd rather you stayed and assisted me yourself," I said, heart pounding and hands clenching in the bed sheets as another cramp hit, my eyes fixed to his face

Kino had said Kev-1 lost control with guests, but that he had never hurt anyone. That was something I could relate to at the moment and anyway it was all but impossible to hurt a Dendärys female in heat. We were built for rough and frequent sex. Kev-1 would be an ideal heatburn partner. Maybe it was just projection but it seemed like he was being denied a major part of his identity by just being locked up in the kitchen. Or maybe I was just a greedy, needy Dendärys in heat, with a prime piece of masculine machinery standing in front of me.

"Are you... asking me to assist you?" Kev-1 said, glancing between the door and I. Was he weighing the power of Avan's requests over mine?

"Yes," I said, holding as still as possible, as if that might get me what I want.

You are definitely an idiot but you might be a genius.

Kev-1's easy, friendly smile reappeared and he finished his path to the bed, knees bumping into the mattress before he came to a stop. "Very well."

There was a brief second where the words sunk in, disbelief an almost audible sound in my thoughts followed quickly by relief.

I must have grown wings in that second because I *flew* off the mattress and into Kev-1's arms, tackling him back to the bed and under me. He laughed and it was a surprisingly natural sound. His hands settled on my ass, squeezing with strong fingers and pressing me down into his lap where I could feel him hardening.

I dove down for a kiss and stopped suddenly, noticing the glasses on his face that were bound to get in my way. I huffed in frustration and lifted my hand to push them out of my way. My fingers slid up the side of his face and into his golden hair as we grinned at one another, but the glasses remained.

"What the-" I tried to push them up again and then realized. A fucking hologram, permanently stuck on his face. "Why are you wearing glasses?" I asked, a smile sneaking onto my lips.

"I like to read," Kev-1 said, gaze earnest.

"You like to..." I stared open mouthed at him for a beat. "Are you supposed to be able to take those off when you want?" Kev-1 nodded and I beamed at him, reaching to scratch at the nape of his neck. "Right. Well I'll fix that for you in exchange for this round of service, yeah?"

He answered by tipping me backwards, mouth kissing a soft line down my throat, hands circling my waist. He held me with care, lips caressing in a slow, sweet path. If this was out of control, I wanted a refund. Well, no. I wanted to continue, obviously, because those kisses felt amazing, but I thought maybe everyone had been making a big deal over nothing. This was a gentle seduction, not a machine gone wild and greedy.

I pulled the shirt I'd borrowed from Kino up over my head and Kev-1's palms slid up my back to hold my shoulders. I rocked on his lap, fingers sliding through his thick hair to pull his mouth down to my breasts. He nuzzled into them eagerly, cheeks filling up with a smile as I groaned and whimpered.

"Come on, Kev-1," I said, grinding down onto his cock, denied by the fabric of his pants. "I need you."

He lifted us up, my legs wrapped around his hips, and turned us, slowly lowering me down onto the bed. His lips stroked over my breasts, kissing every inch, flicking his tongue against my nipples, but there was no savageness to him at all. I slipped my toes into the waistband of his pants and worked them down his hips to his knees before pulling him down against my center again.

His hand met mine on his cock, lining him up at my entrance, nose stroking against mine. He drove in, one long, smooth descent that left me stretching up into the touch like he held a magnetic pull to my skin.

"That's it," I sighed, already rolling beneath him.

His thrusts were light and gentle, nothing like what I'd expected, but I was too far gone to care. If he didn't chase out the heatburn I would call for Avan-8 and let him know I'd tamed his uncontrollable android in the meantime. Kev-1 leaned back onto his knees, smiling in a soft kind of amusement as I worked myself over on his cock, hips surging and pumping him inside me. His thumbs stroked over my nipples, just enough friction to make me feel it running a path down into my cunt.

"You like to watch?" I asked, reaching a hand between my legs to rub at my own clit.

Kev-1 nodded, looking up from where I was touching and into my face. "You're very pretty."

I smiled, laugh catching as I felt that first flutter on the edges. "Thanks, buddy."

"Do you like to come?" Kev-1 asked.

"I love to," I said grinning. He pinched one of my nipples between two fingers for a moment and I moaned and shuddered, release edging closer. "Do that again."

At least he follows instructions, I thought, eyes slamming shut and back bowing up into his touch as he pinched again, the stronger touch creating an echo in my center.

"How many times do you like to come?" Kev-1 asked.

I bit my lip, too busy trying to coordinate every one of the touches together to drive me over the edge. I was going to need

Avan-8 after all. I needed this harder and dirtier and under the command of someone else if I was going to break through this round.

"Tell me, Nötchka," Kev-1 said, my eyes popping open at the hard edge in his tone.

"As many times as I can," I said, breathless.

Kev-1 beamed at me, eyes warm, and then abandoned my breasts, snatching my wrists up in his hands and throwing them up behind my head. His body landed heavily against me and I cried out at the first thrust, deep and heavy, drawing stars out from behind my eyes and a wave of shuddering release from my core.

"Oh! Thank the vekking stars," I gasped as Kev-1 pinned me beneath him and fucked me with all the force and precision I'd been aching for, body grinding against mine, rhythm fast and wild.

My mouth opened but no sound came out, my whole body as taut as a bowstring as I rode out the first orgasm, all while Kev-1 pounded me right to the edge of the next. He'd found the target in my cunt and every thrust hit perfectly on center, lights bursting behind my eyes. The heatburn was wrestling with the fiery, electric repetition of his rutting and the near stinging intensity of my release.

"Don't stop," I managed, voice choked.

My legs rose up, opening myself up to him, and Kev-1's smile was wide and happy as I stared at him, still a little in shock. His nose bumped against mine again, glasses pixellating in the corner of my eyes, and then we both turned enough to make it work, lips parting for tongues to stroke. He released my wrists, holding my face to take control of the kiss, messy and wet and both of us making broken, needy sounds. The bed was starting to creak beneath us as I came again, tearing away from the kiss to clutch at Kev-1's shoulders and bury relieved sobs into his throat.

"Good girl Nötchka," Kev-1 said. "Now, more."

I laughed, breathless and delighted and stunned, as Kev-1's hands wrapped around my hips. My back skidded by inches across the mattress while he fucked me with an unending urgency, the sounds of our bodies chorusing my hiccuping breaths and cries. This is what they meant, I realized, laughing again as my smile stretched so far it hurt my cheeks. Well I didn't care. Kev-1 could carry on to his glitching system's content, I felt *amazing*, stretched and full and body singing as he pounded me through the throbbing pulse of the heatburn.

I giggled as my head fell back off the edge of the mattress, seeing the open door leading out into the hall. Kev-1's mouth landed on my breasts again, biting down hard enough to draw out a low howl from my throat as I held him in place to worry at my nipple with flicks of his tongue. My eyes fell shut again as he suckled a mark into the skin, hips still working in the same, hard, heavy beat. My shoulders drooped over the mattress and I held my breath for a moment. Then Kev-1 fitted a hand between us and rubbed hard at my clit and I came for the fourth time, body slipping down, my hair swinging loose.

I caught myself, a sweaty palm against the floor before I could hit my head, and out the door I could see Avan-8, face white behind the glass of the elevator, rising up slowly from the first floor.

Kev-1 and I slid off the bed, my shoulders taking the brunt of the fall, before Avan-8 made it out of the elevator. I whimpered as Kev-1 slid out of me, my limbs jelly-limp as he turned me over to my belly and then pushed inside of me again. My breasts were pressed to the floor as he held my hips up to take his thrusts. I braced my palms out in front of me and gathered my breath before Avan could run in.

"Don't you dare fucking stop him," I managed, gasping with every thrust as Avan skidded to a stop. "He's—ohhhhh yesssss..." I shuddered, as the heatburn shifted in me, Kev-1 satisfying the hungry edge of the fever. My forehead rested against the cool surface of the floor and I spoke directly to it rather than Avan-8 when I found my voice again. "He's perfect. Don't stop him."

"He won't stop on his own," Avan-8 said, a metallic, anxious edge in his voice.

"She hasn't had enough yet," Kev-1 said, back curving over mine, cock rubbing at the over sensitive front walls of my cunt.

I shouted gibberish praises into the floor, fingers scratching uselessly, voice choking on a repetitive cry as the burn burst and Kev-1 continued through it, even as I soaked his cock until the wetness ran down my own thighs.

"Close the door," Kev-1 said above my head.

"She's done," Avan-8 answered and I could see his shadow coming closer.

"Let him... let him keep going."

The only sound for a minute was Kev-1, still rocking inside of me, hands stroking up my chest and then down again, fingers teasing at my clit and making me shiver.

"I don't want him to stop," I said, whimpering as something almost like an orgasm but quieter left me trembling. "Stay if you want, but close the door."

When the door shut, Avan-8 was still in the room. Kev-1 lifted me from the floor, holding me tight against him, and threw us down on the bed together making me shout and squirm as his hips pushed me down against the mattress, the fabric of the sheets feeling coarse against my swollen, pleasure-roughened pussy.

"I'm going to monitor," Avan-8 said and Kev-1 and I both snorted.

He was totally going to *watch* but I didn't care. Actually, as the bed dipped on the other end, I pushed myself up onto wobbling elbows so I could look at him while Kev-1 planted his feet on the floor and spread my knees far apart. Avan's gaze was bright and almost clinical, fixed somewhere over my head as Kev-1 slammed home and I moaned, clutching at the sheets.

"How's my heart rate?" I asked grinning, hair stuck to my sweaty face, as Avan met my eyes.

"Fluctuating," Avan said, blinking.

"Maybe I need kissing," I suggested, arching my neck for Kev-1 to bend down and nuzzle there. I shuddered, eyes shutting and that not quite orgasm returning again as Kev-1 bit down on the curve of my shoulder. When I opened my eyes again, Avan's blue ones were there, Kev-1 turning me onto my side, propping my left ankle up on his shoulder, stretching me to my limit.

Avan-8 kissed me, tongue stroking in as I came in earnest. There was a hand fisted in my hair, another on a breast, another circling my clit. I gave up trying to keep track of who was where and doing what, and settled for chasing touch, my body constantly writhing toward the next sensation.

A second heatburn snuck up under all the stimulation and between the two of them I rode deliriously through it, shattering on command. Avan-8 held me in kisses until I couldn't breathe and Kev-1 was starting to release increasingly loud groans with every one of my orgasms. I was past caring, riding a new high, far above comprehension.

Somewhere in the haze, I was placed on my back on top of Avan-8, my sweaty hair wrapped around his fist, his mouth leaving sparks along my neck, with Kev-1 still pumping inside of me. His glasses were somehow fogged and his hair swung with every roll his hips.

"I've never seen you like this," Avan-8 said.

I thought he was talking to me but I was out of my own body, the only thing I could touch were the waves of pleasure coursing through my veins like I'd been drained of blood and reborn in ecstasy.

"So wet, so soft," Kev-1 said, words fracturing at the syllables. "She's perfect. Perfect."

I shuddered and Kev-1 made an animal sound, a whimper, his chest falling closer to mine, thrusts turning erratic and shallow, but still desperate, nudging anxiously inside me, driving me to another end.

"Come. Come. Come. Be a good girl."

I twisted, trying to escape even as my hands reached up to hold on to Kev-1, and I came again with a thin scream. This time, finally, Kev-1 seemed to fail in his mission. He shook on top of me, hips freezing and jerking and then freezing again, and Avan-8 reached up to hold him up, keep him from crushing me. He rolled us all to the side and Kev-1 turned into someone new again, arms wrapping limply around me, cuddling me close. His cock went immediately soft and there was a slide of wetness that followed as he fell loose from me. I was too dazed to be embarrassed, even when Avan-8 stroked gentle fingers through the mess.

"I see," he said.

Kev-1 hummed and his thumb rubbed at my cheek as he snuggled closer. There was a kiss on the back of my neck and then a wonderful, numbing, nothing.

ELEVEN
NÖTCHKA

"WHAT THE VEK HAPPENED IN HERE?"

Kino. I smiled into my pillow but couldn't convince my eyes to open.

"She's fine. Just sleeping. I'm less certain about Kev-1 at the moment."

"Huh. Well... okay."

"Is Nötchka okay?" A breathless Romeo.

"She's fine," Avan-8 and Kino chorused.

"Did she break him or fix him?" Kino asked.

I attempted a stretch and the room went quiet. I groaned at the resistance in my muscles and shivered as Avan-8 rolled me over to face the room.

"I didn't even know Dendärys *could* feel sore," I said, grinning. Kev-1 was still at my side, eyes shut behind his glasses and a blissed out smile on his face.

"You're okay though?" Romeo asked.

"I'm excellent," I assured him, drawing up my legs and feeling the dull ache with a kind of triumph. I patted the bed in front of me and then there was a pile of androids surrounding me on the mattress.

"She's perfect," Kev-1 announced, still smiling, still with his eyes closed.

"Quit faking sleep," Avan-8 told him and then a pair of bright blue eyes were shining at me.

"Hey there, buddy," I said, grinning.

"This doesn't mean you can go back into service," Avan-8 said.

"I serve Nötchka now," Kev-1 said, turning onto his back and tucking his hands underneath his head, distracting me completely from his declaration with an incredible display of engineering and design. Also, the biceps. His plating was similar to Avan-8's with a different patterning and a more golden sheen to the synthetic skin.

Around me, the androids stiffened in place and silence followed as Kev-1 and I grinned at one another.

"Can he do that?" Kino asked and my brain started skittering back through the conversation, eyes widening and smile faltering.

Had Kev-1 just told Avan-8 he belonged to me? Or just that he would... service me if he wanted to? Kino and Romeo were waiting for Avan's answer, bodies unnaturally still. Either way, I was upsetting some kind of balance in the house the longer I stayed and I needed to find a way of repairing that too before I did serious damage.

My tablet chimed before Avan-8 could speak and I slid over Kev-1 to hunt for it. He held my hips for me as I hung off the edge, hands scrabbling across the floor until they found my device.

There were a few more missing persons alerts, three women, but none of them were the one I'd seen with the Dendärys pack. Beneath the alerts was a message from *DUCHESSE*.

"I've got a job," I said re-reading the words on the screen. I'd expected another ridiculous prize or invitation but instead Duchesse had come up with an errand for me, this one even farther out on Bandalier than my trip to the Junkyards. "I should get ready."

"I'll come with you."

I was halfway out of the bed, all but straddling Kev-1, when every single android in the room made the offer. Kino and Romeo glared at Kev-1 who was beaming obliviously, and Avan-8 stared at each of his employees one at a time.

You promised Avan-8 you wouldn't be a problem for him and now look at what you've done.

"Avan," I said, finishing my escape from the bed and immediately pulling up my- Kino's shirt from the floor and sliding it over my head. "Will you come with me on this trip?"

I tried not to let Kino and Romeo's injured expressions hit me too hard in the gut. Tried and failed horribly. I was making such a mess of everything.

"Of course," Avan said, and at least he didn't give any indication of winning the argument, his blank expression offering no tease or victory to the others.

I stood, toes curling into the floor beneath me, trying to find the right words to erase the awkward silence. Instead, Gloss' face appeared in the doorway, chin lifting and eyes turning dark, lips parted. Oh shit. He was tasting what had happened in the room.

"What are you all doing in here?" he asked, perfect brow unable to furrow but twitching like it was giving it a shot. "Am I the only one working in this pit anymore?"

"I'm gonna clean up before we go," I said. Romeo caught my hand as I passed him, squeezing it once with a gentle smile on his face. Forgiven when I hadn't even found a way to apologize. The sour knot in my stomach grew more tangled.

"*The Edge of The Universe* is on later," Kino mentioned, rising up from the bed to tower in front of me. "Want me to save it till you get back?"

Nötchka, what have you done to these poor bots?

"Yes, please," I said, thinking I needed my heat to end soon or I was going to risk... I was afraid to put a word to it, but it was more than I'd meant by coming here.

"I'll make you snacks," Kev-1 announced, jumping out of the bed.

I turned quickly away and rushed into the washroom before I could get distracted by all of that.

THE TRAIN out was less companionable with Avan-8 than with my- with Kino and Romeo, but maybe that was for the best. After all I had come out to Bandalier for *work*, and while I couldn't predict my heat finally setting in after all these years, maybe I was letting myself enjoy it a little *too* much.

"What could they want you to retrieve from these parts?" Avan-8 asked, frowning out the window. "It's only waste out here."

"Waste is usually more useful than everyone realizes," I said, with a shrug. I was leaning into his side, using the excuse of looking out the window. Avan accommodated me without a glance, shifting his arm up to make room. He was dressed, looking almost organic, and I found myself missing the hints of machine that decorated him.

"Like me and the others?" Avan-8 asked, turning to me and raising an eyebrow. "Kev-1 and the others would probably be out there."

"Now *that* would be a waste," I said, nodding as my chest squeezed at the thought of Romeo being broken down to pieces, Kino's personality chip erased. I lifted my chin up to stare back at Avan-8. "You bought them before they were scrapped."

Avan-8 turned back to the window. "They only cost a handful of units."

"A handful of units you could have saved toward your own deed," I pointed out.

His face didn't so much as twitch for a long minute and then he said, "I make more money with them on hand."

"Even Kev-1?" I asked. When he didn't answer I pushed. "How many people order a sandwich during their stay?"

"Are you arguing Kev-1's usefulness?" Avan-8 asked, face transforming in small fractions from blank to that teasing edge he tried to hide.

"*Never*," I said, grinning. "I'm arguing your sentimentality."

"I'm an android," Avan-8 said, frowning.

"So is Kino, but he's funny," I said, shrugging. "And Romeo. They only meant for Lover Boys to feel love, not heartbreak."

Outside the train, the Junkyard loomed. We were getting closer to our destination.

"They bought their debt back from me years ago," Avan-8 said, watching my face as I blinked up at him, feeling a jump in the conversation but not following it yet. "They could leave," he added. "If they wanted to. If they were invited."

My brain skidded stupidly over the announcement. Kino and Romeo were free to leave Nuts and Bolts, leave Avan-8... with me.

"You haven't thought of it," Avan said with a tilt of his head. "I guarantee you they have."

"But... the Nuts and Bolts," I said, thoughts scrambling. "Your deed is..."

"I would manage. I can work again, and I have Gloss," Avan-8 said.

He was still owned by Bandalier, constantly trying to save the units to buy up his own deed and just as often having to spend them to save the Cozy house. If I left with any of the others, Avan-8 would suffer for the loss and I hated that thought.

"But it would be hard for them when you finally bonded," he continued.

"What?!" I asked and behind us another passenger coughed in surprise.

Avan-8 blinked at me. "Your mate would not want you to keep them, correct?"

I sucked in a quick breath and then shut my lips hard to resist the urge to shout. I wasn't going to take a mate. And while we were at it, I wasn't going to take Avan-8's bots either. But even if I *were*...

No. I wasn't going to take Romeo and Kino with me.

I was going to try very hard not to take them with me.

"*If* I take a mate," I said, words bitter on my tongue, "It will be one who has enough sense not to go around... you know, telling me what to do." Avan hummed next to me and I jumped up from the seat, resisting the urge to kick at his shin in irritation. I was probably more likely to injure myself that way than to do him any harm.

"We're almost to our stop," I said, moving into the aisle and heading to the door.

I could see Avan-8 reflected in the glass as I stared out, the top of my head barely reaching his shoulders as he followed and stood at my back.

"I did not mean to offend," Avan-8 said, warped reflection frowning down at my hair.

I rolled my shoulders, trying to shake out some of the tension. "I know you didn't, big guy."

"It says in the file that a heat can cause heightened temper," Avan-8 said.

"Shut up about the file before I break you down for parts," I said, hoping I sounded convincing but not sure if I wanted to glue his mouth shut or close it with a bruising kiss.

"What I do not understand, is that the choice of mate belongs to your females. Why not also the choice of profession?" Avan-8 asked.

"It is, it's just... complicated." Avan-8 raised his eyebrows at my lame answer and I sighed, scrubbing my face with my hand. "It's the structure of the culture. The women run things from the nest and the villages—organize the homes and communities. The men mine and trade. If I stayed on Dendärys and really wanted to shake things up I could be a trader but..."

"You would always have to go back there, to the nest," Avan-8 concluded for me.

I nodded. "It's not real traveling. Not like the kind I have now."

He went silent as the doors opened onto the platform. I stepped out and my nose wrinkled. The air was muggy, probably from the hot swamps north of the station, and there was a residual stink of the Junkyards drifting up from the south.

"Come on. We've got a bit of a walk."

Avan-8 followed me with soft steps out of the station and onto the road. There were box buildings up ahead, containers of forgotten storage stacked like a child's building blocks, black silhouettes against an already dark sky. There was a dim lamp flickering behind us at the station and one pulsing further down the road with a long stretch of dark road between them.

"Are you nervous?" Avan-8 asked, voice lowered as if he might avoid my irritation with an adjustment in volume.

"I don't love... being outside, actually," I said, cringing. "You know, in the open like this."

"Dendarys live in nests and clusters," Avan-8 said.

More file information, I thought. But he resisted the urge to point it out so I let it slide.

I nodded and clutched at my elbows, arms folded over my stomach. "Yep. And I live on a tiny enclosed ship. It's not so bad in the city, lots of buildings and crowds. But this is just... not for me," I said, my head whipping around at the first rustle that came from behind us. I squinted into the dark.

"Just a digging mammal," Avan-8 said. "I would defend you within my parameters if anything were to threaten us out here."

He couldn't attack an organic being but he could put himself between me and one attacking if he wanted to. When they'd designed the failsafes that prevented androids from harming organics a committee had been in charge of advocating for the AI. That was the concession; the android made the choice on whether or not to defend an organic, possibly risking harm to themselves.

"Thank you," I said, bumping my shoulder into Avan-8's side. "I would defend you too. And I came armed."

Avan-8 was quiet, eyes scanning the area around us so thoroughly that I barely flinched at the next rustle in the grass. "That was smart of you," he said. "What have we come here for?"

"There should be a disassembled Beast model in an abandoned storage unit," I said. "The lady wants me to grab the manipulator before the unit goes to the junkyard."

I counted the containers as we got closer, trying to pick out which was "the fifth to the east" as it said in the directions. I hadn't expected such a cluster, the parts assembled as if it were meant to resemble a city, rather than tidy rows. Insects buzzed in a cloud around the lamp overhead and made a dive down to my head as we got closer. Avan-8 swiped at them before they could reach me and I smiled. He was applying "threaten" pretty loosely if he was counting bugs, but I didn't mind.

"It's statistically unlikely that a Beast model would have made it this far out of the city, assembled or not," Avan-8 said. "They have the most powerful machinery of the models. When their glitches started they were almost all broken down straight away. Kino made it out because he was still structurally sound, just had a faulty personality."

"His personality is perfect," I said, pointing a finger up in Avan's face. He just raised an eyebrow. "And statistics or not, that's what I was told to come and find so here we are."

"Why didn't they send someone else?" Avan-8 asked. "How did they know you were still on planet?"

I chewed at my lip. That was a decent point. It made sense for me to keep an eye out for model material in space while I travelled but wouldn't Duchesse have people on Bandalier she could source for this without asking me?

"Maybe I'm not charging enough," I said, frowning.

Avan-8 hummed. "I know the feeling."

"You *do* have a thing for charity cases," I agreed. I pointed up at what I guessed was the correct container. "It should be in there. We can just cut through that gap."

Up close the structure turned into an abandoned city, pathways and courtyards forming in the pattern of the containers stacked together.

"There is organic activity here, Nötchka," Avan whispered, a hand landing on my shoulder, slowing my steps as we reached the dark tunnel formed by three containers. "I couldn't see it through the material of the containers."

"Critters?" I asked, keeping my own voice down.

"Hello, Cocheana."

I spun, Avan-8 moving to cover my back, and found the scarred Dendärys male grinning at me from across the courtyard, appearing out of another tunnel.

"It's good to see you again," he said. "I'm so glad you haven't left planet yet before I've savored your heat."

"Don't play with yourself while we're working, Gärys," another voice called from behind Avan-8.

"How many?" I asked.

"Three," Avan-8 said. "Two closing in. I can't act until they do."

"I know," I said, reaching behind my back to take Avan's hand in mine. He squeezed back briefly before I settled his palm against the base of my back where my stun gun was tucked into its holster, hidden beneath my shirt.

"You've been very hard to get ahold of, Cocheana," Gärys said, an obnoxious coo in his voice. As if in the history of males and females, patronizing had ever worked at drawing a woman in.

"You keep turning up where you are least wanted," I said. "My heat is covered. I'm good. I'd appreciate it if you and your friends left me and my friend alone to do our work."

"She doesn't get it," another male said, appearing on my left.

"You're here because *we're* here, bitch," said the one at my back.

Avan-8 had slid the stun gun out of my holster, fitting it into my hand, and he turned to keep an eye on the Dendärys behind us.

"I don't recommend you calling her that," Avan-8 said and I lifted my chin in response. I was jittery and I wanted badly to dart away but I felt safer with Avan-8 at my back.

"You've given us a nice run around while you've been on planet but we'll be taking you in today," Gärys said, calm smile distorting the scar over his cheek. His eyebrows lifted and his smile brightened as he added, "And look, you've brought us a Proto model on top of it. Thank you, Cochie."

"Eww. Honestly, I really hate it when you call me that," I said, nose wrinkled and hand raising the stun gun. I shot it off before he realized what I was holding and Gärys hit the ground with a noisy thump, the other two men shouting around us. "It's going to need to charge," I said to Avan-8, my eyes flicking back and forth between the men on either side of me.

"I understand," Avan-8 said.

The man on my left darted forward first and Avan shifted us, an arm around my waist, as he stepped in the path of the attack.

"Take care of the droid first! Then grab her!"

"You should run," Avan-8 said. There was a grunt, from the Dendärys, as a fist hit a dense, plated chest.

I ignored the suggestion and jumped forward at the man

charging towards me, clipping him in the jaw with my fist just before his hands wrapped around my shoulders. He threw me off to the side, all the breath rushing out of me as I hit the ground, vision spinning for a moment. The men surrounded Avan-8 who did his best to pry them off himself as they grappled blindly for a way to decommission him.

The stun gun in my hand was still in the red zone and my heart was racing too fast. I rolled over on the ground, ready to break open a container in the hopes there might be something useful inside, or at least blunt and heavy enough to serve as a weapon. In front of me lay Gärys, eyes wide and limbs stiff at his side. Peeking out from beneath his rumpled shirt was the handle of another gun. I yanked it free and studied it for a moment before recognizing the web design on the side.

"Avan! Down on the ground!" I shouted, twisting around.

He dropped at my command, his shirt tearing in the fist of one of the Dendärys, both of whom turned in my direction.

"To me!" I said, before firing the net gun. Thin, metallic web flew out of the chamber as Avan belly crawled out of the tangle of bodies just before the net draped over their heads. My stun gun beeped at my side and I switched guns as Avan rolled out of the way. The stunning blast hit the fibrous metal of the net and the men went down in a twitching pile.

Avan ran to me, hefting me off the ground in a swift, smooth motion, and then throwing me over his shoulder as he sped up into an inhuman run. He barely jostled me, even as he raced us out of the courtyard faster than I would have managed on my own feet.

"Thank you," he said, hands squeezing the backs of my thighs, a nipping heat following that I refused to acknowledge in this situation.

"Somebody's trying to fucking capture me!" I said before bursting into hysterical laughter, panic clawing its way up my throat.

TWELVE
NÖTCHKA

"I'M OKAY, I PROMISE," I said, trying to wiggle my way out of Kino's hold. He just kept readjusting his arms around me, gently fastening me to his chest and cradling me there against the vibration of his growl.

Avan-8 had turned off the holo-screens on the front of the house, ensuring we wouldn't be interrupted. I sat surrounded by the droids of the house, every one of them frowning. It felt a little like the time I'd landed myself in trouble for harassing the local repair shop, trying to learn new skills... and for pocketing a couple old tools. The town elders had sat me down and lectured me for hours on finding more appropriate and productive interests, the first of many attempts to correct my habits.

"You are bruised," Kino said, cheek brushing over the top of my head. Kev-1 and Romeo pressed in closer on either side of us, Avan-8's office couch full to the seams with artificial muscle. I rolled my eyes up to the ceiling to avoid seeing Avan-8's reaction to his employees coddling me. Even if his face was blank I would know what he was thinking and I was beginning to wonder if he wasn't a little bit right.

I might be making too much of an impression on these

droids. For that matter they were making too much of an impression on me.

"I could just as easily be bruised from all the sex," I said, huffing and giving up on escape. It was more comfortable anyways to simply relax against Kino. For as firm a chest as he had, it seemed surprisingly supportive, like he'd been built exactly for me to lean my head against. I'd had jitters all the way back to the cozy house and as embarrassing as this display was, it *was* making me feel safe again.

"You are bruised from when one of the men threw you to the ground," Avan-8 said, frowning.

I honestly couldn't tell if he was *trying* to rile the others up or if he just couldn't help being literal. I suspected he enjoyed being a shit stirrer. Kino growled until I heard a metallic clang, and bundled me closer.

I patted my hand over the firm chest where my cheek rested. "Calm down, killer, before you rattle something important out of place."

"What do they want our Nötchka for?" Kev-1 asked.

My jaw worked, brain temporarily absent as I ran over his words. The others rushed to answer.

"To enjoy her heatburn, obviously," Gloss said, pacing in the doorway, arms folded across his chest.

"To mate her and keep her," Romeo said, face falling at the thought.

"They *won't* hurt her," Kino snarled.

Avan-8 looked at me from his desk chair, raising an eyebrow as if to say 'See who I've been dealing with this whole time?'

"It sounded to me like they were taking orders from someone," I said.

Avan-8 hummed as Kino rumbled. "Yes. The premise of sending you out to that location seemed designed for the kidnap," Avan said.

"You think Duchesse was setting a trap for me," I said. It had occurred to me too, although I couldn't imagine *why*.

Kino stiffened and all together the five androids said, "Duchesse?"

"My customer," I said as Avan-8 spun his seat to face his holo screen. "I came to Bandalier when she put a bid in for scrap I found in the outer rings."

"Nötchka, is this the woman?" Avan-8 asked drawing up a picture of Duchesse, probably a few years earlier before she became so enamored with adding lights to her hair and skin.

"Yeah!" I said, trying to lean forward before being pulled firmly back again.

"That's *the* Duchesse. Duchesse of Bandalier," Romeo said, eyes wide and focused on the screen.

"She owns Ecstatic Entertainment Empire. Which owns more than half the planet," Gloss said, staring at me.

"EEE is the company that builds all of us," Kino added, fingers stroking the back of my neck. "And builds all the pleasure houses."

"The invitations to all the parties and the free Sparkle Resort," I said, pieces falling into place. "That was her, trying to get to me."

Gloss let out a dramatic gasp. "You got invited to a Sparkle Resort and you didn't *go*?"

"Nötchka," Avan-8 said, his chair sliding across the floor until his knees bumped against Kino's. "What did you sell to her when you arrived on planet?"

"A Proto model chip," I said, watching Avan frown and tilt his head.

"Maybe they just want her so they can test a new model on her," Gloss suggested.

"If they wanted to do that, they could have just asked," I said. "For that matter wouldn't there be hundreds of women in the city alone who would volunteer for that job?"

"But you have the heatburn," he said.

"Gloss you're the only one obsessed with her heatburn," Kino snapped.

"I'm the only who hasn't felt it yet," Gloss muttered under his breath.

I ignored them both and watched Avan-8. "It has something to do with the pack," I said. "She has them working for her for a reason. Collecting women, like the one on the train," I added, glancing at Kino and Romeo.

"How much did she pay for the chip?" Kev-1 asked.

"One-eighty," I said, and his face went still in surprise. "I only asked for sixty."

"They're only worth forty," Avan-8 said, frown deepening.

"What could be on a proto chip?" Romeo asked. "Did you scan the serial?"

"For my own records, but it wasn't listed in the sale," I said. "She bought it without knowing what specific droid it would have been from."

"Please don't tell me we're participating in a wild conspiracy theory now," Gloss said, body drooping against the doorway, in a sulk after being ignored. "Nobody is interested in Proto models."

"I am," I said, nudging Kev-1 with my toe and making him beam. "Either she's hunting for a specific chip and is willing to buy up any she can find while searching or..." I trailed off, catching Avan's eye.

"Or what she's looking for is in all of us," Avan-8 said. "You should study me."

"And me," Kev-1 said.

"Why don't I just study the chip off my own servers?" They all stared at me and I stared right back for a moment before I realized. "Oh. Did I forget to mention that part? I uploaded the contents into a secure folder until I had time to check it out."

"That's our genius," Kino said, beaming again, at last.

"HOW'S IT GOING?" Kev-1 asked, hand patting at my leg draped over his shoulder. He was sitting in front of a couch in the staff room, on a funny old carpet designed to look like a solar system that had long since burned up. Kino and Romeo were on either side of me, pretending to be absorbed by the space epic playing on the wall in front of us, but they twitched every time Kev-1 asked me that same question.

"Decryption takes a while," I said, reaching down to pat at his hand.

"Do you want sex?" he asked next.

I laughed and slipped my fingers into his hair. I'd found a little spot behind his ears that made him squirm when I scratched there, like some kind of soft cub from home. "I'm all set still," I said. "You really took care of business last time."

Apparently getting fucked till you couldn't see straight was the way to handle a heat. The cycle wasn't over yet, I could sense hints of it lingering in my body, but it seemed satisfied for now.

The screen in my lap flared to life, dozens of little documents popping up from the single file I'd secured, each set labelled with a collection of numbers.

"What are those?" Romeo asked, leaning into my side to watch the documents multiply. "The numbers are... almost sequential."

I hummed in agreement and opened the first. The file was enormous, miles upon miles of coding, far more intricate than the environments I'd repaired for the house. I lifted the screen up and over Kev's head putting it just an inch in front of his nose.

"What does that look like?" I asked.

"Me," Kev-1 said. "And Avan-8."

I pulled the screen back to my lap and opened the second document.

"They look the same," Kino said, reaching over to scroll through the two documents at once.

I slid the files down into the corner of the screen and took another look at the titles of each document.

7.15.9823

9.3.9825

35.4.9826

"Those are dates," I said. "The original file and then… drafts. Spaced apart by a year or more at first and then months, weeks, days." I scrolled down to the bottom of the drafts, from almost fifty years ago. "Stars, you guys are old. Okay." I opened the file and brought up the original. It took a minute and Romeo was the first to spot a change.

"Different," he said, pointing about a paragraph into the code. "There too."

"Pull it up on the screen so we can all look," Kino said.

The lasers firing across the screen in the epic faded, and I loaded the documents up. I scrolled slowly through as the others skimmed and found the new material. Each new file had more changes than the one before, some even replacing previous changes with new information. The final document was almost unrecognizable, adjustments in speech patterns and gestures—traits that might have been written in for allowances in time passing and vocabularies shifting—but also in interests and reactions. It was at least twice as long.

"That's not supposed to be there," Kev-1 said, pointing up at the screen. He reached back and I passed him my tablet so he could highlight the section. It was lines long and too complex for me. "That's an emotion."

"Kev, I didn't know you read code," Kino said.

"I get bored without fucking," Kev-1 said with a shrug, the light of the screen reflecting off his glasses. I ran my toes up the side of his thigh and a smile flickered on his lips for a moment.

"What emotion?" I asked.

"Not one I know," Kev-1 said. "Avan-8 has some. He tries to write them out but they come back."

"Kev, would you know the failsafe coding if you looked for it?" I asked.

He was fast, like Avan, whizzing through the information even as the symbols blurred under his fingers and on the wall in front of us.

"Here," he said, stopping abruptly. "Failsafes remain in place."

Kino leaned forward and added, "Maybe a fraction more allowance for self-defense but some designers were lenient with those codes."

"So this probably isn't about a pleasure model uprising," I said, smirking at the thought. That was a movement I could get behind.

"Those changes aren't updates to our systems," Romeo said. "They must be happening on their own."

I looked at each of them. "Is that not normal? To adapt over time?"

"We're meant to adapt," Romeo said, head swaying side to side as he thought over his words. "But only within certain predetermined parameters. These changes ignore the parameters."

"What I don't understand is what this has to do with them trying to kidnap Nötchka," Kino said, glaring up at the code.

I shrugged. "Maybe they aren't connected." The men all glanced at me so I added, "I never told Duchesse or anyone else that I saved this information. And she had me on the line to collect more of it for her if she wanted me to, so chances are this is about something else. Something she wants more than these files."

"Well you're not running any more errands for her," Kino said, a tinny edge in his voice.

I opened my mouth to argue, hackles raised at the order

and then shut it again. Was I really about to argue my right to work for the woman who tried to have me kidnapped?

"Obviously," I said, raising an eyebrow at Kino. He didn't look very repentant but I'd tackle that later when we were alone. "But that doesn't mean I don't want to know what's going on."

"She's not going to stop," Romeo said, voice soft. His eyes caught mine as I turned to him, an aching worry written in his pursed lips. "Especially now that you've escaped an attempt you can trace back to her."

I slipped my fingers into his and held his hand with both of mine, leaning into his side. "I'll be careful. I promise."

THIRTEEN

ROM-E0

I KNEW before Avan-8 spoke the words. I saw the woman walking up the path to our door, face drawn with a nervous anxiety, eyes a little red and tired. It'd been years since I'd seen one of them, ever since my eyes had given up, but I remembered the look. I loved the women that came to see me, not just because I was designed to. I understood them. I was the same as them.

Heartbroken from unreciprocated feelings. Needing affection, reassurance, touch. Wanting to feel desired and adored. I knew what the women craved and knew exactly how to apply the remedy.

This was the first moment where I was disappointed to see a client walking up that path.

"Room five for you," Avan-8 said but he stood in front of me, blocking my way.

I nodded, moving to pass him. He looked as if he were ready to stop me, mouth parting to speaking and then shutting again with a click. Avan-8 shook his head and stepped aside, returning to his office as I made my way upstairs.

Nötchka was in her room with Kev-1, studying his code or fooling around, who knew. My feet wanted to walk straight to her door, pretend she was my client, pretend it wasn't about service at all. Make love to her like she asked me to. I shivered at the thought of her lips against my ear, praising me.

But I stopped in front of room five and went inside.

The woman sat on the bed, eyes flicking up to me as I entered before falling down to her hands again as they twisted on her lap. She was lovely, older with a shaved head, raised markings running over her scalp and down her neck to her shoulders. Her skin was pearlescent and faintly blue and her eyes were a luminescent yellow as she looked up.

I smiled, my systems warming at her nervous shyness. "Hello, I'm ROM-Eo. What can I call you?"

"Em- Emelle," she said, clearing her throat and pushing her shoulders back, forcing herself to raise her face to me.

I moved slowly, sitting down on the bed at her side, folding one leg underneath me and letting the other hang, facing her. She didn't pull away, but her eyes widened so I slowed my lean into her, one hand tracing her knee, the other soothing down her back.

"You're beautiful," she whispered.

I blushed and then quickly erased the response. I blushed violet now, Nötchka's coloring, and I couldn't explain that.

"So are you," I said, ducking down to brush a kiss over her bare shoulder, trying to ignore the way my structure seemed to resist every infinitesimal movement.

She stiffened at the touch and I relaxed away, relieved for the excuse.

"I'm not sure how far I want to go," she said in a rush.

I nodded, smiling softly. This was common and it was in my design, in my gentleness, to help them slowly find that desire. I was good at it, even when it was talking for an hour or more before we touched, even if it was touching for hours before sex. I was patient, I savored every second, grateful to be with them, not wanting the time to end.

Except now. Now the seconds were painfully long. I wanted to say 'Yes, you're right. We should stop here!'

"Everything is up to you," I said instead and Emelle's shoulders softened, her neck craning to face me.

Those vivid eyes watched me, a greedy kind of stare, and slowly she began to drift in my direction. "Do you love me?" she asked, quieter than a whisper, barely a breath.

"I-" My voice stopped altogether and we sat frozen like that for a beat, our eyes both wide, lips parted. She sucked in a breath, eyes filling up with glowing fluid before slitting shut, a little of the glow sliding down her cheek. I tried again, "I lo-" but the words choked in my throat.

"Of course not, of course not," she muttered, body sagging and turning away from me.

"Wait, Emelle, I-"

"Even a Lover Boy," she breathed.

Oh, somehow this was worse, my entire body feeling at the edge of a fritz. I'd failed my own programming, and hurt someone in the process.

"Wait," I said, risking a touch, wrapping my hands around her arms to hold her still. "I am in love."

She sucked in a breath. "Not with me."

"I fell in love... outside of my programming." I waited but Emelle didn't pull away. "You are beautiful and I..." *Say it*. I needed to say it, to tell her I would be happy to be here with her. That I wanted her.

But I had never lied before.

"Don't say it," Emelle said, a hand swiping at her cheeks. "If I wanted lies just to have a little sex I'd pay for a Sparkle Boy." She turned back to me, a little glow left on her cheeks, and studied me again, this time with narrowed eyes.

"I'm so sorry," I said. "If I'd known I would have..." I had known, hadn't I? I'd known for too long. Gotten away with the last client by never mentioning my model. So instead I repeated, "I'm sorry."

Emelle sighed, shoulders rolling. "It's fine. It's not fine, but it's fine. Does she love you too?"

"No," I said, smiling even at the thought. "She doesn't have to."

Emelle rolled her eyes, squirming out of my hands and over to the headboard of the bed, relaxing into the pillows with a huff. "She ought to. It seems rotten to have a Lover Boy *properly* in love with you if it isn't reciprocated."

I hummed a non-committal response. I'd been in love plenty of times before and it had never hurt less. I knew Nötchka would leave sooner or later. I even knew that I would likely never see her again when she did leave. It didn't change the lightness I felt when I was around her.

"I don't mind," I said facing Emelle. "I'm just happy to know her."

Emelle frowned, wrinkles at the corners of her sweet lips.

"Do you want me to find someone else-"

"No, no. Vek no. This was a bad idea to start with," Emelle said with a wave of her hands, an incandescent webbing stretching quietly between her fingers. "I suppose you've saved me another set of regrets. Tell me about her."

I blinked at her. "You want to know about...her?"

That seemed like a terrible idea, strictly against any sensible way of dealing with a woman. Lover Boy's were specifically coded not to talk about other women with clients. But Nötchka had never been a real client and poor Emelle wasn't about to be one.

She nodded at me, face waiting expectantly. "I want to know why she's worth you."

"*Worth* me?" I asked, mouth gaping. "She's worth... anyone. It's isn't- She's perfect." Emelle's face soured at that so I rushed on. "She's clever and she can fix anything. I couldn't see for years and she fixed my sight. She fixed the house up too. And she's..." My whole body felt like a hundred little signals were firing, as if Nötchka were in the room with me, making me light up.

"Oh look at your dopey face," Emelle murmured, pressing a smile away with firm lips.

"She cares for people. For strangers," I said, thinking of the woman we'd seen with the Dendärys pack. "She's been all over space and takes care of herself, all on her own, but she cares for other people."

"What a star-saint," she said, dryly. "At least you don't go straight for how pretty her face is or how soft her breasts are."

"She doesn't want me to love her," I said and Emelle blinked, mouth hanging a little loose. "But she is affectionate and... wants me. She wants me to feel pleasure as much as she wants to feel her own. And she *is* beautiful. I find everyone beautiful because everyone is beautiful. But my Blossom is made to sing to me, to make my eyes follow her, my skin wish for her."

"Oh you poor thing," Emelle whispered, eyes filling up again.

I smiled and shrugged. I would tell Nötchka, before she left. I just wanted to make sure it came out right. Not as a request but as gratitude.

"You can't be a Lover Boy model like that," Emelle said.

"No, I suppose not," I said, nodding. "Avan-8 will understand. I'll think of something."

"You'll keep my units," Emelle said. When I opened my mouth to object she raised a hand to stop me. "You will. This isn't why I came here, but I would rather believe that real love can exist again, than selfishly take an imitation of love I couldn't return."

"You'll find love again," I said. She was too lovely not to, and too kind.

"Oh, I know," she said, looking down at her lap for a moment. "My kind. The Unneallies. We produce a pheromone that induces a kind of love. But immunities build up over time and they leave. I always hope..." She shook her head, blinking away a new round of tears.

I felt a surge of affection for her. I related to the pattern, saw my own heartaches in the story. If I hadn't loved her a little before, I did now. The thing was, I had loved her, from the moment she started her walk up to the house. I was programmed to. The love from my design was just dimmer now. What I felt for Nötchka wasn't prolonged exposure to a client. It was a glitch in my system. And I loved it. Loved her.

"One will stay," I promised Emelle.

She smiled faintly and looked around the bed before meeting my gaze. "Will you hold me for a little while, ROM-Eo? As a friend."

"Of course," I said, moving to wrap her up in a hug, to tuck us down against the soft bed together.

"She does sound nice," Emelle said eventually, body tucked against mine. "I'm happy for you."

FOURTEEN

NÖTCHKA

I HELD MY BREATH, watching as the last few fractions of the file finished uploading. I was straddling Avan-8's back on my bed with him lifeless and face down in my sheets. I'd uploaded Kev-1 to a folder in my files the day before, but Avan-8 had wanted to replace his old programming with what he had written for himself. And for some insane reason he'd trusted *me* with the job.

"I am going to take it *very* personally if you don't turn on again," I whispered to the lifeless android.

The download completed and I disconnected, sliding off Avan's back to settle at his side, waiting for him to reboot. His face was turned toward me, cheek softened against the mattress in an incredibly organic touch of engineering. For once I could study him without being observed. I reached my hand out to run my fingertips across his smooth forehead, finding soft indents between his brows where he was designed to wrinkle. My finger trailed down his nose stopping at the round end when his eyes opened suddenly.

I snatched my hand back as he stared at me, blue eyes shockingly bright.

"That's not my power button," he said, just as dry as ever.

I narrowed my stare at him. "Don't tell me you spent all that time designing yourself a new personality and it's just as bad as the last one."

There was a grin, a stunningly bright, cheerful twist of his lips and flash of teeth, cheeks full. Then it was gone just as fast, only a hint of it remaining in the corners of his mouth.

"Sarcasm is one of the most complex forms of humor," he said.

My heart was still pounding from that smile and I couldn't even think of an answer.

"What did you find in my files?" he asked, propping himself up on his elbow.

"Umm." I had to roll onto my back and stare up the ceiling to shake off my stupor. "So, you, Kev-1, and the unknown droid all show significant changes on your programming. Gets more extensive over time. I set up some software to scan the files and take note of certain things and what I find most interesting is that there doesn't seem to be any overlap. You aren't making the same developments. They're always specific to you."

"What do you think that means?" Avan-8 asked.

For some reason, maybe it was another heatburn starting, his focus was drawing up a blush in my cheeks.

"I think it means that pleasure droids develop in a way that mimics organic beings over time," I said, risking a glance at his face and finding those wrinkles flexing between his brows. "Does Duchesse build other kinds of droids?"

Avan-8 shook his head and then met my eyes, eyebrows raising. "You think it's *just* pleasure models?"

"I think it's something in your specific code," I said, nodding.

He'd written in expression to his programming. I was watching every little twitch of his features, feeling as if he was suddenly harder to read than before.

"What are you thinking?" I asked after he was quiet for too long, eyes focused past me.

"I always thought our glitches were timed to new models," Avan-8 said. "Now I wonder if the new models aren't timed for these adaptations of our code."

"You were probably right," I said, rolling back to him. "They wouldn't necessarily have known much about the changes with those first new models. Those are in your data servers and probably weren't being spotted until models were recycled."

He made a sound that was somewhere between his old mechanical hum of thought and an effort at an organic 'hmm' like he was practicing the word. I folded my lips between my teeth, resisting the impulse to smile.

"I suppose this makes my own attempt at programming useless," Avan-8 said. "I used my original design so it should mutate as it had been."

I bit my lip for a moment, debating on saying anything, but I was too naturally curious. "Kev-1 said you were trying to write out an emotion."

Avan nodded. "A form of anger. To do with... with being owned. It will come back too, eventually."

"Until you own your own deed," I said, hands clenching in the bedding to control the urge to reach out and touch him. "It will happen."

He smiled, a curious asymmetrical smile that suited his face and made my chest hurt. He reached up and wrapped his hand over my neck, thumb stroking at my pulse.

"Your heatburn is starting again."

I swallowed. The touch on my neck was doing nothing to prevent the heatburn, that was for sure. "Heart rate?" I asked.

"Your temperature has risen," he said. "That's the first sign."

"It can wait," I said, although the longer we talked about it the more pressing it felt.

"It doesn't have to," he said, smile growing. "I do owe you, after all."

There was a breathless hitch in my laugh as he leaned in closer, thumb tipping my jaw up toward his mouth. "Not everything has to be about payment, Avan."

"Why not?" he asked, a new lightness in his tone that had been missing before his upload. "This is a business arrangement."

You know why this hurts, don't you, Nötchka?

But the sting of Avan's correction, a sting I didn't want to acknowledge, was quickly swept under the nudge of his mouth against mine. There was a tickling flick of his tongue against the seam of my lips and I parted them eagerly, already expecting the electric bite of his kiss. I didn't know if it was a glitch or a design specific to him but none of the others had that shock and I was becoming addicted.

His free hand tugged me closer by the front of my shirt until he was rolling over on top of me, settling his weight fully against me. I sighed into the kiss, some kind of soothing shiver running through me at the feeling of being fixed to the mattress beneath him.

"You're making it worse," I said, as he pulled back, his mouth trailing with soft sucks up my jaw to my ear.

"Worse first," he said, voice surprisingly dark in my ear. "Then better."

I squirmed beneath him and he did nothing to stop me, taking his time along my jaw and neck with nips and kisses as I rubbed my hips and breasts against him.

"What happened to making sure I didn't start cramping?" I asked, jaw tense as I tried to bring myself off with friction alone.

"You haven't started cramping," Avan-8 said, a grin in his voice, his fingers pushing my shirt up one inch at a time so that my bare skin met his, cooler and smooth against mine. "We have plenty of time."

I groaned in frustration and pulled his face back to mine, licking my way into his mouth and whimpering as I got a taste of electricity again. He worked my shirt up over my breasts, the hem scraping against my nipples and his hands molded my flesh in his grip until I tore my mouth away from his to gasp and moan. He dove down then, wrapping his lips around a nipple, suckling with a tight grip, teeth tugging playfully.

I pressed my lips between my teeth, holding back a shout as I arched into his mouth, that shocking current feeling like fire on my sensitive skin. When he released me I tried to pull him back again but he caught my hands in his.

"What do you think that would feel like on your cunt, hmm Nötchka?"

It took me a moment to find my voice. "You- you should find out. For science."

Avan-8 grinned, letting go of my hands so he could hook his thumbs into the waistband of my pants and shift them over my hips. "I made a few last minute changes to my programming. Kev-1 has genuine sexual interest," he said, lifting up a bit to slide my pants down over my knees and ankles. "I watched him with you. He found satisfaction in pleasing you. So I wrote in some details for myself."

He pushed my knees up and apart, settling his shoulders between my thighs. "I like the way you feel," he said, reaching up and squeezing his fingers into my soft flesh, making my breath come too fast in my chest. "And the sound of your voice as I please you," he added, running a finger up my slit and making me whimper. "Or tease you. I think I will like the way you taste too, but that is just a guess."

"You didn't have to do any of that," I said, watching his finger spread my wetness over my pussy.

"I wanted to," Avan-8 said. "It was already starting in my old programming. Sometimes I thought of fucking you and developed an erection. I have one now even though I am planning on you coming at least twice before I am inside you."

"Oh for stars sake, Avan!" I said, bursting into laughter. "What are you waiting for then?"

"Begging," Avan-8 answered, grinning, fingertip barely dipping inside of me.

I spent all of half a second considering refusing that request before I realized it was wasting time to think. "Please, Avan-8. Please. Make me come. I wanna come all over that stupid smile of yours," I said, grinning back at him and lifting my hips to bump at his bottom lip.

His hand smeared through my wetness, the heel of his palm grinding briefly against my clit before sliding up and pinning me back to the mattress by my stomach. He replaced his hand with his mouth, tongue immediately lapping, and fire bright sparks biting at my pussy.

"Avan! More, harder. Please! Please, please, please."

I started a chant for him, immediately rewarded when his other arm wrapped under my hips to lift me up and draw me closer to his mouth, tongue sliding up inside of me and making me claw at the sheets with a silent scream as my whole body went wild with the zipping tremors. His nose nuzzled against my clit, bumping in time with the strokes of his tongue. My hands flapped in the air and then I took my breasts in my own grip, squeezing too tight, as if the pain might ground me from the indescribable sensation of Avan's tongue fucking me with an electric current.

"Oh! Fucking stars!"

I came, my whole body trying to fly off the bed and away from Avan's mouth, but he held me fast, my back crashing back down into the sheets, whipping the breath out of my lungs. He licked all around my pussy as I came down with whimpers and sighs, skin goose-pimpled and muscles trembling.

Before I could fully catch my breath, he began his second attack. His mouth wrapped around my clit, the tip of his tongue against me and he began to hum, vibrating against me.

"No, no, no," I squeaked, body already starting to quake again, the burn of pleasure almost painful. But one of my hands was in his hair and my thighs were wrapped around his ears, squeezing tight and holding his face against me. I was more afraid of how I would feel if he stopped than I was of how horribly good it felt.

There was no trick or tease, Avan kept the vibration focused hard on my clit, never letting up, until I was so tense I thought I might shatter into pieces and the fierce, stinging ache had gone on so long I thought there was no hoping of coming. And then something crept up from beneath the pain, something sweet and deeply velvety soft, flexing in a slow pulse until it grew enormous, overtaking the pain and swallowing me under.

I was limp on the mattress, blinking away the stars in front of my eyes. Avan's face was still between my legs but there was no electric sizzle or vibrating burn, just soft lips kissing at every little remaining tremor.

"Are you still hard?" I asked, and I sounded raspy. Maybe I had been screaming after all, the sound drowned out by the rushing in my ears.

"Harder than ever," Avan said, into my oversensitive skin. "Will you come for me like you did for Kev-1? Over and over again."

"Will you fall apart like he did?" I asked. "Will it feel so good to you that you can't stand more?"

"I don't know," Avan-8 said, pushing up on his hands, rising over me like a wave. His mouth was wet and there was an answer of arousal from within me.

"Let's find out," I said and he grinned at me, the tip of his cock pressing at my opening, sliding in easily at first and then needing nudges and thrusts until I was full and panting beneath him.

"Oh," he said, brow furrowing, mouth parting. "I may have overdone it on the coding. I think... I think you feel too good."

I laughed, sweeping my sweaty hair off my face and preening at the declaration. "You've more than proven your prowess," I assured him, reaching up to stroke at his chest as he frowned at where we were joined.

He made a few experimental shifts of his hips, the lines growing deeper on his forehead. "Can you hold me less tightly?"

My smile broke into giggles and I dragged him down to lay against me, taking his face in my hands. "Fuck me until you can't any longer and if I need more I will order you to get hard again. That works, right?"

Avan-8's smile returned. "Yes. That will work. I do owe you for a few tasks now.

I tried to swallow away the sourness, the reminder that this was an exchange of goods. "I believe in you," I said wrapping my legs around his waist and bringing his face to mine to keep him from reminding me that our sex was only business.

FIFTEEN
NÖTCHKA

I WAS IN THE TUB, combing my fingers through fire orange bubbles that reappeared as soon as they were popped, when someone knocked on the washroom door.

"Who is it?"

"Romeo."

I popped two more bubbles, thinking. I was feeling a little raw after my time with Avan-8. Not physically. Physically I felt all soft and fuzzy at the edges. But I wasn't sure how well I could handle the emotional stretch of spending time with Romeo. I was trying *not* to have emotions.

In the end, my desire for a hug outweighed all my good sense.

"Come in."

Romeo slipped in through the doorway, a faint smile on his lips barely visible in the dim light I had set. "Room for another?"

"Sure." I sat up as he stripped and he slid into the slippery, dense bath I'd set, more soap and product than water.

His legs stretched out on either side of me and he drew me back against his chest, already warm to the touch. At first I waited for something to be said, my body tensed as if it expected a blow. But Romeo wrapped an arm around my waist and the other over my chest, content to rest in silence with me. It did the trick, the tension fizzling out of me until I felt drowsy and relaxed. His fingers played with the ends of my hair, floating in a cloud of bubbles, barely brushing my breasts.

"Will you wash my hair?" I asked.

"Of course, Blossom," Romeo said. "Lean forward."

I wrapped my arms around my knees and closed my eyes as Romeo scooped handfuls of the sudsy liquid, massaging it into my hair with careful fingers. He spent extra time on my scalp, working out aches I hadn't even realized I was suffering from until he erased them. I was humming, a grateful kind of purr, as he finished, squeezing out great handfuls of bubbles and then drawing me back to him.

"Want me to rinse you now?"

I shook my head, turning to my side and tucking my head under his chin. "Do you need to get back to work?" I asked.

Romeo was working the tangles out of my hair, not even snagging at the strands, and his fingers stilled at the question. "I told Avan-8 I don't want to service anymore."

I bumped the top of my head against his chin with how fast I sat up and I stared wide-eyed at his announcement. Romeo reached up to soothe at where I knocked my head as I asked, "You what?"

Romeo's lips twitched and he tugged a strand of hair. "You heard me."

I gaped at him. "Is... is this because of me?"

"A little," Romeo said, thumbs brushing at my cheeks. "I suppose. But it's... for the first time since my programming started to unravel, I am happy to love. And even though I know you will leave, I'm happy to know I will carry that feeling. I don't want to pretend I can replace it with someone new just because I am designed to love everyone. This is different and I don't want it to fade."

"But- but what did he say?" I asked, a flutter of panic and...

something else, something almost joyous, gathering up in my chest. "What about the house? Where will you go? Will he let you stay?"

"Blossom," Romeo said, drawing out the word, hands running over my skin to try and calm me. "I can stay as long as I want. Avan-8's... he's a friend to us. Well, Kino and Kev-1 and I. Gloss is a brat."

I snorted, surprised at this summation of the house. I rubbed my hands over my face, the soap stinging at my eyes and Romeo bundled me against his chest. I was... oh, stars, I was happy. What kind of moon-damned reaction was that? I was causing problems in the house, putting Avan's workers into a mood to quit their work and I was *happy*. I didn't want Romeo taking care of other women. It still made my blood boil to think of Kino working and I could only be grateful that Kev-1 was unfit for pretty much everyone but me.

And Avan... well. He was just business.

"I didn't want to make you worry," Romeo said.

I pressed my lips together so hard it hurt. He deserved the truth, to know that I was delighted by the news, but was that really all I could offer?

"Are you sure this is the right decision?" I asked, mumbling the words into his chest.

"Yes," Romeo said, with no hesitation. "I'm not supposed to fall in love until my time has been paid for. But I knew when I heard you. I wanted to be yours."

A shiver ran from the top of my head down to my toes, my fingers clutching at Romeo's chest as something stretched and settled at the back of my thoughts. Romeo lifted my face from his chest, looking down at me with a worried downturn of his lips.

"Are you getting cold? Let's rinse off and get under the covers," he said, lifting me up from the water and turning on the waterfall from above, letting my bath drain away. "You must be exhausted after everything that's happened today."

Now that he mentioned it I wasn't even sure what day it was. How long had it been since Kev-1 had fucked me off the bed? And everything that followed—the trip out and the near kidnapping and all the worry and studying and data downloading, felt fuzzy and distant but also like it'd happened this morning. Maybe the chaos of the week, of the entire stay on Bandalier, could explain the overwhelming wave of feelings that left my knees weak and my skin clammy and my thoughts spinning.

I let Romeo take charge of my body, hands washing away the last of the soap, till my skin was flushed and my hair was squeaky clean. He turned off the water and bundled me up in heated towels, braiding back my hair and herding me out of the bathroom and into the bed.

"Stay," I said, as he started to tuck the blankets in around me. I felt a little better to see him smile at that, and scooted out of the way, curling into his side as he settled next to me.

That thought, the feeling, flexed again inside of me as Romeo wrapped his arms around me and tugged me closer, but then exhaustion took over and let me drift to sleep.

WHEN I WOKE, I understood. This was not just a decision I was making, it was a fact that I *had* to follow through with. And instead of the frustration and resentment I expected to feel, or even resignation, there was relief. And happiness.

I sat up in bed and Romeo was there, smiling at me. He'd set the room environments to the pretty night time planet surrounded by moons and there was a pleasant, cool breeze running through the air.

"You got over six hours of sleep," he said, combing his fingers through black feathers of his hair. "That's the most yet."

"You and I need to go to my ship," I said.

"Alright." He sat up, still smiling.

I was excited, fighting a grin, and I dug around at the foot of my bed for something decent to wear until I found a nice enough shift. It was wrinkled from being stuffed in my bag but at least it was clean. Maybe not up to the usual ceremonial standards but since this would only be between Romeo and I, that was alright. I was happier to have the privacy, the moment just between the two of us.

I led him through the house, our fingers linked, relieved that no one else was out in the halls to catch us. It wasn't that I thought they would try to stop us, not even Avan, only that I wanted to savor the quiet and not spoil the surprise.

"What are we going to get?" Romeo asked as we made it downstairs.

"You'll see," I said.

"Are you kidnapping me and taking me off planet?" he asked and I glanced over my shoulder to catch him grinning.

"Would you try to stop me?"

"No," he said, beaming brighter. "That's just what Gloss always thinks you're going to do with us."

"Gloss clearly hasn't seen the size of my ship," I said. "I barely fit in it on my own."

Oh. *That* was something I would have to put some thought into. Later.

Kev-1 was in the kitchen, reading his own files on a tablet and he looked up as we entered. "Hello, do you need sex?"

"I'm good for now. Thanks, Kev," I said. "Romeo and I are just going to run an errand for a bit."

He watched us leave, and I didn't know if I was imagining the change but I thought instead of blank, his smile now looked knowing.

We escaped into the garage, my dingy little ship sitting in the dark.

"Are we going flying?" Romeo asked.

"Well... no, I wasn't planning on it. Do you want to?" I asked.

"Someday. I've never been off Bandalier. And you never really see the sky here, just the clouds."

I thought of space, of everything I had seen, all the planets I had visited. Even of the brilliant horizons back home. Romeo had never seen any of that. Neither had the others. They'd been stuck here on Bandalier, smoggy and overrun with tourists and criminals, doing the same thing over and over since they day they were turned on. I was suddenly giddy at the thought of the future, I just needed a plan of how to make it happen.

But first...

"Come on," I said, tugging Romeo up to the entrance hatch. He lifted me in and then followed as I turned lights on, checking to make sure I had the backup energy for us to just sit in the dark garage long enough. I nodded over at my bed, "Sit there while I grab what I need."

I had packed the kit at the very back of my storage, not having predicted any immediate use for it in my future. I was doing my best not to make an avalanche of collected junk in retrieving it, wondering why I thought I would need a collection of Rambuleesi toys before I needed my tattoo lasers.

"Got it!" I growled in triumph, carrying the hefty case back to my little bed where Romeo was waiting patiently.

"What are you up to, Blossom?" he asked, smiling with crinkles of humor at the corner of his eyes.

I told myself I didn't need to be nervous, Romeo had already told me what I wanted to hear. But it was one thing for him to say it, not expecting me to take him up on the offer, and another to ask if he meant it for life.

"Romeo... do you- do you have a last name?" I asked, blinking at the sudden thought. He shook his head, smile wavering so I hurried on. "Okay. Okay. Romeo, would you...

would you be one of my mates? And accept my bonding tattoo?"

I held my breath until I couldn't anymore, staring at Romeo's frozen expression. He was turning purple again, fuchsia in his cheeks.

"Nötchka," he breathed, eyes turning wide. "You- do you- you don't have to do this."

"Actually," I said, trying to smile and feeling as if my face might start to crumble with the effort, nerves too overpowering. "I do. It's... the instincts already kicked in. Like, from the beginning, really."

"But you don't want to be mated," Romeo said, a kind of frail terror written on the wobble of his lips. I reached out for his hands and he clutched at mine, grip just at the edge of painful. I didn't mind. Romeo would never hurt me, failsafes or not.

"I didn't want to be mated in the kind of dynamic common on Dendärys. I still don't," I said shrugging.

"I would never expect that," Romeo rushed to say.

"I know," I said, my smile growing stronger. "But it isn't just that. I don't want you with anyone else, just me. And I want us together for as long as possible, traveling, and scavenging, and seeing everything together. I would be lucky, *honored*, to live my life with you."

The shade of purple on his skin was now so bright he almost looked ill, but of course he didn't know that.

"You said one of," Romeo said, eyes brightening. "You mean Kino, and Kev, right?" I blushed and nodded. "Avan?" he asked.

I looked down at our hands and pursed my lips, ignoring the crashing in my heart. I shook my head "That's just business."

Romeo was silent for a moment, finally squeezing at my hands to get me to look up. "His loss," he said. His smile grew stronger with every word. "Yes. You know I am yours. I want your tattoo."

I nearly knocked the kit to the floor as I stretched across the bed to pull Romeo's face to mine for messy, urgent kisses. He lifted me closer, our teeth bumping together as we both grinned and kissed, the kit becoming sandwiched between us as our arms circled each other.

"Now," Romeo said, pulling away for a beat. "I want it now."

And, of course, for a moment I thought he meant sex. I pushed him back on the mattress and light glinted off the kit, on his stomach. Right. Tattoos. He wanted his tattoos now.

"It might hurt," I warned. "I don't know how the laser will react with your...material."

"If I start melting you'll fix me," Romeo said, wearing a boyishly bright smile.

Well, shit. I hadn't even *considered* he might melt.

"Maybe we should just do a little test first," I said, finally opening the case. All the tools looked like they were still in perfect condition.

"Do you know what you're going to draw?" Romeo asked.

"I think so," I said, setting everything up and deciding that my position now, straddling his waist, wasn't going to work. I scooted back and tugged him up, turning him so I had his shoulder facing me. "Any requests?" I asked.

Romeo shook his head, black hair swinging with the gesture. "I want what you choose for me."

I smiled to myself and leaned forward, kissing his shoulder. I lifted his arm until I could reach his armpit. "Tell me if I break you," I said and Romeo snorted. I made a small test spot with the laser, like a black freckle and Romeo's nose wrinkled.

"Just tickles," he said.

I ran my finger over the spot. It was a little hot to touch but the mark didn't rub away or feel like I'd done any structural damage.

"Keep an eye on your internal temperature as I work, okay?"

"Nötchka," Romeo said, quiet and I lifted my face to his, startled by the open vulnerability. "You're sure you want me?"

My breath caught in my chest. *Don't be light, he deserves to feel secure.* I leaned, pressing my lips softly to his, feeling his preternaturally long eyelashes brush my cheek like kisses. "I'm sure, from the moment I had you. From the beginning."

He kissed me back, once, before turning away, spine perfectly straight and eyes wide and expectant. "Ready," he said, adorably impatient to begin.

◻

ROMEO and I were lazing in bed together, my heatburn newly sated again. Romeo was back to admiring the pattern of gretchka blossoms—a bloom that grew around the gates of my childhood home on Dendärys—that now decorated his right shoulder.

"If he's quitting," Kino shouted from the hall, "I'm quitting too!"

The door to my bedroom burst open and Kino stood there in some kind of ridiculous glory, taking up as much space as possible, but grinning like a little boy as he did so. His grin froze as he looked at the pair of us, primarily Romeo's new tattoo.

"You- what is *that?*" he asked, pointing at my flower design.

"A bonding tattoo," I said, Romeo looking guilty and proud at the same time. My eyes widened as Kino's smile crumbled, like I'd just thrown his happiness in a trash compactor. "Do you want one?" I asked.

I'd meant to do the offer properly, not while I was naked aside from a sheet, and just out of the blue. But Kino looked so instantly devastated, like someone had just told him he was about to be recycled.

He gaped for a minute and then glared at me, lips twitching. "What kind of a proposal is that?"

Romeo gasped and I fought off my smile. "Well what kind of knock was that? You just burst in here. How do you know what I had planned?"

Kino slammed the door shut at the first pipe of Gloss asking from the hall, "What's going on?" He grinned down at me on the bed, taking slow, predatory steps to the bed.

"How in starshine do you think you're going to fit me and Romeo with you on that ship?" he asked.

"Kev-1 too," Romeo whispered.

Kino raised an eyebrow at that and I winced. "Haven't gotten that far," I admitted. "There's a few other things to take care of first. But are you in or out?"

Kino snorted and then dove down onto the bed, snatching my wrists and pinning them above my head as he nuzzled into my neck. "I am in, Cocheana," he growled into my skin, the vibration giving me shivers. "Prepare to be mated to within an inch of your life."

"Oh, *now* you act the beast," Romeo said with a roll of his eyes.

I broke into giggles that quickly turned into gasps as Kino began to thrust on top of me, rucking the sheet down out of his way so his body could grind into mine.

"Don't- don't you want the tattoo?" I asked, although my hands seemed more than happy to grab onto Kino's thick ass and hold him in place against me, my mouth opening on an 'o' of delight.

"After," Kino said, biting marks down the length of my neck. "First I will mark you up and fuck you silly. After, once you have marked me, I will fuck you again."

Romeo sighed as I moaned, Kino spreading my legs apart.

"I'm going down to keep the others occupied. The last

thing she needs is Kev-1 coming after her," he said. He patted us both in parting although I was too distracted by Kino sliding his pants down just far enough to slide his hard cock through my wet sex.

"My Cocheana," Kino growled through his teeth that clung to my throat. "My little doll. Say it."

"Yours," I promised on a moan.

SIXTEEN

K1N0

"WHY DID the astronaut break up with his girlfriend?" Nötchka murmured behind me. She'd been focusing hard on the tattoos running up my arms, silly cartoon references to terrible jokes. I loved them.

"She did not clean her hair out of the shower drain," I said, grinning. That was something I heard men complain about a lot when I worked in the Intox bars. I looked forward to bringing it up with Nötchka in the future. She had very long, pretty hair. I liked to grip it in my fist as I fucked her. I didn't think I'd mind cleaning the shower drain in exchange for digging my fingers through that hair.

"He needed some space," Nötchka answered, her thighs squeezing around my hips as if that could serve as punishment for my teasing. Joke was on her, I loved when her thighs squeezed me.

"Terrible delivery," I said and Nötchka's knee dug into my side. The laser stopped on my shoulder, just a faint electric sting lingering and then her body was warming my back, nose nudging along my spine.

"You're lucky I want to keep you," she said, a dark little warning in her voice that made me want to roll us both onto

149

the mattress and remind her who had left her begging just an hour ago.

Instead I reached back, finding her hand and drawing it to my front, holding it tight in mine. "I am," I said.

Nötchka sighed, a shaky sound, and relaxed against me.

"What is it, Cocheana?" I asked, squeezing her hand again and then releasing her back to her work.

"I'm happy," she said, drawing new lines on my back. I waited in the quiet for her to continue. That had not been a 'happy' sigh. Not just happy. "I *am* happy," she said again. "I'm just also... worried about what we do next. And feeling a little guilty about Avan-8."

"I am the best employee he has," I said, smiling as the boast made Nötchka laugh softly. "If you didn't have to worry about the *how*, what would we do next? Where would you take us?"

Her free hand was tracing patterns on my ribs, my sensors almost picking up a tickle from the soft touch. "On an adventure," she said.

"Like the one to the Junkyard?" I asked.

Nötchka's hands stilled for a moment before picking up again. "No, that was just an errand. We'd have a proper adventure."

"Like what? I've never had a real adventure before."

"Umm... well, okay. So, one time, I got a tip on where to find a *major* haul. Like the haul of space pirate legends. And I thought, no way is this real. It was distant, and remote, and dangerous-"

"Dangerous?" I perked up, body bristling at the thought of my Nötchka at risk.

"Well, the planet had this wild climate, right?" she said, voice picking up speed and pitch. I tuned into her vitals too and found her heart rate had increased, body remembering the excitement, the *adventure*. "It was basically a well-documented death trap."

"You were alone?"

"Oh yeah, totally alone, and pretty well prepared. Well, moderately prepared. Well, kinda. Basically the entire planet was automated and absolutely littered with viruses. Every attempt to break-in created a new virus. So I just had to write myself into the permissions software. It worked like... fifty-percent of the time? Thirty-five."

"I'm not sure I like the sound of adventures," I grumbled.

"Oh, but Kino," Nötchka purred, breath warming my back. "I'll be so much safer with you there."

My eyes narrowed. My systems warned that I was being toyed with but the rest of me wanted to preen like a Sparkle Boy with the praise.

"Did you find the treasure?" I asked.

"Nooo, I doubt it was really on that planet, if it exists at all," Nötchka said. "But I did get a lot of tech haul and made a less impressive fortune on that."

"And that's an adventure?"

"It's a kind of one," Nötchka said. "I'm not having, you know, space battles like in Velocious. Although one time I did have to track down a pirate vessel that scooped some of my haul. But they were shaking in their space suits by the time I caught up with them."

"Ah, I see. Are miniature women very frightening in space? I did not know."

"If you're not careful, you'll find out exactly how frightening I can be," Nötchka growled.

"Will you draw something very embarrassing on me?" I asked.

"No, of course not," she huffed. "It would reflect badly on me."

I laughed and Nötchka turned the laser off, shifting away from my back. "Alright. You're all done. Wanna see?"

"Very much," I said. "But first I want my ferocious mate to kiss me."

"You keep saying it like a joke," Nötchka said, crawling

around the mattress to face me. Having her on her knees did wicked things to me, my cock signaling the desire to bury itself inside her sweet pussy. I had always found fucking fun, but with Nötchka the feeling was imperative.

Her eyes were slitted with intent, dark indigo sparkling with the reflections of moons illuminating the walls.

"Is my little mate going to ravish me?" I asked, grinning.

"Keep calling me *little*," Nötchka growled, hands pushing my shoulders back into the pillows.

I laughed, letting her manhandle me down to the bed, her lovely soft legs climbing over mine like I was some great obstacle.

"Tell me what you want, my Cocheana," I said, grinning toothily up at her. "I am yours now."

"You are," she said, chin lifted high, staring down at me like I was a feast for the taking. I was happy to be. Her nails raked down my bare chest and I rolled into the touch, startled to feel it at all. She must have been using all her strength, leaving trace scratches on my skin that would settle again in an hour. "I want to ride you."

I stroked my hands up her thighs, digging my thumbs into the insides and watching her breath catch and her body shift over mine, hips searching for friction.

"Because I am your Beast?" I asked. I had never fit my model before, never felt the tangled possession and rough hunger for my clients before Nötchka. Now it appeared on a regular basis. I wondered how long I could last under her command before the need to have her clinging and bucking beneath me would take over.

Nötchka shook her head, pink tips of her hair swinging against her breasts. She bent down, quiet smile on her lips and I ran my hands up to those breasts, taking them in my grip until she was panting against my mouth.

"Because I want to watch you struggle not to seize control," she said, eyes flashing as she grinned.

I laughed. She was learning me and I loved that too. Did it all mean...?

"Do you love me, my Cocheana?" I asked.

The grin softened and so did the slit of her eyes. She brushed her lips over mine once, then again, until I was demanding more from the kiss, licking in to her mouth, hips bucking, already wanting more.

She pulled away took a deep breath, watching my face as she spoke. "I'm starting to fall in love with you. Is that alright?"

I cupped her face and drew it back to mine, a longer kiss until Nötchka was squirming on top of me, pussy wetting my cock and fingers clutching at my chest.

"If you're asking if starting to fall in love is enough for me, it's perfect," I said, pulling away and grinning at the way her eyes had dilated to black, lips swollen from my nibbling. "I think my code has started to form love for you too."

She laughed, a giddy sound, fuchsia cheeks bright and full.

"Now," I said, propping my head up on my arms and enjoying the way Nötchka's eyes traced the design of my chest and arms. "Ride me, mate."

"Oh, I see," she said with a huff, rising up on her knees and lining me up at her entrance. "You think you can be lazy on your back. Should have mated the Sparkle Boy."

I growled, and my hands flashed out, gripping her hips and holding her still as I filled her up with a slow rise of her hips, watching her breasts heave with her gasps.

"Take that back."

"Make me."

There were better reasons to enjoy the position than just being lazy. Particularly, the way Nötchka moved like a little wild thing when she found her pace and screamed my name when I lost patience and finally flipped her onto her back. We would try it again next time. Life would be fun with my little mate no matter where we ended up.

SEVENTEEN
NÖTCHKA

"CAN'T YOU JUST...PUT on shirts or something?" Gloss grumbled, walking into the staff room the next day and flopping down into an armchair.

Since I *was* wearing a shirt—Kino's—I could only assume he meant my mates. My mates. My lips curled up a little higher at the thought. Kino and Romeo were mine now.

I was spread out over their laps, still feeling lazy after their enthusiastic acceptances yesterday. Kino now had cartoon galaxies spinning up both his arms, moons with grumpy down-turned expressions orbiting around planets with sensuous female expressions. The backs of both his hands sported beaming suns that may have taken after Kino himself if someone pushed me to admit it. Zooming down one shoulder and around his other wrist were little comical spaceships.

"What are you so sour about?" Kino asked. "You just had three clients in a row. Shouldn't you be looking like our Nötchka here?"

"Hey," I said, kicking my foot backwards till it nudged at his temple.

Gloss stared at me and I resisted the urge to squirm, my eyes locked with his as my cheeks heated. I didn't know if it was because he was so pretty he made all the links in my brain just fart and give up. Or if it was because I knew for a fact that, while he'd been following the 'but don't touch' part of Avan-8's policy, he'd definitely been taking advantage of the 'you can look' start of the clause.

I almost regretted asking Kino to close the door on his watching while the others took their turns with me. If I wasn't so dead set on helping Avan take care of his debts with Bandalier I'd be seriously considering blowing the units it would cost me for one run with Gloss. Of course that wouldn't get me off planet with my mates any sooner either.

Kino's hand settled on my ass, sliding under the hem of my t-shirt. "You wanna watch again?" Kino asked, probably trying to taunt the other droid.

My legs parted at the invitation and Kino's fingers slid down to rest at my opening. He made a surprised little hum at my willingness.

Starshine, was I even *in heat* anymore? It was hard to tell when I didn't even have to wait for the burn to start before someone was there, waiting to take care of my needs.

Gloss' jaw clenched as we stared at one another, and his head almost twitched, close enough to a nod for me at that moment, when the cozy house *rattled* and the lights flickered overhead before dying completely.

"What the vek was tha-?"

Before Gloss could finish the question the house rocked again, a dangerous cracking sound following from somewhere upstairs. The lights flared above us once more, blinding me first with the flash and then again with the darkness.

"Basement!" Kev-1 shouted from the hall as Romeo and Kino lifted me up from the couch. Kino's arms wrapped around me, holding me against his chest as we rushed out of the room together. There was another BANG! from outside, this one rumbling the floor more than the frame of the house.

Avan-8 stood in the hall by the front door, silhouetted by

billowing clouds of neon glow smoke, the vapor lit from behind by the city. "Drones," he called down to us before the door slid shut in front of him. "They're circling the house. Get her down to the basement."

I wiggled down from Kino's hold and dove out of the cluster of droids who had surrounded me, dashing into the kitchen.

"Nötchka!"

"I'll be right back," I called as Kino and Romeo chased me.

"It's not safe!" Romeo said, the panic rattling his voice.

As if to prove his point there was a sound of glass shattering and a shout from the hall.

"I just need to grab something!" I called back, adrenaline flooding my veins in a familiar rush.

Kino caught up to me, but rather than scooping me up as I suspected, he simply ran along my side as I made it into the garage. The garage door was dented and there were few things that seemed to have fallen off shelves at the far end of the room, but everything else seemed fine. My ship was safe.

"If the roof comes down I can hold it off you," Kino said, making sure I caught his glare before I unlocked my ship and slid inside. The glare transformed with a flicker of excitement. "Is this an adventure?"

I flashed him a grin. "Feels kind of like it."

It only took me a minute to find my weapons and I made it out before the next blast on the house. Romeo had joined Kino by then and the others stood in the doorway. All together their eyebrows went up as my feet hit the ground, Razer Lazer guns propped up against either shoulder.

"What?" I asked. "I travel through space alone. I'm not running around *unarmed*."

"Hop on, Cocheana," Kino said, turning his back to me. "I'll be your steed and your shield."

I giggled at that and jumped, Romeo helping to lift me

onto Kino's back so that I could just see over the top of his head.

"Watch my back, honey?" I asked Romeo, shouting over the ruckus of the attack on the house.

"Gladly, Blossom."

Kino took me back through the kitchen and down the hall where some of the smoke and debris from outside was drifting in through the open front door.

"I am downloading the file on that weapon," Avan-8 said, fitting in at my left side with Kev-1 at my right. "When I have it—"

"I'll let you play too," I agreed, finishing for him. "But you don't need to worry. I'm a good shot."

A drone was near the doorway, out of sight, but buzzing flight audible even over the next blast that shook the floor. But Kino was steady with me on his back, and so were my droids around me. I took aim through the doorway, watching through the scope. When the drone made to dart past the doorway, I fired, the laser cutting a clean slice through the middle of the flyer, both halves clattering to the walkway below.

"That's my *MATE*!!" Kino shouted, voice loud and joyous, bouncing me on his back in triumph and running to the doorway.

Avan-8 didn't look surprised by Kino's exclamation. Maybe Romeo had already given him a heads up or maybe he'd guessed as much by Kino's new tattoos. Instead he lead the way out onto the lawn, Kino and the others being careful to keep me surrounded. There was a crowd gathering outside the cozy house gates, eyes wide and delighted at the display of destruction, as if they thought it was designed for their amusement.

"Shoot again!" Someone from the crowd shouted.

Did they mean me or the drones? Demolition by demand?

"There, Nötchka!" Gloss said, pointing up at the corner of the house.

A second drone was hovering by my bedroom and I aimed, balancing the gun on Kino's head as he stood stock still for me. The drone spun in the air, a red light catching sight of us and I fired immediately, at the same moment it set off an explosion on the wall of my bedroom. Rubble landed on the ground, kicking a cloud of dust as the damaged drone crashed to the ground. Through the dust, a corner of my bed appeared, leg leaning precariously from the hole in the wall.

"I can hear another one," Kev-1 warned as the crowd screamed and clapped behind us.

"I'm ready, Nötchka," Avan-8 announced, eyes electric as he scanned the area around the house. I passed him the Razer Lazer, patting at Kino's arm to let me down as Avan jogged away, weapon lifted and ready to fire.

There was another bang from the back end of the house and I winced, hoping the drone hadn't just brought the garage down on my ship.

"Hey! Hey, big guy. How much for a fuck?" A woman shouted from outside the gate.

No one answered, we were too busy waiting with bated breath for Avan-8 to come back from shooting down the last drone. A moment later a drink canister bounced off the back of my head.

"I wanna fuck!" the woman repeated, this time picking up a chorus of cheers and other voices echoing the sentiment.

"Ew," I muttered, slipping my fingers through my now sticky hair.

"Let me," Gloss said softly, coming to cover my back, fingers working through the tangles and mess.

Kino growled in irritation, his arm squeezing around my shoulders as he turned around.

"Lemme see your bot cock!" the woman giggled. She was quite pretty, actually. Tall and willowy and decked out with lights clinging to her skin, covering her nipples with illuminated pink replicas. She reminded me a little of Duchesse.

Behind her, a group of female friends laughed and clapped and rolled their eyes at their more inebriated friend.

"I'm. Married." Kino snarled at her.

I was coughing on nothing and Romeo was beaming and everyone else—in what felt like the entire world—was staring at the group of us.

"Whaaaa?" the woman slurred.

I swallowed, glancing up at Kino, and then said, "His bot cock is claimed."

Kino's snarl relaxed into a smile and he ducked down, kissing me hard on the mouth. Behind us Gloss groaned, and I tried to keep any niggling heatburn in check.

"Here comes Avan," Kev-1 said and we left the onlookers to their confusion.

Avan reappeared from around the side of the house, looking a little dusty but otherwise fine. Actually, he looked a bit like a space epic hero with that weapon propped up against his shoulder and I was digging my fingers into Kino's arm to keep from swooning or launching myself at the other droid. *Quit being insane, Nötchka.*

"I got it just before it made it off the property. It looks like they took out our displays, nearly every screen is shattered. There's a hole in the wall of the garage, but your ship is fine, Nötchka," Avan-8 said. "Let's get inside."

"I'll go get your things out of your room, Blossom," Romeo said, stroking a hand over my side. "We can all share one together now that we're married."

Avan-8's eyebrow finally raised at that particular phrasing but he didn't say anything, just stood back and let us trail ahead of them into what was left of the cozy house. I saw the numbers tallying up in my head, all the repairs this would take, all the debt Avan-8 would have to take on, and it made my stomach churn.

"Wait," I said to Romeo, linking his elbow with my arm. "Let me check out the house systems before you go upstairs.

The last thing we need is you getting stuck in the elevator." I turned to Avan. "This is because of what happened in the old container field."

"I thought so too, yes," Avan-8 said with a nod, but there was no anger on his face. "There are not many models left like me. I may have been too easy to find."

"And they saw us with her before," Kino said. "It would be easy to guess which house we all belonged to."

"I'm *so* sorry," I said, chewing at my lip as I stared at Avan.

He was still, paused in thought for a long beat and then he shrugged. "Better the house than you, Nötchka."

My whole body tipped forward a bit, fighting the urge to run down the hall and throw myself into his arms. This was Avan-8. He would probably not understand the gesture, even if I tackled him to the ground and covered him head to toe in tattoo ink. Well, maybe then. The tattoos were certainly covered in that file he loved so much. But he would not appreciate the gesture, that I was sure of. Too much like ownership, not enough like simple business.

"I'll get to work and see what I can fix," I said, squeezing through the others and running toward Avan's office.

"Gloss, can you work?" I heard Avan ask.

"*Now*, after *that*?"

"You heard the people outside. Go and see if you can find a client for us. The house needs whatever we can get at the moment."

"You're going to service?" Kev-1 asked. "I thought you didn't want—"

I closed the office door behind me before I could hear anymore, my chest squeezing, turning brittle, the cracks forming almost tangibly in the pain.

EIGHTEEN
NÖTCHKA

I HARDLY SAW Avan-8 or Gloss for the next few days. I was busy working on all the house systems and hunting for any deals I could get on structural materials and display screens. And they were... well, just *busy*. I tried not to think about it, and when that didn't work I just made sure not to be within *hearing* range.

Now that I was busy trying to work it was clear that my heat was still lingering. It kept popping up while I was studying code or haggling with vendors and it wouldn't be until the cramps started that I'd even realized. Thankfully, Kino and Romeo remained close at hand, more than happy to be of any kind of service. Even if that included Kino using his best growl on a vendor that refused to come down on his wares.

I had yet to hear from Duchesse again, which included any more kidnapping attempts or drone attacks. Which was smart of her because my Razer Lazers had plenty of charge left.

I was out on the lawn, overseeing the installation of new display panels. I hadn't exactly told Avan-8 they were coming in that day. Partly because I hadn't seen him and partly because I didn't want him to know they were purchased with what I'd made by selling a few pieces of haul I had hanging around in my ship. He didn't need to start a tally of favors he owed me. It was *my* fault the house had been attacked in the first place. I was only cleaning up my own mess.

Gloss peeked his head out of the doorway, staring at the installation before looking out at me.

"We'll have them up again soon," I told Gloss. "You won't have to go out to the gate to catch-call anymore."

Gloss swallowed, looking between me and the man at work for a moment before settling on me.

"Nötchka, I think I need your help," he whispered.

I blinked. He did look a little, well, *fragile*... for Gloss at least. His shoulders curled in and his glossy black curls were rumpled wildly, stuck out in odd directions. I wondered if someone had damaged him. If they were still in the house I'd hunt them down and—

"Please," he added, shaking me out of my daze.

"Of course," I said, walking up to him. "Do you want to go to Avan-8's office? My tools are there."

"No," he said, shaking his head quickly. "No. I- can we go to a room? I'd like to keep this...private."

I shrugged and followed him back inside. The hall was empty so we made it upstairs without anyone seeing.

From down the hall I heard a bed squeaking lightly and a feminine sigh followed by "Oh, no, can you- can you not use your tongue, though?"

I followed Gloss into his room before I could hear Avan-8's answer. Who in their right mind wouldn't want Avan-8's tongue tracing every inch of them? Speaking from experience, it was *phenomenal*. She didn't deserve that tongue and I was going to—

"I'm broken," Gloss announced, flopping backwards onto an enormous round bed in the center of the room.

I stopped, door sliding shut behind me, and suddenly looked around. Vek. Gloss' room was... luxe. I don't know if it was the environs he picked out or if the walls really *were* dressed in velvet, but the floor certainly was and I was happily squishing the fabric between my bare toes.

"You're what?" I asked, nudging a flung pillow back toward the bed. The lighting was warm and golden in the room and it even smelled nicer in here than in the rest of the house, like... sweets and perfume and a warm fire.

"Broken," Gloss moaned up at the ceiling. "Completely malfunctionary."

"That's... not a word, I think," I said. Gloss only lifted his head to glare at me, perfect cheeks pink and shining. I sighed and crossed over to the bed, biting my lip as I sank decadently into the mattress. La-de-dah. Even his vekking bed was better than ours. "Okay, what part of you is... broken? I mean... I've seen your clients leaving, they looked happy enough."

"I've been faking it," Gloss said, an arm flopping over his face. "I can't feel *anything* anymore. I'm just like the others now. Just pumping in and out and pretending to like it."

I raised my eyebrows and rolled my eyes up at the ceiling. Clearly he hadn't been in the room when I'd ridden Romeo so hard he'd ended up bucking and gasping to a collapse before I'd even finished. But okay. Sure.

"I don't even tell them I'm a Sparkle model," Gloss continued from underneath his arms, words pitiful and slow and whining. "I'm dull. And barely even good at my job anymore."

"Okay, firstly, shut up," I said, swatting at his thigh and trying not to laugh. "How long has this been going on?"

"Days," Gloss said, sitting up. "Before the drones hit the house. At first it was just... it took a little longer maybe? And then it sort of went in and out, I got distracted. But now it's just... nothing. I haven't felt an orgasm in *days*, Nötchka."

I snorted and didn't bother to hide it this time. I mean, I wanted to feel bad for him, but he was just adorably pitiful. "I'll take a look at your systems, alright?"

"Here, use my tablet," Gloss said, perking up immediately, and reaching under his bed and retrieving a tablet, smaller than mine, but perfectly useable.

"What's this for?" I asked, teasing. "Watching porn?"

"I only tried once, but it didn't work either," Gloss said, eyes wide and guilty.

I managed to stifle my laugh, hopping up on my knees to crawl behind Gloss and hooking the tablet up to his servers. He scooted back, settling his hips between mine, shoulders relaxing.

"Maybe they're coming out with new models," Gloss murmured as I started studying, pulling up some guides to compare his data against. "That's what the others said. The glitches start when the new models come. I'll be replaced and useless soon."

"Look, you won't be useless," I said, trying to find a soothing tone instead of a mocking one. "And honestly, I can't imagine not being able to feel pleasure. *Really*. I'm like you, I'm built for it. But you're wrong about the others. They may not feel it the way you feel it, or I feel it, but they definitely enjoy sex."

"No one feels it like you, Nötchka," Gloss purred, stubbled cheek leaning in my direction. "Trust me."

I blushed and went quiet, focusing. I *did* find changes, but no system failures. Instead it looked more like he'd been creating new drafts, like Avan-8 or Kev-1 or the other Proto models. His ability to translate pheromones and body signals and arousal into pleasure for himself was *still there*, but it had changed. Past my ability to read it at least.

"Hmm, okay, this is... complicated."

"Complicated?" Gloss asked, voice pitching. "How? Why? What's happened."

"Look, calm down," I said, stroking my hand over his back and shoulders, making him still beneath my touch. "We'll figure it out. Tell me how it usually happens for you."

I started to draw my hand away but then he spoke. "Keep touching me."

My fingertips settled at the top of his back, over his spine and against the nape of his neck.

"Usually, like this," he said, voice lowering again, becoming calm and hypnotic. "The woman touches me, or I touch her, and I can feel her. Even if she's nervous or not ready, I get a sense. Come closer, Nötchka."

I hesitated for a moment, there was warmth blooming in my sex, the beginning of a heatburn or just quiet arousal, but either way it was a thing I was not supposed to be feeling around Gloss.

"Please," he whispered. "Just to help."

I sighed and scooted in until my stomach and breasts were pressed to his back, my heart feeling too fast and wild in my chest.

"Yes," Gloss hissed, leaning back against me, his head tilting back, face nuzzling into my neck. I sat, frozen, trying to ignore the way he felt silky and warm against me. I could feel the air stir as he sucked in breaths and every exhale felt like a kiss on my skin. "Starshine, it's *working*. It's you, Nötchka."

"Gloss," I said. I meant it to be a warning although his name caught in my throat and came out needy. "You can't- we can't... *do* anything."

He twisted, shoulder pushing me back until I was unsteady, balancing on the heels of my hands against the mattress as he leaned in, stroking his nose down my throat. "*Nötchka*," he purred into my skin. "Oh, darling, you've fixed me."

"I haven't," I protested, but Gloss' hands were on the insides of my thighs, parting them further to make room for himself as he continued to lean in, sucking up lungfuls of me and nuzzling me like some enormous, shining, cat. "Gloss! I haven't done anything."

My back hit the mattress and Gloss loomed over me, eyes glittering like the skies at night back home.

"I can feel you, Nötchka," he said, smile small and so wicked it made me want to shy away. "You fixed me. Let me repay you."

He dipped down, lips fitting perfectly to mine, and I all but levitated off the mattress to meet the kiss, wrapping myself around him, pulling him closer. A moment later I remembered I was *bonded* and Gloss was off limits. I had cost Avan-8 enough in my time in the cozy, this really was a line I shouldn't cross.

I tugged away from the kiss but Gloss took this as an excuse to leave wet nips down the length of my neck.

"We *can't*," I said, pushing him up.

It was a mistake to think that I could resist him simply by pushing him away. Now I had to *look* at him. The beautifully bronzed skin, black curls framing his face, lips full and begging for me to bite them.

"Nötchka," he said, voice curling over my skin and right down between my legs, making me burn for him. "I knew I would fall apart if I couldn't have you. Craving you like this, for weeks, has been breaking me down. Just this once, and then I'll be better again. Let me repay you. I'll do anything, *anything* you ask me to. I want to be your fantasy."

Well, fuck.

Kino and Romeo had made it clear that I could have anything, anyone I wanted, as long as that included them. They wouldn't deny me this. And if Gloss was right... if I was the cure to his new glitch then...

"Get on your back."

Gloss rolled down to the bed so fast it left me bouncing. His hands reached down to his hips, ready to strip, an erection already pointing sky high inside of his ridiculous little shorts.

If he were mine, he'd have proper pants. Shit.

"No," I said, sitting up and stopping his hands. "Not yet. You've wanted to taste my heatburn. You can start with that."

I pulled my shift up over my head and Gloss' cheeks turned a deeper shade of pink.

"I'm going to make you feel so good," he promised, flush spreading down his neck to his perfect, pillowy chest. "You won't even remember their names."

I snorted and shook my head at him, crawling over to where he lay perfectly still, waiting for his instructions. Silly Sparkle Boy, determined to out do the others. He'd wear himself out trying. It made me smile to realize that after Gloss I'd have sampled every model of the pleasure droids. I had zero complaints all around.

I crawled up over Gloss' chest and his eyes widened as he realized what I wanted.

"Oh vekking stars, yes," he breathed, arms sliding between my thighs and pulling me closer to his face, my wet, aching pussy hovering over his mouth. He stared between my legs until I felt almost bashful and then looked up to meet my eyes. "If I... I don't want you to stop until you've had enough."

I grinned at him, shifting my knees apart until I could just slide myself against his lips, back and forth, teasing us both. "Don't worry. I won't," I said, body trembling at the petal soft touch of his bottom lip against my skin.

Gloss groaned, eyes falling shut, and then his hands wrapped over my thighs and pulled me hard against his face. Thank the stars, he didn't need to breathe because a moment later we were both moaning, my body rocking onto his mouth as his tongue fucked me with hard, quick lashes, just shallow enough to leave me grinding down for more.

A moment later I got the first taste of what a Sparkle Boy could really do as the teasing caress at my opening grew deep and searching.

"Oh! Ffffuuuck," I said, body shaking as my fingers held onto Gloss' curls like a lifeline as I rode his growing tongue. He laughed into me and I shuddered, wondering how I could pay him back for the tease.

I didn't have to worry, the heatburn was chasing up my spine with every sweeping thrust inside of me and soon Gloss was whimpering and groaning. His body was quaking beneath me and I looked over my shoulder, finding him humping his hips up at the air, like a Dendärys in her first heat. I tugged harder on his hair like it was a set or reins and lifted myself off his face, his mouth and chin shining with streaks of my arousal, eyes dilated like I had doped him.

"Nooo," he whined, "No, come back, please, I have to finish you."

"You were keeping secrets," I said, pinching his lips. His tongue, now almost snakelike, a ribbon of threatening pleasure, curled around my thumb and then retreated.

"Wait till you feel my cock," Gloss said, body rolling in a boasting preen.

"Oh I want lots of orgasms before then," I said, raising an eyebrow and releasing. "You've got work to do."

He moaned as I settled and my head fell back as his tongue swept out again, slicking against every little crease of flesh, curling around my clit before sliding back inside of me. His lips mouthed kisses, as I arched back, settling my hands on his stomach, fingertips teasing at the base of his cock. His hips bounced and I rocked against his face with the momentum. His tongue rattled inside me with moans and groans and whimpering sighs until I was echoing them up the ceiling, staring at a glittering imitation of a galaxy I'd flown through once. Soon I was rocking in my own rhythm, thighs burning as I chased release.

The first orgasm affected Gloss more than me, and he nearly sent me toppling to the mattress with his thrashing. But his arms were clamped around my waist, mouth drinking me up like a man left in the desert too long. His tongue made long sweeps, catching up every drop of me, making hungry, slurping sounds that left me blushing. His cock sagged against my hands where I had left them and his muscles loosened.

"Oh no you don't," I said, sitting up and planting my hands back into his hair, pussy rubbing against his chin. His eyes blinked in a daze up at me. "You wanted a heatburn. That was just the beginning."

He made a little whimpering sound but his hands reached up to squeeze at my ass, pulling me to his mouth again for soft kisses, the kind of affectionate pecks you gave a lover in the morning. Within a minute his eyes were widening, feeling that gaping chasm of desire at the pit of the arousal, mouth turning urgent again.

"Yes, yes, Gloss, that's it. More. We need more."

I pulled myself off him, quick enough to turn around and face his bobbing cock before he could catch me and drag me back down again. He nipped at my ass for the maneuver and then bit down hard as I freed him from his shorts, hands circling the base of him and squeezing.

"Vekking kemmrat-" he continued to curse in a variety of unfamiliar languages as I pulled the tip of him into my mouth, testing the clean and airy flavor of him.

I wiggled my hips in his direction and he yanked me back to his mouth so I could only reach him with my hands. I cursed my stupid abbreviated height. His tongue ran a circle around the tight circle off my asshole and I moaned, tugging gently along his length.

"Yess, my little darling likes that spot doesn't she." He licked long lines from clit to ass until I was limp and shivering against his stomach. Then his tongue fucked me again, the stubble of his chin scraping my clit until I came apart, watching his cock flail in the air in front of my face, begging to be tucked inside me.

I had told him I wanted to make him wait but now more than anything I wanted to watch his face as he felt me coming around that cock. I wanted to know what tricks he had other than a tongue that could do things I'd only dreamed of.

"'S better than anything I imagined," Gloss breathed into my thigh. "Hey- wait!"

I smacked his hands away, too needy to explain, as I crawled down and turned to face him.

"Now?" He asked, face twitching with a smile he could barely contain.

"Now," I agreed, bracing myself on his shoulders as he sat up.

"Oh stars, Nötchka," he sighed, as I lined him up at my entrance and sank down.

We were slippery, both of us brushed with my sweat, and our pace was broken every time we became too overwhelmed, hands clutching. I was sure I was now covered in Gloss' handprints and I only hoped the explanation I would give Avan-8 would sound more convincing to his ears than it did when I played it over in my head.

"I wanna- wanna be the best for you," Gloss grunted, hips surging up off the bed, cock drumming inside me. "Tell me how good it feels."

I laughed, thinking of how Romeo turned wild and urgent when I praised him. I shook my head at Gloss, leaning down to mumble against his lips, "Harder."

He groaned, fingers digging into my ribs, and obeyed the order so thoroughly I was shouting a string of 'yes' and 'more' and 'fuck' up at the ceiling.

"Gonna be your best. Make you gush and scream for me," he grunted, bouncing me onto his cock.

He felt so big inside of me, bigger than he had a moment ago, like he was swelling up to fill every spare hair's breadth of me. My eyes widened as I realized. That was exactly what he was doing.

"Gloss, what-" But I could barely breathe, my whole body

tightening up, pleasure coiling like a spring through every inch of me.

He pushed me backwards on the bed, my legs hooked over his arms, pinning me there as he filled me up, brow furrowed with effort, skin glittering brightly.

"Tell me," he said. "Oh vek, Nötchka, tell me- what's this- what's this feeling."

He was so full inside of me now he could barely pump in and out, settling for grinding himself against my clit. I squeezed myself around him and his throat flexed, eyes rolling back and lids fluttering shut.

"You're knotting me," I said, reaching up to pull his shoulders down, taking his face in my hands. "You're bonding me."

I kicked my legs free and wrapped them around his waist, body rolling on the bed as Gloss whimpered, eyes opening to reveal a gaze blacked out with pleasure. I clenched around his cock, forcing myself to slide up and down the length of him, just far enough to keep inside of me, making us both feel the stretch and pressure.

"Who's pleasure is this?" I said, staring down at him and making sure to hold him tight inside me.

"Yours," he moaned.

"Who's cock is in me?" I asked, my voice tight as I held off my orgasm, wanting to hear his answer.

When he didn't answer I gripped his face in my hand forcing his eyes to mine.

"Yours," he said, face twisted in ecstatic agony.

"Who do you belong to?" I asked, fingers digging frantically into his chest.

"You! Notchka, oh vek, oh fuck! Yes, yes, yes."

He rutted so deep inside of me as we came together I bowed completely off the bed, my own voice crying out with his.

"Yours, yours, yours," Gloss chanted, hips pumping wildly as the knot relaxed. I came again, a surprising burst of pleasure, ringing through me, and collapsed onto his chest with a groan and a shudder.

Well. I had really fucked that one up.

▭

"NÖTCHKA."

I scrunched my eyes shut tighter, as if that could stave off being woken up.

"Nötchka," he hissed again.

I whined and rolled over, my forehead bumping directly into Gloss' chest.

"Whha?"

"I wanted to be one of them. The ones you liked," Gloss said.

I squinted and leaned my head back against his arm, searching his face. There was something frozen and frightened in his gaze, too wide and still.

"I do like you," I said, my hand patting limply on his back. "Obviously."

"What will happen to me when the glitches start?"

I huffed and rubbed my face against Gloss' skin and he ran his fingertips down my spine.

"What do you mean?"

Gloss was quiet, just a little faint buzz from his chest that I sometimes mistook for breathing.

"Will you keep me?" he whispered. "Like the others?"

"Will you want to stay?" I asked. "When I'm older and my heats stop?"

His arms squeezed a little tighter around me. "Yes. You're... in my code now. Give me your answer."

I smiled against his chest, for once not having to fight the flood of those soft feelings chasing through me. It was too late to fight the urge to keep Gloss. He'd demanded claiming and I didn't have the strength to stop.

"Of course I'll keep you," I said, kissing his skin.

"But I won't be perfect."

I smirked. He was annoying and petty and jealous and vain. But he thought he was perfect, or at least he felt that he *should* be.

"I like imperfections," I said and he relaxed against me, cuddling closer. "I like change too. It's alright, Gloss. You're mine now."

"I am," he said, murmuring the words into the top of my head. "I already was."

I hummed my agreement as his hands stroked up and down my back, lulling me back into the fuzzy edges of sleep.

NINETEEN
NÖTCHKA

I TRIED to squirm away from the lapping tongue at my cunt, but hands held me still.

"Be my good girl," Kev-1 rumbled. "You keep having fun without me."

I huffed out a laugh, a hand flopping down into Kev-1's soft strands. "I can't again buddy."

"I know," he murmured, licking once more and then dropping a kiss on my clit. "Just taking care of you."

I relaxed again and a different set of arms twined around my waist, pulling me against a broad chest.

"Tell me I'm your favorite," Gloss mumbled in my ear, helping himself to a nibble on my lobe.

I was exhausted. So completely bone tired I was fairly sure that Gloss' ridiculous inflating-dick-turned-Dendärys-knotting had completely obliterated whatever remained of my heat. But if he kept at it with sucking on that exact spot and Kev-1 didn't get his face out from between my thighs we were gonna be in trouble all over again. I pushed them both away, finding a loose sheet on the bed and wrapping it up around me.

I peeked out from a small hole in the sheet to glare at

Gloss. "If this is going to work, you'll have to learn that every one of my mates is equal to me."

Gloss frowned for a moment as Kev-1 hunted for a loose edge in the sheet. The frown only lasted a minute before growing into a smug smile.

"Alright then, *mate*," Gloss purred, leaning in to kiss my lips in the small space I'd left around my face. "Just wait till next time. I was only acclimating this time."

I rolled my eyes but was too busy wrestling Kev-1 for the bedsheets to take the time to tell Gloss off. Let him try. I couldn't complain.

"Come out, little girl," Kev-1 said.

"No sex, buddy," I whined.

"I want my tattoo," Kev-1 said, finally pulling the sheet down over my head and shoulders, turning it into a kind of haphazard gown around my body. He was smiling and I realized I still had yet to get those ridiculous glasses off his face. I was starting to like them too much.

"Oh yes," Gloss said, perking up on the bed. "I demand mine be beautiful. Please. I mean, look at me, they'll have to do this justice."

My eyes grew wide as I looked between the pair of them, Kev-1 with his lazy smile and Gloss lounging entirely naked on the bed, hand gesturing down the length of his body. "Oh vek, what have I done? What is Avan-8 going to do? I can't just *take* all of you!"

"Well you're not leaving me *here*!" Gloss said.

The door to the room swung open and Kino and Romeo stood in the hall, their faces perfectly mirrored, eyebrows raised and faint smiles on their lips.

"Cocheana," Kino said, with a chastising tilt of his head. "What have you been up to?"

My chin wobbled and I fastened my lips tightly together, blinking away stinging tears.

"Oh, Blossom," Romeo cried out, abandoning his teasing and rushing to me. "We were only joking."

"Nicely done, Beast," Gloss said to Kino.

"Shut up, Glitter Butt."

"No, he's right," I said, whispering and swallowing down the urge to cry. I was definitely out of heat, now into the crashing phase. I was so wobbly with exhaustion and the need to sleep for a week that I was near to sobbing. "What are we going to do?"

"Bond Avan-8 too," Kev-1 suggested with a shrug.

"No," Gloss moaned.

"He doesn't want to," Romeo, Kino and I chorused. Kev-1 looked puzzled but I turned back to Romeo.

"We'll figure it out, Blossom," Romeo said, pulling me close enough to kiss my forehead, my breath exhaling in a puff onto his neck as he stroked the back of my neck. "Everything will be alright."

"I've got enough saved to buy myself from Avan-8," Gloss said. "I'll throw in a little extra and he can buy himself a new Sparkle. But you're *not* allowed to have that one. Ouch!"

Romeo shifted, so I couldn't see Kino take Gloss into a headlock, but I felt the ensuing struggle rattle the mattress beneath me.

"First I claim you guys, then the house gets attacked, now this," I said, trying to squeeze the whine out of my voice. "I've just put him in more debt. I wanted to help him get his deed back so he could be independent."

"We've all got some saved," Romeo said, pulling me into his arms. "We'll cover the house. Help him find more models."

A cracking sob broke free and I buried it against Romeo's neck. The room went quiet around me, the scuffle on the mattress dying out.

"It isn't just the money, is it?" Kino asked, uncommonly soft, arm still locked around Gloss' neck.

"Where will we live? What will we do?" My breaths were

coming in brief little gasps. "We can't fly my ship, there's no room for all of us. And we can't stay *here*, with- with him. He doesn't-"

Gloss tried to help me finish the sentence. "He doesn't want to mate you?"

I heard the 'oof' of pain that followed Kino's punch as the tears finally broke free.

"Oh, Blossom," Romeo cooed, bundling me close. "We'll find a new ship. You'll take us to see the stars and the sky, won't you?" I nodded into his chest. "Yes. We'll find a way. It will all work out. Just rest now."

I SLEPT FOR FIFTEEN HOURS, my mates taking shifts at my side, holding me close. When I woke Kev-1 had prepared a strange spread of food, but I dug into it all without a second thought, suddenly ravenous. I'd been running on arousal and sex for the past few weeks and now my body demanded recompense.

"Has- has anyone talked to Avan?" I asked Kino as he washed me off in the shower.

I had never found the act of showering especially strenuous, usually it was very relaxing, but there was something decadent about Kino taking care of all the work for me. He washed my body with a care that bordered on reverence and his hands were just as gentle and thorough as Romeo's had been while he washed my hair, always careful to keep the soap out of my eyes.

"Gloss," Kino grunted. "He just... turned over all his units." We were both quiet, privately wincing at Gloss' complete lack of tact. "But Kev said Avan's not surprised. Cocheana, are you sure-?"

"I'm positive," I said before Kino could finish the question. "He was clear."

Maybe I did need to just walk up to Avan and ask him in plain terms, but I felt so certain. He'd always made the line between us perfectly clear, even in the most heated moments. I didn't want him to reject me *outright*. Not when he'd already done so in subtler ways. I was not a glutton for punishment.

Besides, I had mates. Four. I didn't need to be greedy, right?

"Well the repairs are done and Avan's just now realizing he hasn't even seen bills," Kino continued. "I don't think you can be expected to do more."

"We can't just leave him with a brand new Sparkle Boy and a Cozy House that looks like it's been patched up from a war," I said, shrugging Kino's hands off my shoulders.

"Nötchka," Kino said in a slow, leading tone. I turned my face up into the water so I wouldn't have to see his face, smiling and all too aware. His hands cupped my hips, drawing me backwards until he was framing me entirely in his warmth. I held onto his arms as he rocked me side to side. "We have our own worries, Cocheana. How will you fly us into the sunset when your ship probably won't take off with the weight of Gloss' ego on board?"

I snorted. I suspected Kino was secretly looking forward to the opportunity of hassling Gloss for a lifetime. Also I had caught him staring at the other droid's ass—which *was* delightfully round and perky—and that was definitely something I was going to request we explore when we had the time.

"I'm going to sell my ship and the rest of my haul," I said, turning in Kino's arms to meet his dark gaze. It was a testament to how exhausted I still was that the sight of Kino dripping with sudsy water didn't distract me from all thought completely.

His brow furrowed and I thumbed soap off his cheek. "Cocheana, you buying his deed won't change how Avan-8 feels about being owned."

"I'm not going to buy his deed," I said. If I was going to

own Avan-8 it would be with him dressed in my tattoos, not my name on his deed. "I'm going to pay him back for... for everything. All of the times he... serviced me. The ones from you and Romeo too. The fact that I, you know, accidentally mated all his droids. That the display screens were ruined-"

"Nötchka-"

I waved my hands between us, cutting him off. "No, listen. I pay Avan back, set him up so that he can hire enough help to buy his own deed back within the year. And we... we scavenge the vek out of this planet. Get enough together to afford the first month's rent on a new ship. A *good* ship. A big one."

I held my breath as Kino's eyes scanned my face until he bent down, pressing a kiss to the end of my nose and then another to my forehead. "As long as we are yours, with you, we will be happy, Cocheana," Kino said.

"Don't make me cry again," I warned him.

His palm cracked noisily against my asscheek making me squeak and jump. He laughed, the sound echoing in the shower as I squirmed out of his hold.

"Better?" He asked grinning.

I rolled my eyes and turned off the water. But I did feel lighter, just for having spoken the plan out loud. It would hurt to say goodbye to my little ship, my home for the past seven years. But it would be worth it to have my mates on board with me. I'd have more room for haul too, and better security, plus more muscle and hands to help me when I went hunting on planets. I could teach them to navigate and then the next time I had a heat I would be so well taken care of it actually made me look forward to the experience.

"Better," I said, swatting a towel in Kino's direction and sharing a smile with him.

TWENTY
KEV-1

IT OCCURRED to me that Avan-8 might be better off if I reset him completely. As he was now, bogged down so thoroughly by decades worth of memory and evolving thought and worry and slow gathering resentment, he was getting stupid.

"I haven't found another single Proto model in all my searching," Avan-8 said, not turning to face me from his desk chair.

"When have you been searching?" I asked. "You've taken so many clients."

"While I serviced. Something to do."

"The clients must be so satisfied. I thought *they* were what you were supposed to be doing."

Avan-8 looked up from his screens, turning to me with a furrowed brow. "You're joking. Why?"

"You're scanning files while performing," I said. "I think most people like to be paid attention to during that time. Nötchka does."

"Nötchka is different," Avan-8 said quickly with a shrug.

"Not in that way," I said. My smile was in place and I wondered if I should be frowning like him, but he did that far too much for my taste. I preferred the smile. "Nötchka is different because you like to pay attention to her."

Nötchka was different because she wanted us, our quirks and malfunctions, not just in her bed but in her morning and over her lunch and while she was watching television. She wanted us to feel good when we made her feel good. She wanted us to be happy. Happiness was never on a priority list for any AI, the concept too tricky a struggle for most organics. Pleasure was rare enough, but I felt it in droves with the fierce woman. I liked Nötchka.

Avan-8 was still and silent for a long time. "You're saying I shouldn't do research while I service."

What an idiot. "That's part of what I am saying, yes."

Avan-8 nodded slowly. "Alright. I'll revise. What has Nötchka discovered?"

I pushed my hands into my pockets and leaned against the doorway. "She can't find any listing of available pleasure model chips but she tracked down a few people who sold them. All came to Bandalier, dealt with Duchesse. None of them dealt with capture or drones."

"She's not safe, then. She should leave the planet soon."

"She's selling her ship," I said, watching his face freeze in shock and processing.

"Why?" he asked.

"You'd have to ask her that," I said. Maybe if he did, it would end with them fucking and finally mating. I didn't understand what had taken him so long.

"It's too small for the five of you," Avan-8 said.

"It would be worse with six," I said, raising my eyebrows.

Come on, idiot. Catch up.

"Of course it would," Avan-8 said, puzzled, and turning away. "Look at this list. Low-priority disappearances. All women. Different ages. Not a single race repeated."

I crossed the room, scanning the list and loading it into my data. "They're collecting women."

What could EEE want with women? Gloss' suggestion of earlier, that they were testing a new model, seemed the most likely option, except that Nötchka had also been right. Free service by EEE's latest innovation was something hundreds of women would volunteer for.

"Tell the others," Avan-8 said. "Getting Nötchka off Bandalier should be your priority."

I agreed. It was clear they had their sights on Nötchka. "Is there a common thread amongst the species? Heightened libido?"

"It pops up for maybe a quarter of the missing cases," Avan-8 said. "A higher percentage than normal, maybe, but not a full thread."

"What authority do you call when it is the authorities behind the crime?" I asked.

Avan-8 shook his head, turning away from the screen again. "I haven't decided. I'll do more research on that too."

"As long as you aren't fucking at the same time," I said, cheerful. I would tell K1No about that later, he had the best laugh of all of us.

Avan-8 glared at me, and then his eyes caught on my arms. "What is your tattoo? It looks like code."

"It's my code during sex," I said, grinning. "Nötchka found it for me."

"It's perverse," Avan-8 said, scanning the symbols. He looked impressed.

"Yes," I said, grinning with pride.

"What's it like? Being... bonded?"

"Like being owned. And owning. But this time, with Nötchka."

His gaze was bright and distant as he considered the thought and I left the room quietly. Let him savor the thought, maybe logic would kick his systems back to rights at some point. But if he wasn't smart enough to realize he wanted

Nötchka, he didn't deserve to have her. Less for me to share, anyway.

TWENTY-ONE
NÖTCHKA

I KNEW, sooner or later, I had to face Avan-8. The cozy house wasn't really big enough to avoid him, but I did a fair job of it for a few days, mostly while catching up on sleep. I hoped when I did work up the courage to face him it would be privately.

So of course it was with each of my mates at my side, on our way to the garage.

"You're selling your ship?" Avan-8 asked, eyes sharp and bright on my face. He was in the heart of the kitchen, the new Sparkle Boy at his side.

"Hello, pretty Dendärys doll," said the Sparkle, a towering model with skin that glittered like ice and vividly green eyes, his body almost waifish with thin cords of muscle.

Gloss dived between us, finger pointed in the exotic model's face who blinked sleepily back. "*No.* You don't look at her. We are like bait to her, she can't resist us."

"He doesn't realize how wrong he is, does he?" Kino muttered into my ear and I wrestled with my grin, staring at Gloss' back. I had tattooed him with prismatic lines, the outlines of diamonds glittering across his back and chest.

"Shimmer," Avan said, looking at the new Sparkle. "Go find a client."

Shimmer's marble green eyes rolled at the order but he pushed past us with an exaggerated, slinking walk and went out to the front door to lure in someone for service.

"He's terrible, I hate him," Gloss announced to no one.

I reached up, but Romeo beat me to it, fingers rubbing my temples in soothing circles.

"We're just going to meet the buyer at the shipyard," I told Avan.

He nodded and stepped back, giving us room to pass him, but as soon as I moved forward he did too, nearly knocking into me. I craned my neck back to meet his gaze. I was really starting to wish I'd found much shorter droid models.

His eyes were vivid as I stared up at him. "May I speak with you alone?"

"Of course," I said just as Gloss answered, "No!"

Kino elbowed Gloss aside. "We'll wait here for you," he said, palm nudging me forward at my back and then patting me once on the ass with a wink.

"I'll make snacks," Kev-1 offered.

I smiled at the four of them and turned to follow Avan back to his office.

As soon as we were alone in the hall I wished I had my mates with me. Kino and Romeo were now so in tune with my moods that they picked up on my needs, usually before I'd even started processing them. Gloss was often ridiculous, but his defense of me was sincere and I was realizing that Kev-1 was more observant than any of us had given him credit for. But Avan-8 deserved my focus in this moment and it mattered to me that I give my apology without the others rushing to defend me.

"I'm *so* sorry," I said, as soon as we stepped inside the office.

Avan's eyebrows raised. "Nötchka, it's fine. That's not why I wanted to speak."

"But, I mean, even *Gloss*, and I had promised you that I wouldn't-"

"No, you hadn't," Avan said, sitting down on the couch. There was a small tear on the arm of the couch where my fingers had dug too deep while Avan-8 had been... servicing me. His hand covered the spot, thumb working at the loose threads. "We had assumed he wouldn't need your repairs. But you were too appealing. He told me he stopped functioning for anyone but you. I wasn't very surprised."

All the jittery nervousness, the need to apologize, beg forgiveness, stilled inside of me. I wrapped my arms around my waist as we stared at one another. "Why?" I asked.

Avan's head tilted and my hands clenched into fists, an attempt to control the impulse to touch him. "Gloss is very stubborn. He was determined to have you."

Not, *Because you are irresistible, Nötchka.* Not, *Because I cannot function without you either.*

Stop daydreaming, Nötchka.

"Right. Well. We'll be out of your hair soon," I said, with a jerky shrug.

His eyebrows rose, the faintest smile on his lips. "How? You are selling your ship."

"I'm looking for rentals. We'll figure it out. You don't need to worry about us cluttering up the house."

He blinked and looked around the office. "You're welcome to stay as long as you need. You know that."

"I don't want to be one of your charity cases, Avan," I said, turning away and blinking rapidly. "I'll pay you back for everything."

"That isn't necessary."

"It is!" I swung back to face him, blood buzzing, ready for an explosion of I didn't know what. All the feelings I'd sworn I wouldn't find in this house. "If you hadn't let me stay here, bargained with me I'd be-"

"Mated," Avan-8 said, lips twitching.

All the fight fell out of me with one great breath that quickly transformed into a wavering laugh. I'd fallen into the exact trap that I'd set out to avoid, but now it didn't feel like a trap at all. It was... a home, not a structure meant to contain me but one to provide support and comfort and safety. Not one of my mates would ever ask me to stay in one spot, to settle, and I could go further than ever with them at my side. On my team.

"Yeah, probably," I said, nodding and looking down to the floor. "But not to *them*. So... that means a lot to me. And I'm going to pay you back."

"Very well, Nötchka," he said, insufferably calm. "Good luck with the sale."

"Thanks," I said, wishing I didn't feel so unsatisfied with the conversation. I paused in the doorway and looked back to him. "I sort of ran over you when we came in here. What did you want to say?"

Avan-8 blinked at me for a moment and then looked down at his own lap. He waved a hand in the air. "We covered it in there somewhere. Don't worry about it."

My mates were waiting in the kitchen when I returned, Gloss spread out on the counter with his heels kicking at a loose cupboard door. Kev-1 passed me a sticky, hot to the touch, treat and I bit into it on reflex, humming my approval. It was crunchy and nutty and incredibly sweet.

"He named them nut wads," Gloss drawled to me as I chewed and Kev-1 had to pat at my back to keep me from choking.

***

"SHE SURE IS A LITTLE BEAUT," the buyer said, wrist held out to mine to transfer over the units.

I'd flown us out to the ship lot, all four of my mates huddled together, knees and elbows knocking into one another. It had really proven the point that it would be impossible for us to travel in my little ship as a group.

"She's taken," Gloss said.

"He's talking about my ship," I muttered to my mate, but I didn't shrug him off when he draped a possessive arm over my shoulder. To be honest, the man, a Junker from Gundymia, had been keeping one eye on my breasts through most of the transaction. I wasn't sure yet if it was just a lazy eye, or if he could control its focus, but I leaned into Gloss' side as my wristlet beeped.

Sold. My little baby, my ship, my *home* was sold. So many years later and she was more a product of my own creation than the actual model of ship printed on her belly. And for once since the heatburn ended I didn't blame my rising emotions on exhaustion. I was going to miss my ship.

"There we are," the man said, reaching out to shake my hand. "Pleasure doing business with you. Now I wonder, where might I find one of him for myself?" he asked, gesturing to Gloss.

"Ask for Shimmer at the Nuts and Bolts Cozy House," I said, making Gloss twitch with delight. "Come on, we should find the others."

I stopped to watch as the man wedged himself into the small hatch of my little cruiser. There was a bittersweet ache in my chest, but there was also excitement.

"I told Kev-1 to go find us a good ship to hijack," Gloss said.

And now there was worry too.

I frowned. Gloss was probably telling the truth and worse, Kev-1 was probably taking that task pretty seriously. How hard would it be to talk him out of his goal? Gloss led me in the direction of the bigger, quality ships, boasting noisily about how he'd earned an extra five-hundred units out of the sale for me just by flirting with the Junker. It *had* been an artful maneuver.

"Glitter Butt," Kino hissed, head appearing from behind the thrust motor of the ship ahead of us. "Keep your voice down. Get over here! You need to see this."

I elbowed Gloss' side before he could retaliate the insult, dragging him after me to where Kino and the others were hiding. Through a curve in the ship—a tidy little Star Skipper that had seen some excellent remodeling—there was a perfect window of space to spy on the ship across the aisle. It was the Imerial 480 with the polished tech glass wings, the one I'd drooled over with Kino weeks ago. The wings reflected the activity around the ship in a strange, warped kind of mirror.

"The pack," Romeo whispered, nodding his head in their direction.

And there they were, two of the male Dendärys, standing guard around the entrance of the Imerial as a small trail of women—all different races—marched steadily inside. Near the back of the line of women was the one with golden scales I recognized from the train.

"What are they doing?" I asked in a hush.

"I don't know, but I can tell you for sure that their heart rates are too low now," Kino answered against my ear. "I think they're drugged."

"That's a good ship," Kev-1 said and Gloss hushed him. "It is. We should steal it."

"Too many passengers," Gloss hissed back. "We want an empty ship."

"Where is Gärys?" I asked, studying the faces of the men.

"Who?" Kino whispered.

"The... the kind of leadery one," I said, rising up on my tiptoes. "He's not with them."

"Maybe he's inside the ship," Gloss said.

"Maybe he's behind you."

We all whipped around as one, and a scuffle ensued as

each of my mates attempted to put me behind them while I tried to fight my way through to the front.

"Enough!" Gärys barked, stun gun extended in our direction. "Everyone hold vekking still! Argös! Bindär! Lock up the women and get over here!"

"Nötchka, *run*," Kino growled, hands gripping at my hips. I thought he might try to toss me aside, out of the line of fire, and I was fairly certain his strength could manage it. I was less certain I could outrun Gärys on foot.

"Run and I take apart each of these bots piece by piece," Gärys said in a snarl, eyes locked with mine. "You know I can."

"You want to risk our self-defense measures?" Gloss said, as haughty as ever, but his hand was fisted tightly into the stomach of my shirt, and I stroked his arm to reassure him that I was still there. I wouldn't put my mates in that kind of danger.

"I would love to actually," Gärys said, yellow teeth grinning, scar wrinkling on his cheek. "Never liked bots. Creepy fuckers taking men's work."

"No one is dismantling anyone. We're not moving. Tell us what you're doing with the women," I said.

"Following orders, princess," one of the other men said from behind us. "Women are in custody, Gärys."

"Add these to our cargo," Gärys said, jerking his gun in our direction. "Make sure to put the Cochie with the other women."

Kino bristled, growling, and I ran my free hand down his spine. "It's alright," I murmured. "As long as we're all going to the same place."

"Oh you sure are, princess," the other man said. "Duchesse sure will be happy to see all of you. Takes care of a few points of business all at once."

"Shut your moon-damned mouth, Argös," Gärys said, reaching out and grabbing Kev-1 by the arm. He jerked hard, but his feet only skidded in the gravel as Kev stared at him benignly from behind his glasses.

I swallowed down a lump and took in a long breath. The Dendärys had a slim chance of forcing my mates to go anywhere with them unless they had me in hand too. If I just waited, one of the pack would strike and then my mates—probably Kev-1, whose programing seemed least secure of all of them—would retaliate. We might even manage to get away, if we really did hijack a ship and take off.

But trouble would follow, probably straight back to Avan-8's lap. The last thing we needed was to cause more problems for him. Also, I couldn't help but wonder what was happening to all of those women. I didn't want to leave them in Duchesse's hands and I definitely didn't want to leave them to Gärys' mercy.

"Guys," I said, as gently as possible. "I think we should go with these men."

"Blossom," Romeo started to object.

"We don't want trouble," I said, meeting his eyes and willing him to understand. His gaze was full and watery, but he nodded lightly back. "Let's just...find out what they need from us, yeah?"

"You put her with us or we take your ship apart, piece by piece," Kino said to Gärys, every note in his voice grit and gravel, full of warning. His teeth flashed, bright white and sharp. "You know we can."

Gärys looked past us to his pack friends, head jerking back toward the Imerial. We were herded and shoved, my mates keeping sure to bundle me in the middle of their bodies, safely out of reach of the Dendärys males.

My stomach was tying itself up in knots, squirming wildly as we approached the glossy, high-tech ship. Should we have made a run for it? Fight off the pack and get back the Nuts and Bolts to warn Avan? It might be harder to make our escape from the pack or Duchesse later. But it felt even riskier to potentially lead the fight to Avan-8.

Vek, nothing was easy or safe *now*. I'd just sold my moon-damned ship and they already knew where we'd been hiding. Where else could we go and even if-

My eyes skidded over the custom plating on the wing of the ship as they led us up a set of stairs. Suddenly all my racing worries were distracted.

"Is that reamed thestling?" I asked, my neck arching back to try to see past all the wide shoulders around me and get a better look. Stars, this ship was perfect.

"Careful, little one," Kev-1 said, nudging me gently at my back into the belly of the ship.

It was dark inside and strangely silent aside from our shuffling steps. Romeo grunted in front of me, steps halting for a moment and I bumped against his back.

"Sorry," he murmured.

The lights flared above us and I winced, tucking my face into my shoulder, eyes struggling to adjust back and forth from dark to light again. I knocked my forehead against Kino's dense back and looked up.

All around us women sat, bodies limp on decadent sequined benches that curved around the open space. My breath hitched in my chest as I stared at all of them, at least two dozen women, not one of them from the same race or planet. I could only guess at where a few of them might have been from, but every single one of them stared out at the ship, eyes heavy-lidded and blank, soft smiles drooping over their lips. The one closest to us was blinking huge fluorescent yellow eyes, body dressed in a clingy material that shimmered clouds across the fabric, and only one electric blue shoe. She tipped forward, arms wrapping around Romeo's legs, hands sliding up to the crotch of his loose trousers, a trilling giggle running out of her lips.

"Oh. No, no, " he said, sweet as ever. He leaned into me

and caught her hands, holding them in place in a surprising struggle before finally releasing himself.

She pouted as he tipped her back, leaning her against another, older woman with incredible, heaving breasts. They cuddled together in languid, loose movements, and the younger woman craned her neck back, licking up the other's throat before promptly falling to sleep with a shuddering snore.

"Keep walking, unless you'd rather stay with this lot." Bindär was behind us, gun nudging an uncooperative Kev-1.

I nodded to my mates and as a group we wove through the listless bodies of women, the lights overhead beginning to dance in a rhythm of colors, like some kind of club. *Oh.* Of course. It was the pleasure planet. Imerials were designed to be the height of function and style, meant for military or high commercial use. All that care and form made them expensive, and being expensive they often ended up in use as small cruise ships for the rich, rather than their intended uses. It was a ridiculous waste of engineering in my opinion, but this ship was definitely designed for entertaining. I wondered if it had ever seen deep space.

"Second door on the left," Bindär directed.

I was stuck behind Kino when he opened the door and at first I thought he was going into some kind of malfunction, a convulsive tremor running through his body. Then he started barking out noisy laughs, stepping into the room and swinging his arm wide for me to see.

It was a fucking sex dungeon.

There was an electric pink swing hanging from the ceiling. Not to mention the most colorful assortment of dildos hanging from the wall in what I was *sure* was meant to be decorative. I could not think of a single occasion that could possibly call for so many dicks as lined the glittering silver walls of this room.

"What the vek?" Gloss said, face twisting in horror.

"Get in there," Bindär demanded. "*Now.*" He risked

pushing Kev-1 and together we went stumbling into the room, the door swinging shut behind us and a slow bass beginning to play overhead.

Kino was still laughing as he went leaping into the vinyl sex swing in front of him, legs kicking. "Well, Cocheana. What should we do while we wait to learn our fate?"

I glared at him, fighting my smile so hard it hurt. When Gloss opened his lips I slapped my hand over his mouth as fast as I could. "Don't anyone say anything stupid to me right now," I warned.

Kino raised his eyebrows at Gloss in a challenge and I covered my face with both hands, wondering how on earth I'd gotten myself into this mess and with these adorable doofuses.

"I've contacted Avan," Kev-1 said from behind me, and I dropped my hands, spinning to face him. He smiled, and I could have sworn he was bobbing in time to the music a bit, but given he was the only one of the group with any sense I was happy to overlook it. "He's tracking us," he added, tapping the side of his head, smile growing.

"Oh, come here, buddy," I said, dragging Kev-1 down by his enormous shoulders. I slanted my lips over his and he lifted me from the floor, holding me to his chest and humming happily as I licked my way into his mouth. I pulled my head back just long enough to purr, "You're a genius, Kev."

"Does this mean the sex swing is in or ou-Ouch!"

TWENTY-TWO
NÖTCHKA

THE IMERIAL LANDED NOT long after. Kev-1 said Avan-8 was on his way and I didn't know whether or not to be relieved or worried. Either way I was wearing a bald spot in the ridiculous sparkly shag carpeting with my boots. I was just glad I was wearing boots at all—I shuddered at the thought of walking around barefoot in this room.

"Do we have a plan for getting away or are we just going to let them disassemble us?" Gloss asked. He was spread eagle on a bench, heels hooked into a set of stirrups, talking up to the swirling screens on the ceiling.

"You said females occasionally give up on their mates, yes?" Kino asked me, while glaring at Gloss.

I ignored them both, focusing on the situation. "I want us to get away safely but I... I-"

"Want to know what's happening to the women?" Romeo asked, arm curving around my waist. "Help them if we can?"

I nodded, looking at the others each in turn.

"I won't let them harm you, little one," Kev-1 said, without heat or threat, just his calm smile. When he said it like that somehow the offer felt infinitely more dangerous for the people outside of this room.

"I won't let anyone take you apart," I promised, stepping forward and bending slightly to where he was sitting on the floor, catching his mouth in a brief kiss.

"You could put us back together again," Kino said. He was grinning but his grip was fierce on my hand as I reached for him, still swaying in the pink swing. Any other day and the sight would be too hilarious and tempting to resist.

There were footsteps in the hall and my mates stood, surrounding my back as the steps stopped in front of the door, the five us facing whatever came next together.

"You're ours, Nötchka," Gloss whispered, a hand squeezing low on my hip.

The door opened and Gärys stood grinning in the hall, cheek twisting painfully around his scar, and a line of what appeared to be guards behind him. If guards were oiled up, muscular hunks wearing nothing but little cloths covering their private bits. They *were* armed. And unfortunately they were organics, a fleet of Quentins—a warrior race that bred and sold soldiers to high bidders—which meant that my droids couldn't fight them unless they absolutely had to for self-defense. Or in defense of me.

"Come along, Cochie, nice and slow so you don't spook Duchesse's little toy soldiers, right?" Gärys snarled at us.

I thought I caught one of the "toy soldiers" shoot the Dendärys male a glare sour enough to curdle cream but just as quickly he was focused straight ahead. Kino and Gloss stepped out of the room first, then me with Romeo at my back and Kev-1 last in our line. For each of us, two of the Quentin soldiers flanked our sides, a tight formation that kept our steps even with theirs and ensured we had no means of escape.

Out of the hall and into the main chamber of the ship, the room was cleared away. "Where are the women?" I asked, rising up on my tiptoes.

The Quentin on my right reached out a hand to push me down and there was a loud "click" from behind us.

"Don't touch her," Kev-1 said in that dark, demanding tone that left me in shivers.

Oddly enough, the Quentin obeyed, his hand falling to his side. When I looked up, past miles of gleaming golden skin, he was staring straight ahead as if nothing had happened. They *were* organics, right? Or had Duchesse managed to replicate them so well with her technology it was almost impossible to tell? I was tempted to reach out and tap at one of them just to test their give, but before I could we were being herded down the stairs.

I'd expected the Imerial to land out in the open somewhere, the Quentins leading us into the building. Instead we came out of the ship into a lavish room, similar to the one I had first met Duchesse in, a clutter of lights and lush fabrics and writhing bodies. This one was twice the size and thankfully everyone inside was more or less clothed, depending on whether or not you counted the Quentins. Duchesse must have had the room built to be a landing pad specifically for the Imerial.

I had a strange appreciation for the woman. She was undeniably insane, but I had her to thank for my droids and her taste in engineering was impeccable.

The women from the ship were clustered together inside of another pack of Quentins at the heart of the room. I spotted the gold scaled woman leaning heavily into the side of a soldier, cheek nuzzling at his chest. His arm was at her back and it almost looked as if he were holding her to him, but he was probably just trying to keep her from toppling over. Duchesse was nowhere to be seen but the Thimean, Conmar, who worked for her was taking a head count of women.

"Bring the Dendärys here," Conmar called without looking over.

There was a sudden outbreak around me, my mates struggling against the Quentins at their side and Gärys pushing mine out of his way. He grabbed me by the scruff of my neck, my hair tangling in his rough grip. I spit and snarled and kicked as he dragged me across the room, my toes tripping over dense carpets as Kino roared behind me.

"Just here, please," Conmar said, with an efficient twitch of one his arms to the end of the line of women. He had a tablet in another hand and was busy making notes or checking off the races of women collected in front of him.

"Sir, Duchesse mentioned that my brothers and I would... perhaps have time with this-" Gärys stuttered over the words, hands tightening painfully around my arms as I tried to wrestle him off. I could guess where his request was headed and I would do whatever I could to make sure he ended up a very disappointed man.

"Take it up with Duchesse when she arrives," Conmar said without looking at either of us.

"But, sir," Garys tried again, fingers digging in so hard I could already see the bruises growing around his grip.

"If Duchesse promised you something then *surely* she will follow through on her word," Conmar said, finally looking up at us, layers of eyelids blinking and tone implying that maybe Duchesse's word wasn't worth much. I snorted and Conmar turned to face me. "Miss Uumian, I wonder if you might cooperate to stand exactly here, please."

Gärys held onto me for a moment too long and Conmar made a terrible chattering sound, three Quentins stepping forward from their ranks, one with a woman clinging to his back with a happy sigh. My eyes narrowed at the sudden response. The Quentins were trained in Thimean language. Gärys had called them Duchesse's soldiers, but clearly their commander was Conmar in the moment.

I was released then and I took careful steps to the spot where Conmar was still pointing with his free hand. I covered myself where Gärys had held me, trying to rub feeling back into the bruised flesh.

"Thank you very much, Miss Umian."

I swallowed and turned staring across the room to where my mates were being held, Gloss with a meaty arm around his throat and a deeply offended expression on his face. Kev-1 and Kino both had their arms braced behind their necks, each held by two Quentins, and Romeo alone remained standing between his two guards. His eyes locked with mine and he nodded once, eyes full of hope. I didn't know if he was trying to assure me or himself that we would all make it out of here together, but I was beginning to feel certain we wouldn't. The Quentins outnumbered us by the dozens and this wasn't just a pack of Dendärys males kidnapping women. This was an organization that ran a majority on the entire planet.

"This can't be legal, what you're doing," I said as Conmar stepped in front me, blocking my view. His eyes rolled over my face and body, stopping briefly where Gärys' bruises were blooming on my arms. "Don't you and Duchesse have *some kind* of authority you have to answer to? Galactic laws can't allow for-"

"Miss Uumian, I am to inform you that you have been selected for a very exciting new innovation in Ecstatic Entertainment Empire," Conmar began to drone, voice painful on my ears. "With your participation-"

"My *participation?*" I started, expression twisting with confusion as Conmar recited off his tablet what sounded suspiciously like a *consent waiver.*

"Conmar! Darling, we discussed this," a voice trilled from the doorway.

Her skirts arrived before she did, billowing soft clouds of pastel blue lace, that wafted through the air as if it had a life and will of its own. Duchesse was not far behind, one pristine white arm held in front of her, inviting whoever might be closest to kiss one of the electric light rings she wore on delicate fingers. Gloss snorted at the very sight of her, curls so full around her face I couldn't even see her expression, breasts pushed up nearly to her chin.

She stilled at the sound, sharp gaze narrowing in on my mate. "What's that, Conmar?"

"A Sparkle model, Duchesse," Conmar answered with a bow in her direction.

She tossed her head a little, raising her chin and looking at Gloss down the length of her nose. He preened, and I knew for certain that if he thought he could seduce our way out of this mess he would try. Her lips pursed and she turned to Conmar.

"They're supposed to be *pretty*," she said. I fought my smile at Gloss' pained gasp until she continued, "Have him recycled."

"NO!"

The cry was reflexive, as was my leap toward Gloss, prepared to put myself between him and whoever might try to toss him aside. Unfortunately, the Quentin closest to me was faster than I was, and I was lifted up into the air, his arm around my middle firm but gentler than Gärys.

"Nötchka!" Duchesse clapped her hands with a delicate flutter of jewels catching the light from the room. She floated across the room to me and I wondered if she still had feet or just some kind of elegant motorized wheel system. She took my face in her hands as she reached me, pecking each of my cheeks with a strange kiss, lips oddly firm and sticky on my skin.

"Oh darling, it's *wonderful* to see you again," she said, beaming that bright lit smile directly into my eyes. Her hand travelled down my side and I tried to squirm away until she was petting at the Quentin soldier holding me up. She waggled her eyes at me. "Aren't they *delicious*? Conmar bought them for me for a present and they're absolutely lovely. Terribly dull in bed though, I'm afraid. Stoicism really is overrated."

My mouth was opening and closing but I couldn't come up with a single word. At least not until, "You tried to have me kidnapped."

Duchesse blinked brilliant eyes at me. "Did I?" She turned to Conmar. "Did I try to have Nötchka kidnapped?"

"Yes, Duchesse," Conmar said with a nod.

Her eyes narrowed and for a moment I indulged in the hope that maybe this was all a misunderstanding and we would be released. Maybe she hadn't meant *me* Nötchka, just some other... disagreeable Nötchka.

"And we were *unsuccessful* in the kidnapping?" she asked, acid dripping from the words.

"The Dendärys pack failed to retrieve her, yes," Conmar said.

"Recycle them," Duchesse said in a quick clip. Somewhere in the room a man, one of the pack, shouted a curse word.

"They're organics, unfortunately," Conmar said.

Across the room I caught the eyes of my mates. Kino look half-crazed and Kev-1 was blank in a new and cold way. Romeo's hope was growing dimmer and Gloss looked torn between worry and offense. I hated not being in reach of them. The further away I was the less I believed we would make it safely out of this insanity.

"Well, do whatever it is we do to organics then," Duchesse said with an airy wave of her hand and a roll of her eyes. "Now, where was I?"

"I was reading the Dendärys female the script before the sedative," Conmar said.

"Ah, that's right. But no, we won't. I want to tell darling Nötchka myself. I haven't had any of the fun."

"Duchesse," Conmar said, a new kind of edge arriving in his voice that had me twitching and the Quentin holding me squeezing just a little tighter.

"Conmar," Duchesse barked. "You are my advisor. I pay you to listen to what I say and do what I tell you to do and think of the things I want done so I don't have to. And I am telling you now, it's *my* turn."

I squinted at her definition of advisor. Conmar glanced at

me and I felt a brief and strange kind of kinship. He had been dealing with this woman's particular brand of power hungry insanity for *how long?*

"Yes, Duchesse," Conmar said.

"Good. Scooter," Duchesse said, patting the Quentin's arm and turning in the direction of the enormous velvet chaise. "Bring Nötchka over here, please. And someone get their face between my thighs. I'm exhausted. One of those will do," she waved her hand in the direction of my mates and all four of them looked at each other with a sharp panic.

"You can't," I said, voice too tight, body struggling my way out of the Quentin's hold. He didn't fight me as much as I expected, simply kept me in hand while letting me land on my own feet.

"Of course I can, they're all mine," Duchesse said with a lazy shrug, dropping backwards in an elegant heap onto the chaise, a hand placed limply over her eyes.

"These are *mine*," I said, a dark, possessive anger building in my chest, making my body tighten and ready to attack. Even if Duchesse was built out of the strongest materials now, I was still pretty sure I could tear her up if it came to it. If she threatened my men, tried to claim them. "They're my mates. They only service me."

The hand slid down from her cheeks and sharp eyes met mine. "They're your *what?*"

"My mates," I said clearly, squaring my shoulders even though they were under the hands of the soldier.

"That's not possible!" Gärys shouted from the corner.

"Conmar?" Duchesse prompted.

Conmar scuttled closer, and my body reacted to the insect sound with a soft shudder. "Unheard of," he said and Duchesse raised her eyebrow at me in triumph before he continued with, "But not outside of a Dendärys female's biological imperatives. They have been known to take multiple mates, especially in cases of females finding mates of different races."

Duchesse looked between me and my mates before a smug smile stretched across her lips, the shape turning into a grimace under the strain of the expression on her modeling. "Bring me the Lover Boy model," she said nodding her head at Romeo.

My gut twisted as I watched the Quentins drag him forward to Duchesse's feet, forcing him to his knees in front of her.

"It's alright, Nötchka," Kino soothed, but I couldn't tear my eyes off Romeo's back, shoulders dressed in my tattoos.

"*Stop*," I begged, throat tight.

"I won't do anything he doesn't want," Duchesse cooed as she leaned forward, sharp fingernails lifting Romeo's face up to hers. "Sweet Lover Boy, my darling creation. Your kind was *always* my favorite. The absolute devotion you give. Tell me you love me, darling."

The room held its breath and I blinked through anxious tears. I would win him back. I would make this right when we were safe. Please let us get out of this safely.

"I love Nötchka," Romeo said, voice sweet and simple.

I sobbed in relief, wincing as I watched Duchesse's fingernails dig deeper into Romeo's beautifully soft skin.

"Kiss me," she hissed.

"No," Romeo said, forcing his face to the side, eyes catching mine. "I only want Nötchka. I belong to her."

I grinned through the anxious tears, knowing the kind of possession he spoke of had nothing to do with deeds or serial numbers or even the tattoo I'd inked into his skin. I belonged to him every bit as much.

"I love you," I said, although the words came out in a fragile whisper. Romeo's cheeks filled around the dig of Duchesse's nails and then she released him with a push to the floor.

"You won't be hers when I turn her into a mindless body for the hordes to fuck and fill to their cocks' content and their pockets' limits," Duchesse snarled.

The eyes in the room whipped to her and Kino began his struggle anew, more Quentins taking hold of him to keep him from escaping.

"That's right," Duchesse said, the strange tangle of anger on her face settling back into the smooth sweetness she was designed to display. She watched me with a kind of sharpness that felt like the pricks of knife tips along my skin. "Pleasure models made from organics rather than droids. Real women with real desires and real responses, kept needy and desperate for whoever pays for their time. It's been a challenge, I assure you. Studying where our models go wrong and correcting the errors, but ultimately this was always my goal."

"You... you can't just *drug* women forever to keep them pliable," I said, glancing at the swooning women behind me. Even now some of them looked less peaceful and pleased, and more woozy—faces starting to pout and frown as if they were waking up to the fact that everything felt *wrong*.

"No, I can't," Duchesse said, sweeping curls away from her cheeks. "But I can reprogram their brains. Believe me. It took us some time to find the right keys, what was important to keep open and operating and which parts of the brain to shut down entirely. But it *is* possible. I myself have tested some of the procedure. And Nötchka, I am *constantly* horny." She turned to Conmar, the lights in her hair and teeth and eyes all brightening at once. "Speaking of which."

"I'll bring you a model, Duchesse," Conmar said with a dip of his body. "Just a moment."

"Honestly," Duchesse said, the venom rinsing out of her voice as she relaxed back into the cushions. "If I didn't adore sex so much, I really might start to have regrets."

TWENTY-THREE
NÖTCHKA

"FASTER AND TO THE LEFT, darling. Better. Yess, yes, yes. Alright, but now harder."

I resisted the urge to put my hands over my ears. It would have to be enough that I had turned away from the spectacle of a Quentin soldier making his way under all the poof of Duchesse's skirts, a furrow of concentration on his brow.

The most horrifying conversation of my life had just been put on hold for oral sex. The most perfunctory sounding oral sex I had ever heard.

"His technique is terrible," Gloss hissed under his breath.

Vek, I wanted so badly to be with my mates at this moment. Romeo had been returned to his spot with them. Surrounded by soldiers, each of them kept their eyes on me, aside from Gloss who was taking some kind of perverse pleasure from critiquing the affair on the chaise. The soft stutters of snores were heard from the other end of the room where the captured women had begun to fall asleep against their assigned Quentins. Or at their feet in the case of the gold scaled woman whose Quentin was wearing the tiniest smile as the woman purred like a cub, twined around his ankles.

I chewed at my lip, eyes drifting to the patterns of the rug spread across the floor, an elaborate circuitry written in the softest fibers. We were in over our heads. I was risking my mates' safety and autonomy, as well as my own by coming here. Duchesse was a step further than insane. She was *broken*, undone by submitting herself to her own experiments for too many years. More machine than woman to the point where she had fractured her own mind just to see if it were possible to do the same to others.

In the back of my thoughts the pattern at my feet began to transform from decorative to constructive, a familiar structure to the pattern.

More machine than woman.

In this moment, that might be a blessing. I understood machines and I was good at fixing them! Not that fixing was exactly my mission when it came to Duchesse. I just needed to shut her down. Or off.

I turned in place, following the circuits on the floor, wishing I could push aside the feet and furniture to get a better look. Was I chasing a dead lead out of desperation or was Duchesse really vain enough to design herself into a carpet?

"Oh, Conmar, thank the damn stars," Duchesse cried out in relief, legs kicking under her skirt, shaking the Quentin out. He reappeared, red faced and taking deep breaths, face stoic aside from the wrinkle of his nose. Duchesse's head tilted to the side, curls curtaining over her face for a moment before she tossed them aside. "When I said bring me a model, I didn't mean one of the vintage ones."

"I discovered the Proto attempting to break into the facility, Duchesse," Conmar said.

I spun, chest squeezing so hard I nearly doubled over, and found Avan-8 following Conmar into the room. His eyes scanned over the drooping women, my mates surrounded by guards, skimming briefly against me, before landing on Duchesse who eyed him with equal interest.

"Ahhh, yes, I recognize this one now," Duchesse said, lips

curling as her eyes traced over Avan-8's chest. "Our little experiment."

Avan's feet stalled for a moment in his path and my neck hurt for how quickly I snapped my head to stare at Duchesse.

"How does a model react to the *prospect* of freedom when you dangle it at a length in front of them, an incentive they can never reach," Duchesse said, watching Avan's face.

He gave nothing away. All the little quirks of expression he'd been developing since his upload were frozen now.

"And are you one of hers too?" Duchesse asked him, with a vague wave in my direction.

He was passing me on his way to her, almost close enough to touch, and I wanted badly to dive between them, to claim him in front of the room as I had with the others. My stomach churned with keeping silent, fists clenching painfully at my side.

"I am not," Avan-8 declared.

The pain was greater than heartbreak. Everything in me hurt at once, like a great crack had echoed through my bones, turning my knees weak. A whimper strangled in my throat and Avan's back tensed in front of me.

"Who do you belong to, Proto?" Duchesse said, smirking growing tighter, more twisted with every slow second.

"To Bandalier," Avan-8 said.

Duchesse sat up pin straight, eyes glaring. "No. Bandalier is just a planet. Who *owns* you?"

There was quiet for what felt like a long time but when he finally spoke, there was none of the anger I knew he must be feeling. None of the rage *I* was feeling.

"You."

Duchesse relaxed, her skirts sighing around her, and her smile smoothed with satisfaction. "Very good. Now, let's see what your old bones can do, hmm?"

It occurred to me then, watching Avan take those slow but steady steps closer, that if she owned him, if she *created* him, she was every bit as old as he was and then some. My eyes flicked from Avan-8's back to the floor, determined to find an answer or solution and just as convinced that there was nothing for me to find, the cause was lost. I was so distracted I almost missed it.

Avan-8 kneeled in front of Duchesse and I was queasy watching her hands trace over his shoulders, paying special attention to where I'd reattached his arm.

"I'm glad she fixed you up," Duchesse said, quiet and intimate and only audible as the room seemed to hold its breath. My heart pounded in my ears like a drum.

"So am I," Avan-8 answered and I recognized the tone, could imagine the way his face was softening as he looked back at her. He was more seductive than he realized but I hated knowing he could turn it on for her just as easily as he did with me. He leaned in closer to her, skirts floating up to her cheeks as he reached beneath them. "Now I can do this."

Duchesse's face had been turning soft and dazzled until all at once her eyes widened and her lips parted. She went toppling backwards with the chaise in a noisy storm of activity, Avan-8 rising up off his feet and shoving the chaise aside with a great heave.

I was not thinking as I watched what happened around me. I didn't understand what he had done, what he was *trying* to do. I only saw the Quentins run to him and reacted in instinct by running with them. I squirmed through the charging soldiers and Avan-8's arm hooked around my waist, lifting and turning us both so the first strike landed against his back.

"Escape with the others," he said, as soldiers tried to untangle us from each other before continuing their assault.

He was holding me tight against his chest, my feet dangling above the floor, our noses nearly touching and my eyes locked on his electric blue stare.

"Escape with us," I said, wincing and yanking my arm

away from a Quentin. Another nearly pulled me loose, but there was an 'oof' of pain at my back and a grimace on Avan-8's face as he kicked the man away.

"Conmar!!" Duchesse screeched from the floor, skirts billowing around her body, mechanical feet kicking in the air like a baby.

"Your failsafes," I whispered, eyes widening as Avan-8 elbowed a soldier off his back.

"Flexible," Avan-8 grunted, ducking us beneath the swinging fist. A moment later a body was tossed away from us and Kev-1 was at my back, grinning like a child while throwing a quick punch at another soldier.

"You are ours, little one," Kev-1 announced. "Self-defense!"

Romeo and Gloss and Kino were a part of the fray now too, not fighting exactly, but taking blows and distracting the Quentins from Avan and I. It might have been funny if I was more convinced that we would make it out successfully.

"Take me over there," I said pointing in the direction of where the women were more or less all asleep, just a handful of Quentins left to guard them, not looking entirely sure of where they should be focused.

"Someone fucking pick me up off this floor!" Duchesse screamed.

Too many of the Quentins responded to the order, giving us room to run out of the ring of soldiers that had formed around us.

"Statistically there's no viable exit this direction," Avan-8 told me, still carrying me in his arms.

"I'm not looking for an exit, I'm looking at the carpet," I said.

"Is now the time for an interest in interior decorating?" Gloss asked and then hissed in irritation. "Save your punches for the people trying to recycle us, Roughie."

"What part of the carpet, Blossom?" Romeo asked, skipping the logical question of *Why?* and instead settling on being perfectly supportive as usual.

"There, under the sleeping Bilutian," I said, pointing out the girl with gossamer wings that were batting in a lazy, uneven tempo as she nuzzled into the carpet. I wiggled down out of Avan's hold to run closer.

Kev-1, Avan-8 and Kino took care of the interference with the Quentins while Romeo and Gloss moved the girl aside for me.

"Here," I said, tracing my feet along the lines of pattern. "This is the conductor, and back there was the load."

"Little one, it is only a carpet," Kev-1 said, his back nudging mine as he wrestled against a soldier.

I shook my head, nudging them both to the side and Kev-1 making room for me as I followed a path. "It's functional."

"It's fiber," Gloss argued, running ahead of me and pushing women out of my way even as he groused.

"It's a *replica*," I bit out, trying to concentrate and follow the logic of the design rather than worry about the chaos around me.

Conmar and a few of the Quentins were pulling Duchesse up from her chaise. Gärys and the pack were thankfully missing from the room, probably having taken the opportunity to escape before Duchesse remembered she wanted them punished for failing to catch me the first time around.

"I think I have the layout, but I need to find the switch if I'm going to get this right," I said, knowing that the others were only following my instructions because there was nothing else we could do in the moment. Because they trusted my word. If I was wrong about what this circuitry mimicked then I was wasting a possible opportunity of escape. But if I was right it would buy us time or even better, keep all of us, including the women, safe from Duchesse and all her plans.

"We should be searching for a safe route out," Kino said, more to Avan than me, I suspected.

"I came to give you the opportunity," Avan-8 answered, words grinding in his throat as he struggled to hold a Quentin out of my way.

"Are you an idiot?" Kino asked, body squaring like a shield in front of me. "Nötchka's not just going to *leave* you here."

"It's illogical," Avan-8 started and I cut him off.

"He's right, you're coming with us."

"I belong to-"

I swiveled and snatched Avan-8's face in my hand. He had thrown off every soldier that approached him, ignoring his failsafes entirely, but when I gripped his face he bent to me, docile and obedient.

"I don't fucking care about the deed, Avan," I said, words rushing out in a near blur, my body all but vibrating with tension. "Did you hear what she said? They've been manipulating you for decades! Intentionally making sure you could never afford your own deed. The virus in the house was probably them. Maybe the rough customer who tore off your arm was them too. Fuck the deed! You're the only person who can say who owns you."

"I'm a droid, not a person, Nötchka," Avan murmured as the others struggled around us, trying to afford us a moment even as the previously occupied Quentins joined the fight and we were outnumbered again.

"You're a person," I said, holding his stare with my own. I would believe it for him if I had to. "That's what they're watching in those Proto files. You change and evolve like an organic mind. You cannot be owned."

Something like pain flashed across his face, and for half a moment I thought it was him coming to terms with what I'd said. Then I realized a Quentin had grabbed up a terrifying erotic statue from a shelf and jammed it into Avan-8's shoulder.

I grabbed the base of the statue, where a tangle of bodies fucked each other in a complicated circle, before the soldier could pull it free. We wrestled for a moment, my face snarling as I tried to keep the statue in place so it wouldn't rip anything important loose. The Quentin frowned at me and then rolled his eyes, and I yanked Avan-8 against me, the soldier falling back a step, as if he wasn't really interested in winning. My mouth opened, confusion on my tongue, when I spotted the pattern in the carpet just over his shoulder, the entire piece working together into a complete picture in my mind.

"I have it!" I shouted. Avan-8 was leaning too heavily on me. "Are you alright?"

"What do we do next?" he asked, a hollow rattle in his voice as he ignored my question.

"I need to get to Duchesse," I said under my breath, rising up on my toes to try see through the sea of soldiers surrounding us. "I can turn her off."

"I think the Quentin was doing that earlier," Gloss said from behind.

"She's barely organic now," I said to my droids, trying to keep my words below the racket of fighting around me. "I'm pretty sure she has a switch."

Kino and Kev-1 made their way ahead of us, clearing a path. If I hadn't been so focused I might have wondered why this seemed easier than it should have, like the Quentins were falling back, barely putting up the appearance of a fight against us. But I had a goal now and it, and the way Avan's feet dragged strangely against the carpet, were my only concerns in the moment.

Duchesse was doing a terrible imitation of weeping when we reached her back at the chaise, Conmar standing mildly at her side, not looking concerned about the fact that the room was now in shambles or that his boss was distraught.

"You. Are. Horrible," Duchesse sobbed, fingers wiping mimed tears from her cheeks as she blinked with over-bright eyes at me. "You don't even understand what I am offering you. A lifetime of ecstasy. Constant heatburn. Endless pleasure. With just a few snips and snaps of technology you've never imagined, I can leave you breathless and aching for a lifetime."

I gaped at the woman for too long, my thoughts skidding away from my goal at the ludicrous offer.

"And you wouldn't need half the physical reinforcements that most of the other races would require," Duchesse pointed out. "Dendärys are so resilient when it comes to sex."

"You're acting like I should be pleased to let you *profit* after turning me into a slave to my sex drive," I said.

"WELL DOESN'T IT SOUND LOVELY?" Duchesse screamed, rising up from the chaise in a flutter of fabric.

"No!" I shouted back. My plan was forgotten, my fist rearing back and flying forward to land squarely against Duchesse's dainty nose.

We both screamed at the contact. I'd forgotten she was made of stronger materials than my hand, but she wasn't built to withstand strikes. I remembered in a rush what I'd wanted to do and I jumped her, tackling her back to the couch, her fingers clawing down my arms and her body bucking wildly beneath me. I didn't know if I was fast enough to avoid the Quentins and Conmar, but I managed to pin her shoulders beneath my knees, my left palm pressing her head into the cushions.

If the carpet was correct, whoever had designed her form had needed to place the switch in the least sexual place possible, to be certain it would never be accidentally pressed. I cringed as my right hand fumbled at her nose, resisting the urge to look away as I jammed my index finger up her left nostril, wiggling it wildly and praying to absolutely anything that I was right in my guess. Gloss made a dramatic gagging noise behind me. Duchesse screamed like a wild animal beneath me, face taut and distorted with rage. My finger slipped against nothing, until suddenly there was an indentation and-

Click.

All at once her voice broke and died off, face going slack. In the next beat every light, in her her hair, her eyes, her teeth, her rings and clothes, went dim as her body went limp.

The room was silent and I held my breath, finger still jammed up the other woman's nose.

"Is she dead?" Conmar asked, and I looked at him, trying to gauge what response he was hoping for.

"Umm, just...off at the moment, I think," I said, blinking and taking harsh breaths to recover from the struggle and panic.

Kino lifted me up off Duchesse and huffed as I wiped my hand off against the leg of his pants. Duchesse's nose had been as pristine as the rest of her but, I mean, *still*.

Conmar turned to Duchesse, staring at her for a long stretch of quiet. I nudged at Kino with my elbow and as a group we began to back up, no one making a move to stop us.

"Very well," Conmar said, turning to the room. "This accelerates my timeline, but it will do. Ecstatic Entertainment Empire has been under investigation by the Galactic Commission of Physical Trafficking and is now seized. The business and all its assets are hereby frozen and all present parties will be required by Universal law to submit to an interview. Authorities are informed and will land shortly, so if you'll just arrange yourself in a tidy line and wait, you may be released without penalty after a review of your case."

What the vekking fuck was going on?

"Blossom," Romeo whispered at my back. "It's your call."

The Quentins were following Conmar's orders, lining the snoozing women up along the wall. Of course they were. Duchesse had said it herself, Conmar had purchased the Quentins. As a gift to her. Except that you couldn't *gift* a Quentin. Their contracts were financial, not based in honor or promises. They were bought and paid for and that was who they served and Conmar was...

"I've been undercover with EEE for over a decade," Conmar said to me. "Ever since we caught wind of the programming evolutions made by their droids. It was a bit of a windfall when Duchesse set off on this new kick of altering organics. Made it easier to shut her down."

"But... but you let dozens of women be captured first," I said, pointing to where those very woman rested in drugged slumber. "Physically seduced under your orders."

Conmar blinked at the sight of them. "I expect the GCPT would have intervened before the procedure. Maybe during, just to be sure the laws were thoroughly broken and we couldn't end up tangled in the legal red tape."

Maybe... maybe they would have waited until women were under the knife. Not having done anything until they could be certain a charge would stick. As if the trauma of having been collected for the experiment wasn't enough on its own.

"Fuck this," I said to my mates. "Run for the Imerial."

TWENTY-FOUR
NÖTCHKA

I HAD my hand wrapped firmly around Avan-8's wrist, just in case he tried to turn himself in or remain in custody or whatever his misguided set of justice might prompt him to do. Kev-1 and Kino were shouldering soldiers aside while Romeo and Gloss helped me drag Avan-8 to the set of stairs leading back into the belly of the ship.

Conmar began to click, throwing his head back and revealing a strange segmented shell along his neck. The sound echoed painfully from the ceiling and back down to my ears, making my knees wobble. But Gloss had his arm around my waist and the sound didn't irritate my droids. In fact, it did more harm to the Quentins we were fighting, making them wince and squint, battling the effect of the horrible call as well as us. And not just them. Soon there were the soft cries of women whimpering and waking. As I pushed Avan-8 ahead of me up the stairs those whimpers turned into complaints.

"Someone shut the vekking alarm off!" one woman said in a slow, grating whine.

"Where. The. Vek. Am I?!!"

My feet stumbled at the soft sob from the corner and Gloss pushed me along. "They're safe," he said in my ear. "The authorities will take care of them. Let them distract Conmar for us."

"But if we stayed-" I started. Could we make sure they made it home? That they weren't taken further advantage of?

"Avan-8, Kino, and Kev-1 would be downloaded and recycled for breaking their failsafe protocol," he said and my blood froze at the thought. "We need to go."

I nodded and rushed the rest of the way up. Gloss was right and I was selfish enough to refuse risking my mates. Down on the floor something shattered.

"Somebody tell us what the fuck is going on!" a woman bellowed, and I grinned at the sound of footsteps rushing in the opposite direction as us. Conmar's rattle died abruptly at the interruption. He would have his hands full now that he'd woken the women and that afforded us the perfect opportunity.

Inside the Imerial again I found the controls by the door for the stairs, letting Gloss and Romeo take over with Avan-8 as I studied the panel.

"Little one, we have a problem," Kev-1 said at my back, sounding calm.

"Just a small one, and then we'll be headed to the horizon," I said in a rush. "Can you crack this panel for me, babe?"

"Sure thing, Cochie."

My heart skipped over the sound of the voice. Not these assholes again.

"You didn't think you'd get away from me that easily, did you cub?" Gärys asked, sliding closer until his chest brushed against my back. Kino growled, but the sound was muffled and when I glanced over Bindär had him in a headlock, an electromagnetic pulse gun pointed at my mate's chest.

"I'm naturally an optimist," I murmured, staring at Bindär's finger poised against the trigger. I could fix this. I could fix this. I could. I just needed to figure out *how*.

Gärys reached past me to the panel I'd been studying, a

laser cutter slicing through the material to reveal the innards I needed. I bypassed the passcode requirement and the stairs began to slide up, doorway closing on the chaos in the room beyond. Women were staggering wildly through the room as the Quentins tried to herd them back into order and Conmar flipped between two tablets.

"You don't know how to pilot the ship, do you?" I asked, refusing to look at the pack.

"It's... gadgety," Argös grumbled.

"You didn't think I was going to leave this planet without getting a taste of you, did you?" Gärys growled in my ear. I kept my eyes on Kino as his shoulders shifted and tensed, fighting his own urge to take on the pack around him. With the EMP gun against his neck he didn't stand a chance.

"You know if you actually gave me room to take a vekking breath I might have this ship in the air by now," I said.

"Gärys, let's just get the fuck out of here before the authorities show up," Bindär muttered.

"Yeah, Gärys, I don't think they'll look too kindly on your recent activities," I said.

He only stepped closer until I was forced to press my cheek against the wall and his mouth was brushing my skin. I held my breath, the smell of him sour and hot on my skin.

"Get us off this planet and maybe some of your little animated dildos will still be functioning at the end of the ride."

He stepped away, finally, and I pushed past him, stopping in front of where Argös was holding Kev-1. Romeo and Gloss had propped Avan-8 up against a wall, his body turned so that the figurine lodged in his shoulder wasn't pressing deeper.

"I'm taking Kev up with me," I said, taking Kev-1's arm in my hand. Argös made to release him without any further argument before Gärys spoke.

"Not a vekking chance, Cochie."

"The name is Pilot Uumian," I spat back at the man who tried to make himself taller as if that was the kind of thing that might leave me wilting. "And you and your crew know shit all about flying this ship. Kev-1 at least can upload the manual for me. Now get out of our way."

There was a pounding sound at the door of the ship and Argös pushed Kev-1 in my direction as Gärys glared at him. I pulled my mate to the cockpit with me as the pack bickered behind us.

"You have a plan?" Kev-1 asked under the sound of arguments.

"Barely half of one," I admitted.

"I have some suggestions," Kev-1 said, grinning and my heart swooped with adrenaline and joy.

▭

IT DIDN'T TAKE us long to get the Imerial detached from the roof of Ecstatic Entertainment Empire. I caught a brief glimpse through the front window of two women tackling a Quentin soldier to the floor and then the hatch sealed shut after us.

"Authorities are seven ticks out," Kev-1 said. He'd skipped the scanners and simply hooked himself up to their wavelength.

"I can miss that, easy," I said. I chewed at my lip, hands squeezing around the flight controls with a nearly erotic joy. I loved this ship. It was dreamy. I was going to ask my droids if it could count as one of my mates. "Our detour might cost us an escape," I warned.

"It might not," Kev-1 said. "Avan's online with me. Any thoughts on the EMP?"

"None I like," I said. The gun probably only had enough charge for one shot, *maybe* two. But one shot was enough to fry one my droids, possibly beyond my ability to repair them. That wasn't a risk I was willing to take. "We're almost to the container yard."

I had minutes to come up with something and my brain felt like it was scrambling through thorns.

"Gärys is baiting Kino with what he plans to do to you," Kev-1 said. "Avan is concerned he may-"

"Okay, I've got it," I said, already feeling queasy at the thought. And what would happen if it went wrong. "Keep us in the air and try to keep the boys calm."

Kev-1 frowned at me, sliding into my seat as I rose. "Nötchka... you're smarter than them," he said finally with a nod.

I was feeling like I might be pretty stupid, but Kev-1 was right. Stupid or not, I only had to be smarter than the pack. And that shouldn't be too much trouble.

I pinched my cheeks until I felt them burn and then staggered out of the cockpit to where the pack held my mates... and Avan-8. Shit. That was a conversation I was going to have to have soon, wasn't it? *Ditch the pack first. Beg Avan-8 to have you as a mate after.* It was good to have a to-do list.

"What are you doing out here?" Gärys snarled.

"Heat," I whimpered, stumbling against the wall, making sure to avoid his touch. "I thought it was over but-" I groaned, bending at the waist as if a cramp was taking hold of me.

Gärys laughed, slow and deep and pleased, and I peeked up long enough to catch my mates' eyes, offering the smallest smile I could afford them.

"Should've realized a droid could never break a heatburn for you, Cochie," Gärys purred as I kept myself out of his reach, walking in halting steps to the others. I faked a long whine and Gärys laughed. "Well, don't worry, cub, I'll take care of you."

"No," I snarled jerking away from him and up against Argös who still had the EMP gun against Kino's chest. "Pleee-assee, I need you."

I caught Argös' blush from beneath my batting lashes and almost felt sorry for him. He looked like I'd just offered him his first tattoos. Kino growled and I slipped my hand up Argös' chest until my fingers brushed against the back of Kino's neck.

"Not a fucking chance," Gärys snarled from behind, and I rubbed up against his packmate as he made a dive for me.

"Hey!" Argös snapped, releasing Kino in order to scoop me up and away from Gärys. "Lady's vekking choice, man."

"You cod-swapped idiot, no woman would choose you over the either of us," Bindär announced with snarling teeth until I was surrounded by the Dendärys pack.

"Landing now!" Kev-1 called from the cockpit.

Avan-8 surged up from the floor, steps unsteady but determined and he pulled Bindär off of me by the throat. I caught the EMP gun out of Argös' stunned hands as Gloss and Kino rushed to copy Avan, Kino tackling Gärys away from me and dragging him off by the shoulders.

"Romeo, the door," Avan said.

"Third and eighth circuit at the same time," I told Romeo as I ran back to the cockpit.

Kev-1 had piloted us to the container yard where the Dendärys pack had first tried to kidnap me.

"Authorities three minutes out," Kev-1 said, voice neutral.

"You're vekking dead, Cochie," Gärys howled as a breeze from the ground swept into the cabin of the ship.

"Toss 'em, boys," I called back as I got the controls ready to take off again, as fast as we could possibly fly.

"There's a message alert that's been going off the last few minutes," Kev-1 said.

"I'm not sure it's something we want to hear," I said, listening to angry shouts and screams of my mates tossing out the Dendärys pack. We were two containers up off the ground. That was a good fall those assholes were feeling and I wasn't the least bit sorry for it.

"That's how I thought you'd feel so I disabled the tracking system on the ship," Kev-1 said.

I grinned at him as the door sealed shut after the third

enraged howl. I shouted back to the others. "Get in here and hold on. We've got a horizon to hit!"

I shot us into the sky at high speed, feeling a special kind of satisfaction knowing I'd just hit the pack with a good wave of desert dust on our way out. The others came staggering in one at time, bracing themselves against the pace I'd set with the ship.

"Are we going to make it off Bandalier without getting caught?" Gloss asked.

"Authorities one tick off and coming from the opposite direction," Kev-1 told me.

"It'll depend on how badly they want to catch us," I said. If they prioritized EEE over a handful of rogue droids, we'd be all right. I could only hope and push the Imerial to its limits. Luckily those were pretty high.

"Get ready for the view," I said, with a glance over my shoulder at Romeo whose eyes were fixed to me instead of the window in front of us.

The clouds above Bandalier were dense and black inside, leaving a nasty film on the window that I burned away with speed and a snap of electrical wash.

"Give us that sunset, Nötchka," Kino said, crouching down at the side of my seat. Avan-8 and Gloss stood close at hand and for a moment everything felt frozen and quiet. The engines on the Imerial were buttery and smooth and there was hardly any tremor even with the way I pushed harder, faster. I was in love.

Then we broke out of the clouds into a fiery, electric brilliance, stars burning bright and gassy green above us in a sky that wavered like flames. Just ahead, sinking around the edge of the clouds, a lightning blue sun flared so hot and stark I had to wince.

"Just like in the epics," Avan-8 whispered.

TWENTY-FIVE
NÖTCHKA

"NO ONE IN PURSUIT," Romeo said, popping his head into the medical lab I'd found while exploring along the long corridor of the ship.

Avan-8 sat on a table in front of me as I repaired the kinks and tears of the injury in his shoulder.

"Kev-1 said the auto-navigation is working like 'a greased cock in a ready woman,'" Romeo added with a faint violet blush on his cheeks. "We should be at the first trading station tomorrow."

I laughed and nodded, "Perfect. We'll unload what we don't need from Duchesse's collection and gear up."

"We're scavengers now!" Romeo said, grinning and leaving us.

I returned to my work on Avan-8's back, finishing the damage inside and taking a look at what I could do for the exterior.

"If we temporarily patch this I can find the right synthetic for a serious weld, probably tomorrow when we land," I said.

"You should sell me for parts at the trading station." Avan-8 didn't turn to face me as he spoke and I felt like he'd just put my brain on pause, until I could dig my way out of the shock.

"That's insane. I would never do that," I said, pushing at his shoulders to force him to face me. I looked hard into his eyes. "Did they damage your systems?"

"Nötchka, you're going on the run with four droids-"

"Five," I corrected. He hadn't counted himself.

"And no supplies or any of your usual gear. You have to completely start fresh."

"There's food," I said, because the kitchens were well stocked. "Also, drugs, and some of them are even legal. We'll flush the ones that aren't before we get to the station. And there are, like, fancy clothes. Not to mention all the sex toys we decide not to keep." The swing was staying. "Plenty to sell."

"Including me."

"I'm *not* selling you, Avan," I shouted, jumping up from the table. Except that when I did it left me at least a head shorter than him again and I had a difficult time feeling stern from that angle. Not to mention this line of conversation left me with a distinct kind of panic.

He stared at me for a long time, bright blue gaze almost tangible on my face. "I'll make my way from there then. I won't trouble you any longer."

"Stop!" I said, flapping my hands uselessly in front of me, like I was resisting the urge to smack him for making me feel so tied up in knots. "Were you going to kick us out of the Nuts and Bolts before we were kidnapped?"

"Of course not," Avan-8 said with a puzzled tilt of his head.

"Right, so. So you're not kicked off the ship, okay? You're one of us."

"They are your mates, Nötchka," Avan-8 said. "I am not."

I sucked in air and the breaths didn't seem to catch in my lungs for a moment. "Right. Yeah. I know." I covered my face with my hands, trying to rub away the urge to cry, or at least hide the evidence if I started.

"It will be awkward if I stay," Avan-8 said. "Unless you

would like it if I stayed long enough to repay the service I owed you. We can count the shoulder if-"

"Stop, stop, stop," I chanted, a frantic high pitch in my voice, turning my back to him. "I get it, okay? The sex was an exchange. You aren't one of my mates. I get it."

I heard Avan-8 slide down off the table and there was a ringing in my ears along with a faint buzz from his throat.

"What was it that made the difference?" he asked, softer. "Between them and me."

I turned, peeking up at him through stinging, watery eyes.

"Why you picked them as mates," Avan continued, staring at my face with a plain neutrality that flinched at the end of his question.

"I... wait," I frowned, forcing myself to study his face. He was too good at hiding any sign of feeling, but Kev-1 had said that Avan-8 developed emotions. I knew about the bitterness, the resentment of being owned. He did his best to hide that. What if it wasn't the only feeling he'd been disguising?

"Avan, do you think I don't want you as one of my mates?" I asked.

The buzzing stopped and Avan-8 blinked. "Do you?"

"You kept saying it was just business," I said, eyes growing wide. My heart in my chest was a wild, caged animal, and I thought I might collapse. "Just service in exchange for repair."

What if I had been wrong? I tried to bury the hope. It would hurt too much to be wrong again, but the feeling was crawling up my throat, making my chest feel swollen and bruised. There was a bright ringing in my ears, like an alarm that warned I was in danger of breaking my own heart again.

"Nötchka," Avan-8 said, the corners of his mouth twitching as he took a step forward, forcing me to crane my neck back further. His fingertips skimmed down my bare arms. "Forgive me if I've been obtuse. I may not have programmed myself with enough emotional cognizance, but-"

I punched at his stomach and the words came out in a tumble faster than they arrived in my thoughts.

"Of course I want you as a mate! I've been trying to claim you since you offered that *stupid* trade. Avan, I love you."

His hands were pulling me up to my toes, fingers spread across my shoulder blades, as his head ducked down. Our lips met, crashed, connected, in a kiss so deep it felt like a grip through my entire body, drawing a needy whine right up from my throat. Aching, anxious, heartbreak turned into a warm flush in my blood and I wrapped my arms over his shoulders, a soft scratch where his injury brushed my skin.

"I tried to write out my feelings five times," Avan-8 muttered into my skin. I kicked his shin for that and then grunted when it only hurt my toe. He lifted me higher against him, arms bundling tighter around me. "I love you, Nötchka Uumian. You are my favorite virus."

I pulled away, my head falling back with a loud laugh. "Sweet talker," I said. "That new personality is growing on me."

"You are written in me," he said, taking hold of my face in one hand, blue eyes holding mine until I felt a current running through me down to my dangling toes. "I don't think there is anything that could untwine you from me now. You own me."

"No. We belong to each other," I said. "No deeds required." I stretched, taking that electric kiss I craved so much, feeling the vibration of Avan's groan against my chest.

Avan-8 indulged me until I was pressed against a wall, too dizzy to say for sure how I'd ended up there. He held me fast, the both of us catching our breath together. My hands traced over his back, nails finding the thin grooves of plating and memorizing the routes they took.

"Will the others mind?" he asked, lips running a pattern across my cheek, down my jaw and back again for another sweet, searching kiss.

"Would it stop you?" I asked, when he broke away. My

breath stopped short as he started to suck along my neck, right over the pulse point that made me squirm.

"No," he said, voice dark, and his teeth scraping over the spot until I was limp and trapped in his arms.

"They'll be happy," I said, smiling at him as he lifted his head to look at me. "They know how much you mean to me."

Avan-8 beamed at me, hands sliding down my waist to my thighs, hiking me up against his chest, my legs wrapping around his hips. "I won't make love to you in a med lab," he said.

A strange, girlish giddiness struck me at the statement. It wasn't as if he hadn't done just as well before when we were only "business" but hearing the change of terms gave me a full-body high of happiness.

"There's bound to be a not entirely terrifying bedroom somewhere on this ship," I said, cupping his face in my hands and tilting it up to kiss his throat.

Avan-8 squeezed me against him. "Come, mate. Let's find a soft surface and I'll show you how much you mean to me. After, I want you to put your name on my skin."

▭

THE BEST BED, a decadent round mattress big enough to hold me and all my mates, was in the worst possible room. The ceiling had an enormous and horrifically erotic mural of Duchesse. We ended up in the shower of the connecting wash-room, with me clinging to a hand hold in the wall as Avan-8 took me apart first with his mouth, then his hands, and finally all of him.

The only other place the bed fit was in the main chamber of the ship, but since it was only us together my mates decided that was as good a place as any to sleep, and ended up wrestling the thing down the hall.

I woke from a nap with Avan-8 draped halfway over my

chest, face pressed into my neck. Against my other side lay Gloss, Kino still fitted up against his ass from where they'd both collapsed after wrestling for my entertainment as Romeo worshipped me with his mouth. Romeo nuzzled at my belly button now, feet dangling off the mattress, toes wiggling aimlessly.

Kev-1 came in from the cockpit, arms folded across his chest and a smirk spread across his lips. My smile bloomed in response to his.

"They do alright without my help?" he asked.

"Mmmm," I lifted my hand in the air and wobbled it side to side.

Avan-8 caught the hand in his and dragged it down, cuddling it against his chest. "Brat," he muttered.

"Conmar's been trying to communicate with the ship every five minutes since we broke orbit," Kev-1 said. "We're almost out of range."

"Think I should take it?" I asked.

Kev shrugged. "Might be worth knowing if we're about to be pursued by the full force of the galaxy or not."

I groaned and detangled myself from the bodies around me, stumbling off the bed and over to Kev-1.

"Mate, clothes," Avan-8 said, words gravelly and making me shiver.

It wasn't that I felt like I was in heat again, exactly. Just like I was never going to be bored with my mates.

Kino rolled away from Gloss and tossed me his shirt. "Do we come too?" he asked, but the others were already rising, grabbing up pants for themselves and following Kev-1 and I. Kino was quick to follow.

Just as we arrived the comm started to blink again. I curled up in the pilot's seat, surrounded by my mates, and feeling a kind of happy that even the threat of universal justice upon us couldn't shake from me.

"Conmar," I said in greeting as the window in front of me

flared with the image of the Thimean. There was no one with him and it looked as if he were in an office. I wondered if it was his at EEE or on a GCPT ship that was chasing us across deep space.

"Miss Uumian, Models," Conmar said with a nod. "Authorities are working to dismantle EEE and the situation with the women is..." there was static in the background and sudden, muffled, argument. "Working on a resolution," Conmar settled on eventually.

"I'm... glad you have things in hand back there," I said, slowly. "Did you find the Dendärys pack?"

"They were apprehended while attempting to steal a ship from the yard and have since been charged," Conmar said. "I've been promoted to a Director position."

It was difficult to tell for certain with the way the comm connection was fragile at this distance, and Conmar's naturally layered voice, but I thought I detected a hint of pride.

"Congratulations," I said, resisting the urge to glance at the others. Had he called to let us know? It seemed trivial to me but I wasn't about to say so.

"I am now in the position to assign upwards of eight dozen fleets to hunt you and your mates across the galaxy and have you arrested for obstruction of justice, as well as synthetics breaking their failsafe protocol."

I gaped for a beat and then made to dive forward and disconnect the conversation.

"I am also now in the position to grant you all pardon," Conmar continued and I froze with my hand over the end call button. "As well as declare the now missing Imerial ship a non-issue."

"I see," I said, very slowly, as if it might keep him from making too hasty a decision.

"The decision will, of course, be dependent on how much of a problem you create for me in the future," Conmar said.

My shoulders dropped in relief. "Understood. Very much so. Of course."

"Enjoy your travels, Miss Uumian."

"Best of luck in your work, Director," I said, fixing a nervous smile to my face.

There was a twitch on his face and a hint of terrifying fangs that must have been a result of a smile. Then the line disconnected and I collapsed back into the chair, body weak with relief.

"We're safe," Avan-8 mused, sounding every bit as surprised as I felt.

"We have to behave," Gloss said and I wondered if I needed to worry about how disappointed he sounded at that.

My fingers stroked aimlessly over the surface of the control panel in front of me.

"Look at her," Kev-1 said under his breath. "She's more in love with the ship than us."

"It's a good ship," I said, lips curling. It was a perfect ship. And it was *mine*.

"I knew you would do it, Blossom," Romeo said, bending and pressing a kiss to my temple.

Kino turned his back to the window and grinned down at me, the smile infectious. "We're going to have so many adventures."

THE END

AFTERWORD

Thank you so much for reading and I hope you enjoyed the ride! This book was something that I wanted so badly to read, I felt like I had to write it just to satisfy the urge. I would very much like to come back to this outrageous, playful universe in the future, (Quentins, anyone?) but it was important to me to wrap this story up and not leave readers hanging on a ledge while I worked on my open series. If you liked the book and want to see more, feel free to reach out. For now, just imagine all the hilarious and terrible hijinks Nötchka and her mates are getting up to while unsupervised! Keep reading for a look at what's coming next from me!

ALSO BY KATHRYN MOON

COMPLETE READS

The Librarian's Coven Series

Written - Book 1

Warriors - Book 2

Scrivens - Book 3

Ancients - Book 4

Summerland Series

Summerland Stories, the complete collection plus bonus content

Standalones

Good Deeds

Command The Moon

Say Your Prayers - co-write with Crystal Ash

The Sweetverse

Baby + the Late Night Howlers

Lola & the Millionaires - Part One

Lola & the Millionaires - Part Two

Bad Alpha

Sol & Lune

Book 1

Book 2

Inheritance of Hunger Trilogy

The Queen's Line

The Princess's Chosen

The Kingdom's Crown

SERIES IN PROGRESS

Sweet Pea Mysteries

The Baker's Guide To Risky Rituals

The Knitter's Guide to Banishing Boyfriends

Tempting Monsters

A Lady of Rooksgrave Manor

The Company of Fiends

ACKNOWLEDGMENTS

Lindsay, I'm so grateful that I shouted your name in front of a class of 100+ people and made you sit at the back of the room with me. One day we're gonna be some crazy old ladies living next door to each other (so you can have 50 dogs and I can have 50 cats) but until that time thanks for sticking with me every second of the way. And for making me put on lipstick and do my hair and actually talk to people in real life, even if I always adopt the strangest ones at the bar. Ride or die, Earthquake.

Moongazers, I love you all so much! I promise my head is full of stories and I hope this year to share so many of them with you! Thank you for sticking around and for being so amazing, each and every one of you!

Gratitude always to the writing friends who brought me into the fold and introduced me to the perfection that is RH. You've shared your amazing stories with me and your incredible support and I'm so grateful for you! Big hugs to Penelope, Joelle, and Sierra <3

Thank you to my beta team for their high fives/butt pats/squees and of course, the 8 million corrections it takes to clean up a draft from me, LOL! Alicia, Megan, Emily, Meri, Ashleigh, Sue, Cassna THANK YOU SO MUCH FOR YOUR HELP AND ENCOURAGEMENT. I'm very lucky to have you and I never forget it!

Ariel Bishop deserves major KUDOS for the incredible work she did on the gorgeous original cover and for being a champ every time my brain flip flopped on a decision. And equal undying thanks to Lana Kole for the new cover!!

Sara B. is my wonderful editor and, even better, super awesome friend. Thanks for being a sounding board and smart eye and giving me real talk. Also thank you for being my hair-dyeing buddy! I loooooove youuuuu!!

Waffles, this book wouldn't exist without your filthy perfect brain and your enabling and your magic powers of being a muse. Long live the pornpire!

ABOUT THE AUTHOR

Kathryn Moon is a country mouse who started dictating stories to her mother at an early age. The fascination with building new worlds and discovering the lives of the characters who grew in her head never faltered, and she graduated college with a fiction writing degree. She loves writing women were are strong in their vulnerability, romances that are as affectionate as they are challenging, and worlds that a reader sinks into and never wants to leave. When her hands aren't busy typing they're probably knitting sweaters or crimping pie crust in Ohio. She definitely believes in magic.

You can reach her on Facebook and at ohkathrynmoon@gmail.com or you can sign up for her newsletter!

 facebook.com/kathryn.moon.9022

www.ingramcontent.com/pod-product-compliance
Lightning Source LLC
Chambersburg PA
CBHW032228050726
47591CB00001B/309